PALACE
OF
SHADOWS

Also by Ray Celestin

The Axeman's Jazz
Dead Man's Blues
The Mobster's Lament
Sunset Swing

PALACE

OF

SHADOWS

RAY
CELESTIN

MANTLE

First published 2023 by Mantle
an imprint of Pan Macmillan
The Smithson, 6 Briset Street, London EC1M 5NR
EU representative: Macmillan Publishers Ireland Ltd, 1st Floor,
The Liffey Trust Centre, 117–126 Sheriff Street Upper,
Dublin 1, D01 YC43
Associated companies throughout the world
www.panmacmillan.com

ISBN 978-1-0350-1907-6 HB
ISBN 978-1-0350-1908-3 TPB

1 3 5 7 9 8 6 4 2

A CIP catalogue record for this book is available from the British Library.

Typeset in Adobe Caslon Pro by Jouve (UK), Milton Keynes
Printed and bound by CPI Group (UK) Ltd, Croydon, CR0 4YY

Visit **www.panmacmillan.com** to read more about all our books
and to buy them. You will also find features, author interviews and
news of any author events, and you can sign up for e-newsletters
so that you're always first to hear about our new releases.

For Yannis and Petros

PART ONE
Memoir: Samuel Etherstone

1

It is said that all religions have in common a creation story. That they give meaning to the world by explaining how it came to be. But I am of the opinion that religion's defining feature is the apocalypse story, the account of how the world will end. For a universe that continues on eternally, adding ever more souls to creation, diminishes the worth of every soul. And so religions provide meaning by providing an end. They fix themselves to a future inferno, and from it build back the scaffold of their belief into the past.

And so too it is with artists, who see a vision of some future object, reach into the darkness of time yet to come, and pull it back into the present, making their vision a reality in a creative process that likewise runs against the flow of time.

It is on these matters that I dwell as I sit here, an old man, and embark on telling my story, wondering if it too runs against time. For though I am reaching into the past to recount events long since over, I am also that younger man of decades ago, reaching into the future through these words, pulling himself from the rubble of a dead century, into the light of another.

It makes it hard to know where to start this strange tale of mine. For not only does the story run both ways, it does so because its thread is tied to itself; the beginning and the end are one.

But if there *is* a knot that marks the join, it's the day I first received the news that was to set in motion all the horror that followed.

It happened thus:

On a chill, foggy morning in the summer of 1899, I received a note from my agent, Douglas Carmichael, to meet him at the art market on Piccadilly on a matter of great importance. It was an unusual request, for in all the years Douglas had represented me, he had never sent me such an urgent note.

I left my rooms and made my way down the Whitechapel Road, where I caught an omnibus into the West End. The fog had clasped the streets in an oily embrace, reducing visibility to an arm's length. Heedful of the conditions, the driver kept the horses moving at a four-beat gait, until suddenly shouts arose from outside the carriage and the 'bus came to a juddering halt.

'We might be some time, sirs,' shouted the driver from up above.

I looked around at my fellow passengers – a group of sombre businessmen – and we all descended to see what the holdup was. An accident. Strewn across the great intersection of Shaftesbury Avenue and Piccadilly Circus were the remains of two carriages that had collided head on, and were now mangled into a single monstrous heap of metal, wood and flesh. It looked as though a much larger, four-horse brougham had pummelled a one-horse Victoria into the cobbles, before toppling over onto its side.

Further on, through the cauldron of mists, I could make out a clutch of policemen directing traffic. They had set their bullseye lamps along the roadway, but the light cut feebly through the fog.

I heard a sound and realised the Victoria's horse was still alive, its hind legs trapped in the wreckage, too weak and injured to free itself. If I was feeling low already, the sight of this poor animal plunged me further into the abyss.

Just then a policeman approached through the gloom with a revolver in hand. He walked carefully towards the horse, traversing the black grease that had been deposited onto the road surface by the fog, and had certainly played a part in the accident.

When he reached the horse, he lifted the gun to its head. In the moment before he fired, I thought I saw a look of fearful resignation in the horse's eyes. Then a loud report shattered the morning quiet and the back of the horse's head opened up and showered the street with gore. The poor beast collapsed into the debris, and the bonfire scent of cordite drifted into the air. The policeman kept the gun raised, blood dripping off the muzzle, speckling his sleeve. Then he lowered his arm and trudged mournfully back into the mist.

I turned and saw that the other 'bus passengers were staring at the scene with the same horror and depression of spirits I felt in my own breast. One of them looked at me and muttered something in what I guessed was Hebrew, for he had mistaken me for a fellow Jew. I am often confused for one; my father was an Englishman, my mother Chinese, leaving me with dark features of an indeterminately foreign character that throughout my life people of various races have assumed to be their own. I smiled at the man and shrugged. He nodded, seeming to understand his error. Then he and his companions turned and headed in the direction of St James's.

I looked once more at the dead horse, then feeling queasy and faint, ventured off towards Piccadilly in search of food, for I had not eaten that morning, or much of the previous day. When I reached the other side of the Circus, I went into the ABC and ordered tea and buttered toast and took a seat by the window. As I ate, I watched the sun rise above the rooftops, dissolving the fog, revealing the full width of the great thoroughfare of Piccadilly, which, as time passed, filled with people in their Sunday best.

I downed the dregs of my tea and left for the art market, passing by the Criterion and its electric light display, the statue of Anteros, the entrances to the Underground station. Despite the weather and the early hour, there were a few Mary-Anns loitering about the railings near Swan & Edgar's, lilies in hand, enticing other like-minded men to the public conveniences and back streets beyond.

Eventually I arrived at the park and the art market, which was filled with crowds. I cast my eye over the works for sale and could find nothing that chimed with my own art, a discovery which produced the usual mix of feelings. The stalls brimmed with Bible scenes, Shakespeare scenes, postcard views of Britain's stately homes, an avalanche of Pre-Raphaelite derivatives. All were still in vogue at the time. While France forged ahead with Impressionism, neo-Impressionism, and Symbolism, the English still lingered over high Victorian art. A backward-looking art, insular, moralising, sickly. It put us a quarter of a century behind the rest of the Continent, as we always were when it came to such matters.

I stepped past two men in silk top hats bartering with an artist over a charcoal sketch of Beckford's Folly and in the distance I spotted a tall, portly man standing by a watercolourist's stall.

'Douglas!' I shouted, raising a hand.

He looked up, grinned and headed in my direction.

'Sam,' he boomed. 'How are you, dear boy?'

'Well,' I replied, heaving a smile onto my face.

We shook hands and looked each other over.

Douglas Carmichael had been my man since just after I'd left the Slade. A dilettante gallery owner and artists' agent, he'd managed my career and supported me through all my years of scandal and failure, when galleries had refused to show my paintings, and I couldn't even find work as an illustrator.

He was attired that morning in a magenta necktie and an ulster overcoat in a herringbone stitch. In his hand was his trademark walking cane topped with an ivory skull. It was heartening to see my friend still dressed how he wanted. Such was the insulation provided by great wealth and a well-established wife. While the rest of the aesthetic art movement had fallen ever further into poverty and destitution – myself included – to Carmichael it was as if the last four years had never happened. He continued to buy his silks from Liberty, his wool from Jaeger, his furniture from Whiteley's; he dined at Kettner's and the Café de l'Europe; he covered his walls with *ukiyo-e* prints, Whistlers and Beardsleys. After all the calamity that had befallen us, he was still the epitome of an aesthete.

'Shall we get some food?' he said, looking me over and finding cause for concern.

'I've just eaten. Buttered toast at the Aerated Bread Company tea house,' I replied, motioning back to the other end of Piccadilly.

'Well, maybe come with me to lunch later,' he suggested. 'I'm meeting Ransome and Markino in Bloomsbury. Pixie'll be there, too.'

'Thanks, Douglas, but I have other plans. What did you want to see me about?'

He looked at me with a gleam in his eye.

'Come, let's take a stroll through the park,' he beamed, waving his cane towards the greenery beyond the market. 'An upturn in your fortunes may be on the horizon.'

2

We entered the park and walked along a path that snaked from the art market to the Palace in the distance, which was just visible through the last of the fog.

'I've received a letter from a social secretary in the employ of Mrs Henry Chesterfield,' Carmichael said. 'You've heard of her?'

I shook my head and Carmichael seemed surprised by my ignorance.

'She's the owner of the Chesterfield Gun Company,' he said. 'The sole owner. Although the name is misleading for they're not just an armaments manufacturer. Munitions, poisons, industrial chemicals, agricultural equipment. Probably a dozen other products I'm unaware of.'

'And what does she want?'

'Apparently, one of your prints turned up at an auction in Leeds, and from there, somehow, it came to Mrs Chesterfield's attention and she was much impressed. The secretary requested you call upon her employer. You, my boy, after years of struggle, might well have landed yourself a patron. And one of the richest in the country at that.'

I should have jumped for joy, but the words left me cold, and even in the moment I wondered why. Maybe after so many years of hearing only bad news, my mind could no longer accommodate itself to something good. Like a man who has been beaten

8

for so long he continues to flinch at the touch of a nurse. Or perhaps, even then, I had some premonition of what was to come.

'Did the letter say why she wants to meet me?'

'I assumed to arrange the purchase of more of your work.'

'But she can purchase from a catalogue. Or a portfolio. There's no need for me to travel up to Leeds.'

'Perhaps she has a commission in mind.'

I nodded and we fell into silence. As we walked I realised something – Carmichael should have been happy about this news too, but his levity rang hollow. Beneath it he seemed uneasy: there was something he wasn't telling me.

'Which print did she see, Douglas? I'm a little surprised that some matriarch living up in the provinces would be interested in my work. You saw what the great British public was buying back there.' I waved a hand towards the market.

My own art was much darker than anything I had seen that morning. It was gloomy. Gothic. Macabre. I specialised in 'impossible objects' – optical illusions that played tricks with form and perspective to depict things on paper that couldn't possibly exist in reality; staircases that went upwards yet ended below where they'd started; rings whose inner surface somehow looped about to become their outer surface; squares and triangles and other shapes whose geometry I distorted so they likewise defied reality, and thereby befuddled both mind and eye.

These illusions I combined with a dark palette to give my work the hellish tone of a nightmare, taking inspiration from all the past masters of the gruesome in European art: Goya, Bosch, Bruegel, Dürer. Before I fell into disgrace, art critics declared me the Piranesi of London, a modern-day Fuseli. But despite all this praise, and the positive reviews in the *Art Magazine*, I'd never managed to exhibit at the Royal Academy, let alone the Paris salons. The totality of my impact on the art world was the inclusion of a few prints in a group show at the Grosvenor Gallery. In over ten years of working, I had no patrons, and hardly any buyers, despite Carmichael's best attempts to promote me.

'Mrs Chesterfield doesn't live in Leeds, Sam,' Carmichael said. 'She lives on the North York moors. You really haven't heard the stories, have you?'

'What stories?'

'The kind that require a bench.'

We stepped off the path and walked over the spongy, wet grass to a bench. We wiped it clean of dew and sat and looked out over the park once more. On our right was the distant bustle of the art market, on our left was Buckingham Palace. In the park itself people promenaded, dressed in their finery. Gentlemen, families, nannies pushing prams.

'I know the story because of my wife,' Carmichael said. 'She was at finishing school in Geneva with one of the cousins. When the note came she filled me in on the finer points.'

'Which are?'

'Let's start with the generalities. The Chesterfield Gun Company was started decades ago by an Oliver Chesterfield, who had the patent on the mechanism for the original automatically reloading rifle. The company ended up as supplier to the British Army and made its fortune in Afghanistan. During the first Opium War there were rumours of profiteering, of Chesterfield selling the gun to middlemen supplying the enemy. Nothing was proved, of course, but the family assets grew and grew, seemingly without end. As if old Chesterfield had the Midas touch.

'He was a dyed-in-the-wool bachelor himself, more interested in engineering than starting a family, but he had a soft spot for his nephew, Henry Chesterfield, whom he was grooming to be his heir. Henry was in his early twenties then and had married a Miss Evelyn Baker of Lambeth, daughter of a merchant, in a love match. Miss Baker became the Mrs Henry Chesterfield of today. Two years into their marriage, with the company booming and Henry's future looking assured, Mrs Chesterfield gave birth to a baby boy, and that's when the trouble began. Within a few months Oliver Chesterfield died suddenly of a stroke. Keeled over in his withdrawing room in Grosvenor Square and fell through the window onto the railings outside.

'The company passed into young Henry's hands, but not long after, he too perished – an explosion at a munitions factory. And so the company, and all its attached fortune, changed hands again, passing to the infant son, who they'd named Oliver in honour of the uncle. But a few months later the baby contracted diphtheria and died as well, God rest his soul. All three owners of the company deceased within a year of each other, leaving Mrs Chesterfield alone and in charge of the company. This was all before the Married Women's Property Act, of course, but Henry had set up a trust to guard the fortune in the event of his death – one of those legal structures the aristocracy have been using for years to protect family assets from wayward sons-in-law. So Mrs Henry Chesterfield, twenty-two-year-old shop girl from Lambeth, ended up in sole charge of one of the greatest concerns in the empire. All this is of public record. Reported in the newspapers decades ago. What I recount next is based on rumours and on what my wife knows of the affair. It's from here the story gets stranger.'

'Stranger still?'

'Indeed,' Carmichael replied, smoothing his hands over the top of his cane. 'Within a few months of being put in charge of the company, Evelyn Chesterfield went mad. I daresay the three sudden bereavements caused an excess of grief. She descended into monomania, went off in search of the *au-delà*, trying to commune with her dead family. This was during the period when mediums and spiritualists were all the rage. After becoming prey

11

to various charlatans she was introduced to a psychic by the name of Gosterwood, of whom nothing much is known at all. Gosterwood succeeded where all the others had failed and somehow convinced Mrs Chesterfield that he could contact poor dead Henry. During one of the seances, she asked why everyone who'd owned the company had been killed, and Henry's spirit – or rather, Gosterwood speaking as Henry's spirit – told her all three of her relatives had been taken by the vengeful ghosts of the soldiers who had been killed by the family's guns. According to Henry, the whole sorry tragedy had some reason to it – comeuppance for the means by which the family had made its fortune.

'Mrs Chesterfield asked if she was in any danger too and Henry told her she was. That the spirits of the dead soldiers would be coming after her now that she was in charge of the gun company. But he also said there was something she could do to protect herself. That she would be safe if she moved out of London and began building a family home, the family home the young couple had never had the chance to enjoy while they were alive. But only if construction never ceased. As long as someone was working on extending the house, no spirit could harm her.'

Carmichael raised an eyebrow again and smiled faintly.

'Why would Gosterwood tell the poor woman such a lie?' I asked.

'Perhaps he was as mad as she. Maybe madness attracts madness. Either way she took him at his word. She sold the property she had in London and scoured the country for suitable places to build. At last, she settled on a plot along the Smugglers' Coast in North Yorkshire, hemmed in by sea-cliffs on one side and moors on the other. She couldn't have picked a more desolate spot in all England. She hired an architect, a mad Italian refugee who'd fled to London from some dark scandal in Venice, and together with Gosterwood – who had by now inveigled himself into the household – they all decamped to Yorkshire and started building the house. Not long after, Gosterwood disappeared and the Italian architect took his own life, but construction continued without them.

'That was fifty years ago and the house is still being enlarged. After such a great span of continual construction the place is supposed to be a sprawling mess of a thing. Disjointed, confused – one might even say insane, built as it is in the image of its maker. Doors open onto walls; staircases lead up to ceilings; rooms encase courtyards; courtyards encase rooms; there are dead ends and trapdoors and storeys which are completely inaccessible; flights of stairs go up only to return to their starting point; corridors march on for hundreds of yards only to loop around and likewise return to their beginning. Every two years a new wing is added, so that by now the house is a tumorous thing, tumbling blindly across the moorlands and cliffs, connected by a spider's web of corridors.

'Two competing theories have arisen to explain the house's bizarre form. The first is that it has grown unruly because no proper architect planned its enlargement. The second is that the house is meant to be confusing: so as to befuddle the spirits who are so eager to wreak their revenge on Mrs Chesterfield. She has turned the house into a labyrinth. This second theory is furthered by the fact that old Mrs Chesterfield has filled the house with religious art from around the world. Some of the only outsiders allowed to enter are antiques dealers and curiosities-men. Which is where, Sam, I suppose, you come in.'

He fixed me with a look.

'Don't you see? Doesn't this house remind you of your own art? Your optical tricks and bewildering perspectives? Your "impossible objects" made real? Perhaps this is why she wants to meet you. She wants to fill this confusing house of hers with art that matches its own nature.'

13

A shiver rattled down my spine. I had been listening to the tale as if to a ghost story around a roaring fire, with a sense of distance. Carmichael's comment reminded me that I had a connection to the place. That I was expected to go there. My future prosperity depended on it.

'She wants to buy my art to decorate this . . . madhouse?' I said. 'My art is born of an interest in optics and physics, of exploring how the human mind perceives its surroundings. This house is the product of a madwoman being exploited by a charlatan. Of grief-stricken, religious mania.'

'But whether through an interest in science or an excess of religion, you and Mrs Chesterfield have arrived at the same place.'

I gave him a sharp look. Perhaps too sharp, for he paused, shifted his body, changed tack.

'Your art is challenging,' he said. 'It's not the kind of thing you can sell in Sunday morning art fairs.' He nodded at the market in the distance. 'When someone rich comes along and shows some appreciation of it, you need to grasp the opportunity.'

I sighed. At last a wealthy patron had expressed an interest in my art, but she was afflicted with an insanity of the most pitiful kind.

Carmichael rested his cane against the bench and took from his pocket a cigarette case of finely embellished silver. He offered me a cigarette, took one himself and we shared a match. I inhaled the rich, heady smoke. Turkish tobacco, scented with spice. I looked at the maker's stamp: Bradley's of Oxford Street. The pack probably cost more than my weekly rent.

'There's more,' Carmichael said, exhaling smoke. 'Few people are allowed to visit the house, and those who do, never talk about their experiences. Chesterfield keeps a pack of ravenous solicitors on her payroll, extinguishing any rumours before they see the light of day. No doubt you will be made to sign some contract during your visit which will ensure your silence.'

14

'That's not a problem.'

'I'm sure, but that's not what I meant to tell you. I suppose when there is an absence of information, people will make up their own stories.'

'Such as?'

'The type you would expect – that the house is haunted. There have been a number of unexplained deaths there. Construction is a dangerous business, of course, and when a building project has been going on for fifty years there are bound to have been a few casualties. But the house being what it is, these deaths have been multiplied by wagging tongues. The other well-worn rumour is that the house drives people mad. As well as the Italian architect there have been numerous other suicides. The rumours say staying in the house too long unhinges people's minds. That the house is dangerous.'

I stared at my friend.

'And you believe all this?' I asked.

He pursed his lips.

'I don't believe the house is haunted. But there may be some truth to the idea that the place drives people mad.'

'A house cannot drive people mad.'

'Can you be so sure? Doesn't the environment one lives in affects one's state of mind?'

'Of course. But to the point of making one insane?'

'Imagine, then, living in a desolate location, in a house of strange angles and confusing architecture, decorated by the demonic artwork of a hundred foreign religions. Imagine whilst staying there you are working for a madwoman, on a project equally mad. Could not being surrounded by all this madness cause one to become mad, too?'

I considered his words, and realised his concerns were not as outlandish as they had first seemed.

'What if she wants you to work on something in the house?' he continued. 'A commission that requires you to stay there for an extended period?'

'Douglas, I believe I am strong enough of mind not to be infected with the morbidity of the architecture, no matter how long I stay there. You said yourself that there is a similarity between my artwork and this house. Perhaps I'll consider it home.'

'That's what I'm worried about.'

I looked at him, not sure if he was serious. Then his solemn countenance was fissured by a smile.

'So you'll visit her?' he asked.

I was unsure of what to do. Even then, before I had ever set eyes on the house, I felt a vague repulsion for the place, a chill fear in my veins, merely from its description.

'I'll think about it,' I replied. 'How long do I have to decide?'

'I've no idea. But it might be best to strike while the iron is hot. If her interest cools you may lose the opportunity.'

I nodded and we settled into a silence rustled by the wind in the trees, the low murmur of people passing in the distance.

We finished our cigarettes then rose and walked southwards through the park. When we reached Constitution Hill we stopped and looked across to Buckingham Palace. There was no flag flying above it. Queen Victoria was not at home, and hadn't been for a very long time. Just like Mrs Chesterfield, she too had descended into grief-stricken madness after the death of her husband and was rarely seen in public now. She too had fled north and taken up residence in a palace of shadows.

'Where would the empire be were it not for rich, old eccentric women?' Carmichael said, turning to me. 'I think I'll catch a cab to Museum Street from here. Are you sure you won't come for lunch?'

'No thanks, Douglas.'

'Very well. Pixie'll be disappointed.' He took a moment, then asked softly, 'How long has it been since Rose died? Seven years?'

'Our son would have turned eight this past spring.'

'That's too long for a man as brilliant as you to be alone.'

I smiled awkwardly and said nothing, hoping my silence would signal that I didn't want to discuss the topic.

'Well, maybe your new patron will effect many changes in your life,' he said.

He raised his hand to a group of jarvies whose cabs were parked along the side of the road. One of them waved back, jumped onto his carriage and manoeuvred it towards us. Carmichael tipped his hat at me and hopped inside.

I watched the cab trundle off then turned again to look at the Palace. Two years earlier I had been standing in a similar spot for the Queen's Diamond Jubilee, helping a cinematographic producer film the event. The Queen had been forced into attending the celebrations by a young Prime Minister in a bid to increase her popularity, and the gambit had worked – crowds flooded the streets, cheering for a monarch who'd been despised just a few years before.

I recalled the old woman, near blind and racked with rheumatism, doing her best to wave at her subjects from an open-topped carriage. She looked close to death even then, and now two years had passed. How long did she have left? Coming so late in her reign, that last pageant seemed like a final flash of beauty, and it reminded me of something Oscar had said once: that society was like the summer, its colours most vibrant just before its end.

Soon the century, and the whole Victorian era, would pass away, and what lay beyond was, of course, unknowable.

Or so I thought at the time.

3

I sat by the window on a District Line train and watched the darkness streak backwards through the tunnel, mulling over Carmichael's news, Mrs Chesterfield's mad threnody of a house. Even then, before I had ever met her, she seemed like a figure from history, a crazed pharaoh or Caesar or Morgana Le Fay. The English countryside was littered with the architectural follies of aristocrats and parvenus alike – Fonthill Abbey, Cragside, Akroydon and Saltaire. But even compared to these, Mrs Chesterfield's house seemed the most complete testament to a disordered mind. I wondered if it really did resemble my own art, and what that said for my own sanity.

I lit a cigarette and turned my gaze to the interior of the carriage, its wooden panels strewn with advertisements for Pears Soap, Nestlé Milk, Slazenger Tennis Rackets, Smith's Sparkling Champagne Kola. I wondered how much the illustrators who designed them had been paid. Then I thought of how I would spend the following week, trudging around editors' offices looking for similar work, handing over my portfolio to some secretary, before sitting down for the long wait in reception. Then the secretary returning with the inevitable shake of the head.

On to the next advertiser, magazine, illustrated newspaper, lithograph firm. And so it would be on into the future, competing each year with the ever greater horde of art graduates being churned out by the Slade, Saint Martin's, the Goldsmiths' Institute, South-Western Polytechnic. None of them tainted as I was. None of them associated with the now disgraced aesthetic art movement.

My mind jumped back to those dark days when it had all collapsed. At the head of the movement had been Oscar, our most prominent member, his name known across the Continent and in America, too: Oscar *Wilde*. But then he was sent to prison and everything changed. In the immediate aftermath of his conviction, crowds gathered outside the offices of the magazine we used to publish and they rioted, stoning the building. When Oscar's belongings came up for auction, a mob ransacked his house. For weeks afterwards, the *National Observer* and *Punch* and the *Daily Mail* all crowed in editorials and cartoons about our end.

Oscar's conviction not only destroyed the aesthetic art movement, it also led to anyone associated with him becoming unemployable. Many of us had to flee to Europe. In my case, lacking the funds for such an escape, I stayed on in London, where the illustration work for magazines and advertisers quickly dried up, and I was reduced to painting sets for the theatres on Drury Lane, and then for the producers of cinematographic reels who were springing up all over Soho. Time-consuming, joyless work that earned me so little I often had to choose between paying for my board, my food, or the coal to heat my room.

I closed my eyes and struggled not to let such musings seep through the mode of my being, focusing instead on the metallic rattling of the train as it charged through the perfect fit of its tunnel.

I got off at Whitechapel, and walked the rough-paven streets to my lodgings, passing by the slum's rude grotesquerie of old-clothes stores, pawnbrokers, pubs, off-licences, tripe shops, cloggers.

Outside the Church of England mission, prostitutes and destitutes were queueing up for a bowl of soup. On a corner, a gang of young men had taken a break from battling the area's other gangs and were arguing with each other over the trading of Guinea Gold cigarette cards. I nodded at a few of the boys I recognised and they nodded back without taking the risk of smiling at me.

Less than an hour earlier I'd been outside Buckingham Palace, the centre of an empire that took in nearly a quarter of the world's population. And here, just a short Tube ride away, I was in a slum as poor as the shanty towns of Cairo, Lagos, Bombay, or any of the other despairing cities in the Queen's domain. There was a reason the London Missionary Society sent their trainees to Whitechapel to get them used to the poverty and filth they'd soon experience overseas.

I skirted a ganglion of railway lines and approached my lodgings, passing by an ageing lemonade man. He'd put down his dispensing can and stack of cups, laid his sign against a wall, and now he sat on the kerb, surveying the street, sipping from a brown bottle of Beecham's cough syrup.

I scraped the mud from my shoes, unlocked the front door and stepped inside. As I trotted up the stairs, my landlady hobbled into the hallway.

'Welcome home, Mr Etherstone.'

'Mrs Tiverton.'

'A friend of yours came to visit while you were out. I showed him to your room.'

I frowned. I had few friends and they rarely visited.

'I see,' I replied. 'Thank you.'

'Shall I brew you some tea?'

'Perhaps. I'll call down if we require some.'

I rushed up the stairs and opened the door to see John Fitzpatrick sitting uneasily on my bed. An obese Scotsman, Fitzpatrick was a producer of cinematographic reels, the same producer I'd helped film the Queen's Diamond Jubilee.

'Sam, my boy!' he boomed, a grin on his face.

It was then I noticed there was a large leather case by his feet, the type he used to transport his cinematographic cameras.

'Fitzpatrick,' I said wearily. 'Would you like a cup of tea?'

He waved away the suggestion and took a hip-flask from his inside pocket.

'The sun is over the yardarm,' he said, holding the flask in the air.

I went to the sideboard, found a pair of glasses and wiped them clean. He poured us both drams of whisky and I sat on the chair by the wardrobe.

'How did the editing of the South African reel go?' I asked.

I'd last seen him three weeks previously, when he'd been filming on Hampstead Heath. He'd bought some reels of Boer warriors from South Africa to distribute around the country, but the canisters had been damaged by seawater on the ship back to Liverpool. The middle sections were lost so he decided to fill in the gaps by dressing up some vagrants to look like African irregulars then filming them charging up and down Parliament Hill like the Grand Old Duke of York's ten thousand men.

In the handful of years since the cinematographic camera had been invented, most film producers had been 'embellishing' their news film reels in such a manner. Like many of the men who'd rushed into the nascent industry, Fitzpatrick had a carnival background; journalistic ethics were hardly his concern. Especially when the rewards for a popular reel could be so large – the most successful were duplicated and passed along ragged distribution chains that generated royalties from all over the world. Yet almost a month on from the shoot on Hampstead Heath, Fitzpatrick still hadn't paid me.

'Grand, grand,' he replied. 'We filled in the missing segments.

It's not something I enjoy doing but war reels do good business. People want to catch a glimpse of the enemy, now more than ever.'

'Why?'

'Do you not read the newspapers, lad? We're going to war. It's only a matter of time.'

I nodded. There was always a war brewing, because there was always the empire, which was really nothing more than a machine in which bullets were shovelled in at one end, and gold coins spat out at the other.

'Newspapers are a luxury I can sorely afford,' I said.

'You should read them regardless, boy. Regardless. A society without a well-informed citizenry is at risk indeed.'

I thought of how well he was informing the citizenry with his faked news film reels, the bedraggled phantom of an enemy he'd cobbled together from the gin-soaked vagrants of Kentish Town.

'All that is necessary for the triumph of evil is that good men do nothing,' I conceded, quoting Burke, or possibly Mill.

He grunted his approval. I took a sip of the whisky, rich with peat and smoke, warming my chest.

'A war,' Fitzpatrick said. 'And for the first time, cinematographers will be there to document it.'

He was close to gleeful, and I almost understood his excitement. Film could capture the present. With the twirl of a projector, there was the world, immediate but mediated, filled with light and movement. What better subject for it than war?

'What is it you wanted to see me about?' I asked.

'Here,' he said, rummaging around in his pockets. He produced a few coins and handed them over. My missing back pay. Now I knew for certain he was after something.

'You came all the way to Whitechapel to give me my wages?'

'Not just that, lad. You are a suspicious one. I came to make you an offer of work.'

22

'Again, not something you've ever travelled here to do.'

'It's lucrative work, lad. Something a little different.'

I said nothing. Clearly he was embarrassed by whatever it was he'd come here to ask, and after being so mistreated by the man over the years, I was happy to let him stew in his awkwardness.

'Well, the thing is, lad, I learned of the commission you received today.'

'I received no commission.'

'Well, if not a commission, then you've at least piqued the interest of a certain Mrs Chesterfield?'

He raised his eyebrows and smiled mischievously. How could he possibly have found out so soon? Did he know someone in Carmichael's gallery, perhaps? My eyes darted to the cinematographic camera at his feet, and the reason for his visit became clear.

'One hears things,' he said.

'And?'

'Well, there's millions around the world who would pay good money to see inside that house, lad. The strangest house in all England. Perhaps in all the world.'

'Are you thinking of arranging tours?'

'Damn it, I want you to film it! Take the camera with you and film it. The reel would be worth its weight in gold.'

'And how much of that gold would I see?'

'Half,' he said. 'Fifty-fifty. Straight down the middle.'

I nodded, but there was no way he could be trusted. He would be the one receiving the payments from all the distributors around the world, declaring the revenues, inflating his expenses. Fifty-fifty in Fitzpatrick's language probably meant something closer to ninety-ten. If that.

'And what of Mrs Chesterfield's lawyers?' I asked. 'I hear she hires them by the dozen.'

Fitzpatrick waved his hand through the air.

'The reels will be all over the world before she has the chance to shut us down,' he said. 'And as for damages – accounting, lad. We'll set up a separate company to receive the payments and make it look like we made a loss. She'll not see a penny.'

The same dubious accounting that would see my share of the profits reduced to nothing.

'You know how the camera works,' he continued. 'You've used it before. Take it with you, film the house, and we'll both be rich.'

'But I'm still not sure if I'll visit her.'

'What's there not to be sure about? You're hardly in a position to be turning down offers like this.'

'Beggars can't be choosers?'

'Exactly.'

He spoke before he'd had a chance to realise what he was saying, and when he did realise, a look of embarrassment crossed his features.

'I meant—'

'I know what you meant,' I smiled.

We settled into an uncomfortable silence. I sipped my whisky and listened to the sounds of the slum seeping in: the rumble of a distant train, the lemonade man shouting his wares, the mournful lowing of cows left in a railway siding, their journey to their slaughter in an East End abattoir arrested for a few short hours.

Fitzpatrick turned to me and grinned.

'I say, you're not afraid of ghosts, are you? Is that why you won't go?' He boomed out a laugh.

'Nothing like that.'

'What then?'

'I feel the work might be immoral.'

He gave me a confused look.

'The woman is mad,' I explained. 'She's surrounded by people exploiting her madness for their own gain. I might not want to become yet another green-eyed courtier at her insane Versailles.'

'Is it not a little arrogant of you to make yourself the judge of her madness?' he said. 'If I wanted to pay someone for some work, and that person told me I was too mad to make the request, I might feel insulted. Sorely so. I might feel the person insulting me was pompous, arrogant, self-righteous.'

He raised his eyebrows and downed the last of his whisky. I was loath to admit he had a point.

'If the reel does well,' he said, 'perhaps we could make more of them. Of all the grand houses in England. It's an apt subject for the camera. Cinema is an art of movement and space; so too is architecture.' He paused to mull over his own words, which displayed a sensitivity that I had rarely seen in the man. 'So, what will you do? I can't leave the camera with you if you're not intending to go.'

'I'll think about it,' I replied. 'If I decide not to go, I'll drop the camera off in Dean Street.'

This seemed to satisfy him, so we drank another quick dram, then he gathered up his things. As he was heading out of the door, he turned to me.

'You'd be a fool not to go, Sam. Even if you decide not to work for her, film the house and you'll make a pretty packet on your return.'

When he had gone I lay down on the bed. The day had waned on and I had eaten nothing since my buttered toast that morning in the ABC. I looked around the room: the ancient wardrobe, the stained yellow wallpaper, the scuffed floor. It really was a hovel. I thanked God that Rose was not around to see me in such diminished surroundings.

4

Three days later I made my way to King's Cross station. As per the telegram I'd received from Carmichael, I crossed the vast concourse to a W. H. Smith & Son bookstall. It was covered with books, magazines, snacks, refreshments, and other odds and ends that travellers might need. At the centre of it all was a salesman in a waistcoat, shirt and sleeve-bands.

'Good morning,' I said. 'I believe you have a letter left for me by a Mr Carmichael.'

I handed over my card. The man rummaged around in a box behind the counter, pulled out an envelope, and passed it to me. Inside was the letter from Carmichael, a set of train tickets, and a crisp five-pound note. I unfolded the letter:

Dearest Sam,

Please find enclosed tickets for your trip. You'll journey on the Great Northern from King's Cross to Selby, where you'll change to the North Eastern Line and catch the train for Scarborough that runs up the coast. Descend at Filey, which is a few stops after Bridlington. Engage a cab to take you to the village of Lunham. You have rooms at the Black Lion pub for the night. In the morning, a man will pick you up and take you to the Chesterfield house.

PALACE OF SHADOWS

In bocca al lupo,
Carmichael

He'd made no previous mention of leaving money for me, but I was glad he had. I made a mental note to thank him and repay the money on my return. I checked the station clock and saw I still had some time left before the train departed, so browsed the wares at the bookstall. Amongst the periodicals, penny fictions, sensation novels and railway books, I found a copy of *Blackwood's Magazine*.

Five minutes later I was aboard my train as it chugged out of the station. My fellow passengers all had their heads in books and newspapers, making me the only one to look through the window as we travelled across the country. It was a bruised land that passed by, scarred by industrialisation, sliced by railway lines, canals and telegraph wires. Nameless towns came and went, slumbering in the pollution of factories and mills, around which tenements, terraces and slums spread in red-brick ripples.

At some point I must have drifted off to the rat-a-tat chanting of the train, for I awoke to a carriage already dim in the afternoon light, alone except for a train guard shaking me by my shoulder.

'We're at Selby, sir,' he said.

I thanked the man, gathered my luggage and stepped off the train.

Selby station was a sprawling thing, two dozen railway tracks spread across an expanse of wasteground, surrounded by warehouses and factories.

I found the station's tea room, which was pleasant enough, sat at the counter and ordered a cup of tea and a glazed bun, and spent the half-hour I had to kill eating and drinking and watching the steam hiss out of the kettles, the people coming and going, the blur of the station beyond the condensation-covered windows.

My connecting train was smaller and slower than the express

from London. It crossed the River Ouse then wound north-east out to the coast, before turning north towards Bridlington. On one side, the train chugged past a constantly whirled-up sea that foamed against the rocks like a beast displaying its strength. On the other side, fields and barren moorland stretched serenely into the night. We stopped at several silent coastal towns where no one seemed to board or descend. Were it not for the shouts of the railway staff I could have mistaken myself for the only human being on the entire line.

When we reached Filey I descended into the chill night air, which was made all the more bracing by the proximity of the sea. The station was small and badly lit by paraffin lamps and seemed to be deserted; I could find no booking clerk at the ticket office, nor even a porter or stationmaster, and there were certainly no other travellers. I stepped outside to where the rank of cabs should have been, but was confronted with an empty, gloomy street.

Some long seconds ticked by as I wondered what to do and then I heard a noise and saw a wagonette approaching. It stopped at the rank and I asked the driver if he would take me to Lunham. He nodded and helped me with my luggage and we made our way out of the town. We took narrow, winding lanes bordered either side by tall hedgerows which cut off the view, so that I could make nothing of the moors or the sea that I knew surrounded us.

After half an hour or so, the driver whipped the horse onto a muddy path that descended sinuously to the coast and I was finally afforded a view of the landscape: plunging hills and valleys; hard, chalky fields; lines of stunted trees that hobbled through the moonlight all the way to the shore, where a tiny fishing village nestled in the slopes of a grey cove.

We continued on towards it, our descent slow. Eventually we entered the village's lanes, which were narrow and swollen with mud, the cottages either side packed so tightly they were almost tumbling onto each other. Everything was dilapidated, cramped, slanted, mean-looking.

The driver stopped the carriage in front of the Black Lion public house, which differed from the cottages adjoining it only by its signboard, and the lights in its windows.

I descended the wagonette, took my luggage and paid the driver, who whipped the horses off into the darkness without even a goodnight.

I turned and studied the miserable surroundings and realised that the scene would not have looked out of place in an old master painting of three hundred years ago. I had left a modern city of moving pictures and dynamism, of advertisements and Underground trains, roaring pubs and pleasure palaces, to come here – a gloomy, fixed, unchanging place. It felt as if I had gone back in time, into a world of stasis.

I steeled myself and entered the pub. It was tiny, no more than a bar at which a couple were serving drinks, and a few tables scattered about where groups of fishermen sat. Everyone in there turned to look at me as I stepped inside, and the boisterous conversation that had filled the place died out. The woman behind the bar smiled broadly.

'You must be the artist,' she said, in a thick Yorkshire accent.

As she walked towards me, the background chatter renewed, but at a more subdued level.

'I'm Mrs Kell,' she said.

'Samuel Etherstone.'

'This is my husband, John.' She gestured to the man who'd been behind the bar but was now approaching us.

'I'll take your things up, sir,' he said.

He swooped down and picked up my luggage and we shuffled through the tables to a staircase at the rear. He led me up to a narrow corridor and through into a bedchamber. It was modest, but homely, with a fire already lit and a bed piled high with duvets and quilts. There was a cabinet, a wardrobe, and a window looking out onto the beach.

'My wife has a fish stew on the stove. Shall I bring you up a plate?' the landlord asked.

'I'll eat downstairs, please. I've spent most of the day on my own in a train carriage.'

He paused, as if put out by my request.

'Right you are,' he said. 'Come down when you're ready. There's water on the cabinet.'

Ten minutes later I was sitting at one of the tables in the bar, tucking into a heartening fish stew, a crust of brown bread smeared liberally with butter, and a tankard of ale. As I ate, I studied the place. The patrons were indeed all fishermen, dressed in thick cable-knit jumpers, tough cotton trousers and wellington boots.

When I finished my meal, I ordered another drink from the landlord, and sat supping it and smoking a cigarette, reading the magazine I'd bought at King's Cross, particularly taken by an African story. I couldn't help but notice, however, that now and again some of the fishermen would look my way and whisper to each other.

At some point, one of the younger fishermen turned to me and smiled.

'Excuse me, sir,' he said in a halting Yorkshire accent. 'What's your business with the house?'

'The Chesterfield house?'

'Round here we just calls it *the house*.'

'I've been asked to come up and see Mrs Chesterfield. Although I don't know quite what she wants from me. I'm an artist and I'm assuming she wishes to buy some of my paintings.'

The fisherman nodded and looked back at his friends. It was then I noticed that both the landlady and her husband were absent from the bar, and I wondered if the men had been seeking this opportunity to engage me in conversation.

'We wish you all the best in your business, sir,' the fisherman said. 'But, please, make sure you don't spend too long in the house.'

As the man finished his sentence, the landlord strode back into the bar. He must have heard the tail end of the fisherman's warning, for he glared at the man and a heavy hush descended.

'Pay no heed to the lad,' the landlord said. 'They're a beef-headed lot that drinks in here.'

Unsure of what to do, I smiled and returned to smoking and drinking, trying not to show how perturbed I felt.

Over the course of the evening the customers departed in ones and twos, till eventually I was left alone with just an old man sitting at the table next to mine. His head was bowed heavily over a pint jar, his face filled thickly with wrinkles. He turned in my direction and we smiled at each other.

'I allow myself a single pint at the end of the day,' he said, tapping the jar in front of him. 'For beer is both medicine and nectar to me.'

'A sound view.'

'You're worried about what the lad said?' he asked, waving his pipe towards the table where the young man had been sitting.

I nodded.

'It's just their way,' he said.

'Why did he warn me not to stay in the house too long?'

The man hesitated.

'That's a very long story,' he said.

'I only have this for company,' I replied, holding up my magazine.

31

The old man paused and turned to the bar, which was empty, the landlord having gone to the rooms at the back of the building on some errand.

'Come,' the old man said, waving me towards him. 'Drink does loosen the string of my tongue.'

I took my beer and joined him at his table.

'People that go to work at the house don't come back with their minds together,' the old man said, speaking in a low voice, even though we were sitting close. 'It gets into their heads, makes 'em do things they wouldn't normally do.'

'Such as?'

'Some kill themselves. Some kill each other. Two of my childhood friends went for building jobs there decades ago. Within a year the one had murdered the other in a brawl and was dragged to the gallows screaming it was the house that made him do it. And I don't doubt it. There's a cruelty there. That's why none of the locals'll go near the place. Doesn't matter how much she pays, they're not so shuttle-headed as to take her coin. Now she has to rely on outsiders. Not that it bothers her. Old Mrs Chesterfield has enough in her to brave Satan himself.'

'There's a cruelty in the house?' I asked.

'Not just in the house. On the moors. Under the earth. In the rocks and caves. It was there long before Mrs Chesterfield came. Why d'you think she chose this place? It's a time-haunted land. When they dug the foundations, they dug right into those caves, and that's when the Marsden girls disappeared and Varano lost his wits.'

I remembered Carmichael's account of Mrs Chesterfield's history, his talk of a mad Italian architect who'd fled to England from a scandal in his home country.

'Varano was the architect?' I asked. 'Mrs Chesterfield's original architect?'

'There was only ever one.'

'And he lost his mind as well? Because he stayed too long in the house?'

'Nay, lad. Because he *built* the house. And it was only after he'd built it that he realised why he'd done so. That's what drove him mad. Him and Gosterwood both.'

'I don't understand.'

'They lost their wits because they discovered the real reason the house is being built.'

'You mean to repel ghosts?'

The old man smiled thinly.

'If she's building it to repel ghosts like people say she is, then why are the Marsden girls calling people to their deaths? Singing at night so men are drawn off the safe paths to drown in the sticking mud that fills these moors. Men who know these lands like the back of their hand. That house she's built cries at night.'

'So why is she building it?'

The old man looked at me, his eyes bright. Just as he was about to speak, we heard footsteps and turned to see that the landlord had returned, a scowl on his face.

'That'll do, Tobias Clarke!' he scolded, glaring at the old man. 'I think you've had enough to drink tonight. Best you go home and sleep it off before you speak any more foolishness.'

The old man paused, rattled by the landlord, his words, his presence. He suddenly looked chastened. He downed the last of his beer and stood up. As he opened the door, he paused and turned to me, as if to say something. Then thought better of it.

When I returned to my room I was relieved to find the door had a sturdy lock. I made use of it, then sat on the bed, my thoughts a whirl of anxious speculation.

As I tried to think it all through, I heard a dog barking outside, incessant and panicked. I rose and crossed to the window. Below my room was the pub's yard, where I spotted the dog, standing in front of a gate in the low stone wall which separated the yard from the beach beyond. It seemed to be barking at something further along, where the ground gradually sloped up before meeting the dark curve of the moor in the distance. Though from what I could see in the moonlight, the beach was completely empty, and the grey mass of the sea was calm.

After a few seconds, the rear door of the pub opened, spilling light into the yard, and the landlady stepped out. She went over to the dog and stroked him, but the dog didn't cease his agitated barking, never took his eyes off the same spot further on.

The landlady trudged over to what looked like a coal shed, opened its door and took from it a large bundle. Then she walked through the gate and out onto the beach. When she separated something from the bundle, I realised what it was she was carrying – branches cut from a yew tree. She took the first branch and jabbed it into the shingle that covered the beach, so it stood upright, rising a couple of feet into the air. She walked a few paces along and jabbed in the next branch, and so on, until she'd formed a semicircle of branches that stretched around the gate like a protective wall.

Then she returned to the barking dog, and together they watched the beach, their gazes fixed to the same spot further on. In an instant, the dog stopped barking, and their gazes moved in unison, as if they were watching something retreat along the shingle, up the slope, back to the distant moor. I strained my eyes, but could not see what they did.

And then, just for a moment, I saw something at the brow of a hillock further on – the veil of mist that hung there moved, as if disturbed by something walking through it, although the thing itself could not be seen, only the emptiness where it should have been. But as soon as I had comprehended the vision, the pale mist was rolling over, filling the void, settling, its moonlit shroud complete and motionless once more.

A few seconds passed, then the landlady turned to head back into the pub. As she did so, she happened to look up and catch my eye and I jumped away from the window, such was my angst.

I crossed my room and checked my door was fast, even though I knew I had already locked it, for a chill fear was pumping through my veins – the strange episode on the beach, the old man's stories, the fisherman's warning. It was all there. The danger had been spelled out to me. And yet I did not heed the signs.

5

The night passed without incident and early the next morning I rose, readied myself and descended to the bar. The landlord was not present, but Mrs Kell made me tea and prepared a plate of bread and cheese. She made no mention of what had happened the previous evening, though her manner was undeniably cooler.

After I finished my food I waited in the bar until I heard the noise of a carriage outside. I took my portfolio and stepped out into the shivering dawn. There was a light drizzle in the air, and the lanes were empty save for the phaeton awaiting me. The driver – a middle-aged man with bushy orange hair under a black hat – nodded at me and I hopped aboard. We started off down the path, and at the racket of the phaeton's wheels a murder of crows lifted itself off the hawthorns that stood across from the pub.

In the daylight, the buildings had lost their gloomy aspect, and the village looked almost picturesque. But within a minute we had left it behind, and were moving northwards along a narrow track that rose steeply towards the headland. When we completed our ascent, the high ground afforded us a panorama of the locality; to our right was the sea, a mass of grey waves lumbering in to shore, while in front was a wide expanse of hilly moorland, rolling pastures bounded by drystone walls, and scarps of shale and limestone.

We continued on through this landscape, taking a long, meandering route. The further we travelled the more pleasing the surroundings became, the ground covered with bracken and grasses and heathers, ablaze in their summer finery, speckling all with a rainbow of colours. Here and there light shimmered off the surface of marshes, and sedges swayed in the wind. I wondered then if the path took so many turns so as to avoid the dangerous sinking muds the old fisherman had mentioned the night before.

Eventually we descended into a narrow valley, crossed the stream that gurgled through it, then climbed the slope on its far side. When we reached its brow, the landscape on the other side came into view – a wide valley wherein a small town spread from the edge of the sea-cliffs all the way across the moor as far as the eye could see. I wondered why I had spent the night in Lunham, rather than here, which surely must have been in closer proximity to the house. The driver turned the phaeton and steered it down the hill, heading towards the town.

'Are we to make a stop?' I asked, for I had assumed we would be going straight to the house.

The driver turned to frown at me.

'A stop, sir?' he said in his thick Yorkshire accent.

'At that town down there?' I said, pointing down the hill to the buildings below us.

The driver stared at me a moment, then he smiled slyly.

'That's not a town, sir. That's the house.'

I stared at the man, surprised that he would joke with me thus. But he held my gaze and I realised he was in earnest. I turned back, straining my eyes, gazing once more into the valley below. A sense of revulsion shivered through me as I saw that the driver was right; it *was* a house. Not a grouping of separate buildings as I had initially thought, but a single, coagulated structure. Monstrous and abhorrent, it rippled haphazardly across the moor in

37

an unbroken wave. It flowed over depressions, crested hills, and ran madly all the way to the cliffs, where it disappeared in a mist of fog and sea spray that hid its full extent. It was as if some Morgana Le Fay had stitched together a blanket of roofs, walls and windows, and with a great flick of the wrist, had unfurled it onto the land.

Disbelieving my own eyes, I rose in my seat to get a better view, causing the driver to snigger, but I paid him no heed; a blade of fear was running through me, my mind stumbling.

How many rooms did it contain? How many miles of corridors? How much money had been spent on its construction? How many lives?

I shuddered, as if approaching something unholy, repugnant. But I could not look away. My eyes stayed fixed on the leviathan looming ever larger. As if in a nightmare I had the feeling I was marching towards my own damnation, and there was nothing I could do to stop it. I had an urgent desire to instruct the driver to turn the phaeton around, to take me back to Lunham, the railway station, the safety of London.

And yet, I didn't.

We continued to descend the hill, coming ever closer to the house, and I began to see more of its details – wings, extensions, annexes, buttresses, cupolas, railed widow's walks. The tangled tiers of roofs were an *omnium gatherum* of different styles: monitor, gambrel, hipped, mansard, all glued together; the windows were a similar mix: apsidal, lancet, dormer.

And then I saw that not all the house was like this. At what must have been its front, the haphazard wooden design gave way to a regular, more ordered, stone section, built in the neoclassical Palladian style that was so popular in the Georgian era. There was a well-proportioned central block, fronted by Ionic columns and a pediment, from which two long colonnaded wings extended.

Were it not for its vast size, this part of the house would have looked normal, unremarkable even, just another example of the type: Stowe House, Holkham Hall, Buckingham Palace, the British Museum.

Yet from behind this ordered facade emanated the sprawling, chaotic, wooden section, as if the frontage was just a gatehouse to the shanty town beyond, which sprouted like a growth from the otherwise regular stone segment to eat up the countryside further on. I recalled Carmichael calling the house tumorous, and I realised he was correct; it was a gluttonous tumour of a building.

The phaeton reached the bottom of the hill and turned at a right angle, winding its way round the perimeter of the estate. The house disappeared from view behind a copse, and in its absence, I began to wonder if I had really seen all that I had. Then I wondered how it was that no photographs or paintings or lithographs of the house had ever circulated, for surely it was the most singular building in existence.

When we emerged from the copse we turned so we could approach the house from the front, the driver steering the phaeton onto a long, straight avenue of elms, at the end of which lay a fountain, and beyond it, the house. From this aspect, it looked entirely normal, for the ordered stone frontage now hid the wooden sections behind, so that there was no sign of the monstrosity further on, making me wonder again if I had imagined it.

We reached the end of the avenue, rounded the fountain and came to a stop. I peered up at the huge columns towering into the sky and realised that the entire facade was made of Portland stone, and was such a fine example of classicism that I could have been standing in front of a temple in Ancient Greece or Rome, making me feel once more that there had been a dislocation in time.

39

Worse still, I knew in my bones that as I looked up at the house, the house was looking back at me.

After a few moments I became aware of the driver's presence. I turned and saw he was staring at me, wondering why I hadn't descended. I hopped out and took my portfolio from the footwell. The driver nodded and moved the phaeton on, its wheels crunching on the gravel like a wave breaking onto a shore.

I looked up at the house once more, and it was then I noticed the sculptures running along the pediment and entablature above the columns. Parthenon friezes depicting a race of savage, mythical beasts, their features so grotesque that the effect was entirely unnerving.

As I studied the images, the sound of footsteps disturbed me and I turned to see a rotund man in his late sixties approaching down the front stairs. He was smartly dressed in black, with the weather-beaten appearance of an outdoorsman. His most notable feature, however, was his missing right leg, amputated below the knee, from where a wooden peg extended beyond the ankle of his trousers.

'Mr Etherstone?' he said. 'I'm Frank Waylett. I'm the major-domo here. Good to meet you, sir.'

He had a Yorkshire accent, but not as strong as those of the fishermen in the pub. I wondered why he had used the Continental term, *major-domo*, and not the English, head butler.

'Mr Waylett,' I said, trying to regain my composure.

Waylett held out his hand. He had a firm grip and a vigorous shake.

'I trust your journey was comfortable?' he asked.

'Very much so. Thank you.'

'Good. Mrs Chesterfield is attending to some other business at present. She asked me to take you into one of the reception rooms till she is free. This way, please.'

I followed Waylett up the steps, surprised at how easily the man traversed them on his wooden leg. We reached the portico and I noticed that black crêpe and ribbons adorned the top of the front doors to symbolise mourning.

'Welcome,' Waylett said, gesturing to the interior.

I expected to step through into a grand hall, and yet, not five feet behind the front doors was a wall running parallel to them, cutting off my path. I stopped and frowned, wondering again if a joke was being played upon me. The wall, made of grey marble, rose some twenty or thirty feet into the air and stretched a similar distance lengthwise.

'A ghost door,' Waylett explained.

He held up a hand to the right, and we turned and walked with the wall to our side.

'In Asian religions there is a belief that spirits cannot turn corners,' Waylett continued. 'So their temples are built with a wall just behind the entrance to keep them out. Mrs Chesterfield is partial to the design.'

We reached the edge of the wall and stepped around it so that the full extent of the hall came into view. Like everything associated with the house, it was of gigantic proportions. The walls on either side felt as if they were miles distant, the roof dizzyingly high. It was as if I'd entered the nave of a Gothic cathedral, although the space here was not as encumbered by columns and vaults, giving a sense that the hall was delineating an immense cube of unbroken air and light.

This sense was added to by all the giant mirrors fixed to the walls. Set at odd angles, in unexpected locations, they bounced illumination and reflections around so wildly it was unclear what was an actual door or window, and what was simply the image of one captured in glass. In a few instances I thought there was a fireplace or statue placed yards up a wall, only to realise it was actually a mirror, angled so that some feature lower down was reflected higher up.

The overall effect made it hard to understand the true size of the hall, its boundaries, its lines, the location of its contents. It was almost as if I had stepped into a prism of broken glass, a kaleidoscope of a room.

'We call it the Great Hall,' Waylett smiled.

He gestured towards the far depths and we started to cross its expanse, the bang of Waylett's leg on the tiled floor echoing across its immensity. Despite the hall's colossal proportions, it was hardly furnished at all – there were a few life-size statues standing either side of some doorways in the distance, a few tapestries and paintings, but in terms of furniture, there was nothing. Neither was there anything which suggested it had a history: no heirlooms, no family portraits, no escutcheons or coats of arms. It made the place feel new, perfectly, cleanly new, as if it had sprung fully formed out of the void and settled itself onto the land as unsullied as a newborn.

As we journeyed, a few people passed the other way – two labourers, a man in a business suit, a gaggle of laughing maids with coils of rope slung over their shoulders. It was as if the house was a public space and I made the comparison yet again to a cathedral or some other opulent temple.

When we were roughly halfway through the hall, Waylett turned and headed towards the right-hand wall, in which countless archways and doors had been inset. Above them the stonework was broken by mezzanines and balconies and so many staircases it was as if a waterfall of them was cascading down from the upper storeys. Further up, in the impossibly high ceiling, a few windows had been fitted so that shafts of light cut in from above, dispelling the shadows from some parts of the space, while leaving others untouched.

As we neared the side of the hall I could see in greater detail the statues which flanked the doorways; Far Eastern and demonic, muscled men with red or green skin, holding aloft scrolls and flaming swords. Temple guardians, far from their homelands. The paintings and tapestries hung on the wall behind them were of a similar type.

Eventually we reached the opening that Waylett had been aiming for; an opening which, to my eye at least, was indistinguishable from all the others. We stepped through it into a long, dim corridor, and I was glad to be out of the disorientating vastness of the Great Hall, although here too there was a profusion of mirrors. Some of them stretched from floor to ceiling, multiplying the turns and passages, so I was never quite sure if we were turning an actual corner, or walking straight into a wall.

After a few minutes we approached an open door and Waylett paused outside it, gesturing for me to enter. I stepped into a spacious room, as sparsely decorated as the Great Hall, with just a table and two armchairs in one corner and a cabinet in another. Again there was no garniture to make the space feel lived in, no paintings or hangings or tapestries. The only points of interest were the fireplace, where a feeble fire burned, and two great windows looking out onto the grounds in front.

'A drink while you wait, sir?' Waylett asked, approaching the cabinet.

He swung open the door to reveal a set of decanters and fine crystalware. I thought the offer strange: it was still before nine in the morning.

'The house can be a little cold at first,' Waylett said, sensing my confusion. 'Visitors find a drink warms them up.'

'No, thank you.'

'Very well. If you change your mind, the drinks are in the cabinet. Mrs Chesterfield will be with you shortly.'

He crossed the room and smiled at me before stepping out, closing the door softly after him. I listened to the knock of his leg receding and shivered in the cold. Looking around I noticed one of the windows had been left slightly ajar, so I walked over to it and pulled down the sash. As I did so I noticed the scenery beyond the window and was filled with a rush of intense disorientation.

I was on an upper storey. But we had ascended no stairs. We had turned right out of the Great Hall and down a corridor and then into this room. We had encountered no staircases nor any slopes along the way, so how had we travelled up multiple floors?

I felt the chill from earlier even more strongly, despite having closed the sash. I backed away from the windows and my eyes alighted on the drinks cabinet. Succumbing to the power of suggestion, I poured myself a brandy, then dragged one of the chairs next to the fireplace and settled myself in front of it, hoping the drink might calm me and wash the confusion from my head.

I stared at the flickering flames and drank and settled into drowsiness. Just before I fell asleep, I noticed the fireplace's mantel, a carved design of intertwining poppies and asphodels, both flowers associated with death.

6

I slept fitfully, my mind prickled by images of yew trees, mirrors, bonfires, caves, the sense of someone at my shoulder.

I awoke with a jolt and wondered where I was. How long had I been asleep? I looked at the brandy tumbler in my hand and saw it was empty. I rose and put it down on the mantelpiece just as I heard footsteps approaching in the corridor outside.

The door opened and two women entered. The first I could tell was Mrs Chesterfield. She was into her seventies, but straight-backed, with a sprightliness to her step. She had milky hair and eyes to match, and was dressed in mourning attire; a dress of black Parramatta silk and cashmere, jewellery of jet, a lifted veil, a crêpe shroud of the type that well-off widows in London wore, bought from Courtaulds at great expense. All this was cut to a fussy style that had gone out of fashion when I was still a boy. Even though her veil was lifted, the weight of her clothes, and their lack of trimmings, suggested she was in first-stage mourning. But her family had died decades earlier. I thought of the crêpe and ribbons above the house's front doors, the asphodels and poppies on the fireplace. Had the house, too, been placed in mourning ever since its construction? And yet, none of the house's copious mirrors had been covered in a shroud.

'Mr Etherstone? I'm sorry to have kept you waiting. I'm Mrs Henry Chesterfield,' she said. Her voice was sharp, her enunciation brisk, her accent hard to pin down; part Lambeth, part Yorkshire, part elocution lessons.

She fixed her gaze on me and I studied her face, which was lined and creased by much sorrow. Her eyes were devoid of colour, the cataracts in them having smothered her pupils entirely, making me wonder how she had managed to stride into the room without a walking stick, for she must have been utterly blind.

'And this is my lady's maid, Miss Thornwick,' she added, stepping to the side to reveal the second woman, who was about ten years her junior, darkly complexioned and heavily disfigured, her face possessing a twisted, lopsided quality to it, as if one side was held in a painful clench, and the other side was being pulled downwards by some hellbound force. In the middle of this churning disfigurement I could discern a pair of small, incredibly dark eyes.

I nodded and turned the best smile I could on the maid. She flashed me back one of her own, stinging and mean. As her lips rose they revealed a set of teeth discoloured in the same way Oscar's had been, through regular doses of mercury.

'A pleasure to meet you both,' I said. 'No need to apologise for any delay.'

'Good,' Mrs Chesterfield said. 'We don't stand on ceremony here. I trust your journey was a comfortable one?'

'Yes, indeed. Yorkshire makes a pleasant change from London.'

'I daresay anywhere makes a pleasant change from London. I expect you're curious to see the house. Come. We'll talk as we walk.' And with that she turned and exited the room. I made to pick up my portfolio but she pre-empted me. 'You won't need your portfolio. You can leave it here.'

'My letters of reference?'

'I already know all there is to know about you.'

I followed them out and we turned a corner, heading towards

the interior of the house, Mrs Chesterfield striding along the corridor as if she was fully sighted. I wondered again how she could do so with her eyes clouded by cataracts. Did some vision still remain? Or had she committed the house's layout to memory? The notion made me think of a spider gliding along its web.

'No doubt you're wondering why I called you here,' she said. 'It will be easier to explain when we're *in situ*, if you don't mind the wait.'

'Not at all. Mr Carmichael, the man who acts as my sales agent, mentioned you saw some of my work at an auction?'

'Not I, but our local vicar, Reverend Hartington. He has a passion for these kinds of things, though not the means, so he squanders his time at art auctions in Leeds and York. Always looking and never buying. He saw one of your etchings for sale and thought it might interest me. He brought me the catalogue which contained a thumbnail facsimile. I bought the piece, and several other works, and I asked one of my secretaries to contact your agent. You may have noticed, Mr Etherstone, that your art, particularly your architectural conceits, bears many striking similarities to my own work of art.'

She waved a hand into the air to indicate the house.

I nodded and turned to look around me once more. In the short time we had been walking, the nature of the house had changed, making me wonder if we had moved from the stone-built front to the wooden sections at the rear, for the corridor we were traversing seemed less soundly made.

Eventually we reached the corridor's end and stopped. In front of us was a closed door, and nailed to the wall next to it, a cabinet. Miss Thornwick opened the cabinet, revealing a collection of oil jars, lamps, splints and matches. She took out a lamp, checked it for oil and lit the wick with a flint lighter.

'Many parts of the house have no windows and are in constant darkness,' Mrs Chesterfield explained. 'Other parts have windows, but the light that should shine through them was blocked out when we built adjoining sections. So we leave means of illumination about the place. Come.'

She nodded at Miss Thornwick, who opened the door and we stepped into a space that would have been entirely dark were it not for the oil lamp. Its light was too weak to illuminate anything more than our three figures, and the splintery, unvarnished floorboards beneath us, so I had no inkling what the rest of our surroundings looked like. The atmosphere was close, however, suggesting we were in another corridor, yet there was a chill in the air which made me think of mineshafts, tunnels, caves.

The two women strode on, side by side, and I followed as best I could, occasionally falling into the darkness outside the lamp's orb of illumination, making me realise that if my fast-moving guides abandoned me, I might never get out of this cavernous world.

'You mentioned you already knew everything there is to know about me,' I said.

'I think it prudent to make enquiries about all the people who visit my house before they do so.'

'You made enquiries?'

'I did.'

'And what did they reveal?'

'Your unsuccessful career as an artist in London, your fall from grace as a member of the aesthetic art movement, the death of your wife and child. We even uncovered the details of your birth in China and the great scandal that attended it, your return to England and your upbringing in . . . somewhere in Surrey, was it? I must say, for someone with a Chinese mother, it's not much apparent in your features. You look just like any other sallow European artist.'

As she recounted this dry summation I was struck with a sense of having my privacy violated, of having been wronged. Furthermore, she'd recounted this cherry-picked biography so emotionlessly it was almost as if she was belittling me; a sense compounded by her offhand comment about my appearance.

I was on the point of making some protest when Miss Thornwick turned around to observe me, revealing the side of her face that was scrunched into spasm. The oblique rays cast out by the lamp pitched her features into high relief, accentuating her disfigurement, making it look almost as if she was wearing a theatre mask. I couldn't be sure if she was smirking at me, but I was certain she was revelling in my discomfort.

'I might say your whole life has been a scandal,' Mrs Chesterfield mused. 'But do not vex yourself; so has mine.'

Miss Thornwick studied me for a few seconds more, then turned back around.

'May I ask whence you derive your inspiration?' Mrs Chesterfield asked. 'Do these images you commit to paper come from dreams? Do they appear fully formed in your consciousness? Or do you sit in front of a blank piece of paper and work them up in increments?'

The protests I had been forming fell from my mind at the abrupt change in topic, and it took me a moment to compose my response. I wondered if I should tell her the truth – that I suffered from brain fevers as a child, that they caused hallucinations, visions of strange structures, alien geometry, nightmares; that ever since, I had dedicated my life to capturing them on paper, to make their madness real.

'I think my artwork appears to me at first in dreams and moments of stillness,' I replied. 'Then I work up the images, applying my own sensibility until I am happy with the outcome.'

'I see.' Her tone was flat, emotionless, so I couldn't tell if my answer had pleased her or not.

She asked no further questions and we journeyed on in silence, the women striding along with surety and confidence, while I still brooded over the way Mrs Chesterfield had made enquiries of me, had violated my privacy. I thought again about how she had commented on my appearance, and wondered once more on the extent of her blindness.

At some point I noticed there were no longer floorboards beneath us, but bare soil, and again I had the sense of travelling through a mineshaft or a cave; an effect added to by the stale smell of dry, rotting wood that emanated from the walls. I thought it a good job there were no lamps or gas jets installed here, for if a fire were to start, the whole shanty town would be ablaze in seconds. Maybe this was another reason these sections were kept in constant darkness.

As we continued on I wondered how much ground we had covered – a quarter-mile? A half? And still we were encased in the dark womb of the house.

Eventually, we turned a corner and came to a stop in front of a door, its outline edged with bright light that was seeping in from its far side.

'Here we are,' Mrs Chesterfield said.

Miss Thornwick opened a cabinet fixed to the wall, similar to that of which she had made use of at the start of our passage. She extinguished the flame of the oil lamp and plunged us into darkness that would have been total were it not for the thin lines glowing about the door. I heard Miss Thornwick stow away the lamp and close the cabinet. Then she swung open the door and dazzling light poured into the corridor, burning my eyes. I stepped out into this new, blinding space and after a few seconds my vision adjusted and I saw that I was standing in a vast, windswept field.

7

'We are in the very centre of the house,' Mrs Chesterfield said. 'On all sides, in every direction, the house stretches for almost a mile.'

She raised her hands into the air and I looked about my surroundings. In the distance the house's inner walls traced a rough circle around the edge of the field. A field in the very heart of a house, with mud, moss and bracken underfoot, with tall grasses and sedges that whipped about in the wind, while up above was the broad expanse of the heavens, marbled grey with clouds.

I looked again at the distant walls, as if to assure myself they were not a mirage, and I noticed they had doors set into them at irregular intervals, making me wonder how many passages wound through the building to end up here, if the whole house was actually a maze, with this airy penetralium at its centre.

'Clara, a cigarette,' Mrs Chesterfield said, addressing her lady's maid with an informality that surprised me.

Miss Thornwick shuffled about in the layers of her dress and produced a silver case. She opened it and handed over a cigarette, then lit it with the same flint lighter she'd used to light the oil lamp earlier.

Mrs Chesterfield inhaled and seemed to relax. When I caught the smell of the smoke I realised why, for it was a scent I recognised from the aesthetic gatherings in London – the cigarette had been dipped in an opium solution, laced cloyingly with the stuff.

'I will be blunt, Mr Etherstone,' Mrs Chesterfield said. 'I am dying. I have a swelling in my brain. Two years ago the doctors gave me four months to live. I knew they were underestimating me, but I can feel it now, inside me, growing. I do not have much time left, and I cannot confound their predictions for very much longer. And so I contemplate my legacy. I've made arrangements for enough money to be put into trust to keep the house maintained eternally after my death. As long as the company exists, there will be this house, and surely the company will exist since it sells weapons of war, and there will never be an end of war. I will be laid to rest, for all eternity, here, in the centre of my house, in this space which has been reserved for my mausoleum. A mausoleum that you will build for me.'

She looked at me through the opium smoke, and an eerie smile contorted her features.

'As I have already remarked, there are many similarities between the impossible artworks you create and the house I am building. I do not believe this to be mere coincidence. Your art is the closest thing to my own that I have seen in all the long years I have wearily trodden this Earth. And so I want you to build my mausoleum and I want it to be as beguiling, confusing and impossible as anything ever dreamt up by man. One of your hellish prisons made real, a pyramid of ancient devilry. I want you to create your masterwork, Mr Etherstone.'

I frowned at her, baffled by her offer.

'Mrs Chesterfield, I am not an architect or engineer. Neither am I a sculptor. Furthermore, I make images of optical illusions, impossible things that do not exist, that *cannot* exist in reality. I'm unable to build you a real-life representation of something that is, by definition, impossible.'

'I'm not asking you to build something impossible. I'm asking you to build something that contains all the strangeness and

confusion that you can muster. And as for engineers and architects and stonemasons, I will supply them; all you need to do is
create and draw the plans. I've been searching for someone to
build my mausoleum for decades, and now, just before my end, I
stumble across you. It cannot be mere coincidence.'

I felt uneasy at her suggestion that I had arrived at the house
through the workings of providence, for it echoed my own sense
that something had been drawing me here against my will, possibly the house itself. I took her in once more, this remarkable
old woman in her widow's weeds, white-eyed, frosty-haired, her
face sunk in its sea of wrinkles, standing upright and rigid in the
centre of her spider's web.

'I want the plans ready within eight weeks,' she said. 'So that
the mausoleum can be finished before the year's end. You will be
free to design what you wish, but I will have the final say. If your
plans do not meet with my approval I will pay you your expenses
and nothing more. If I accept your plans, I will pay you a lump
sum of three thousand pounds, and an annuity of a further two
hundred a year to be paid to you semi-annually until your death.
My offer will not only give you an opportunity to create the greatest artwork of your career, it will also make you a very rich man.
All you need to do is draw up the plans, and act as an overseer of
the works until the mausoleum is completed, at which point your
payment will be released to you. In the meantime, you will be
given a room here at the house, three meals a day, and a stipend,
if you can find somewhere around here to spend it. As part of the
contract, you must attend dinner each evening, and stay in your
room each night. So . . . do you agree, Mr Etherstone?'

I am not ashamed to say that foremost in my mind was the
money she mentioned. The sheer amount of it. Enough to make
me rich, to get me out of Whitechapel, to have Rose and Thomas's
graves moved, to buy headstones for them, to allow me to spend

the rest of my days painting and drawing whatever I wanted, without need of patrons and customers, or having to trudge to editors' offices day after day, only to be refused entry because of past scandals that were not my own. I thought of paying back all the kindnesses shown to me by my landlady and my friends. Next I thought of the opportunity she offered, the means to produce an artwork that would last for centuries.

Almost against my will, I surveyed the field and imagined it filled with a mausoleum, a giant stone construction greater than any other funerary art in the country. But behind these thoughts, edging into them, were the practicalities of the thing, the impossibility of it.

'I do not believe it is possible,' I said. 'To build a mausoleum big enough to fill this space in just six months.'

'Time is a matter of money and manpower. I have both, and so I have mastery of it.'

'Mastery over time? Granted, with abundant resources you can reduce the time it takes to build, but only by so much. In the meanwhile, time shall move forward regardless.'

'Shall it? I never thought of time as moving forward, I always thought of it as falling into the past, each moment shed as soon as it's born, flung back like spray from a boat, sparks from a fire. I feel sorry for time, always dying and discarded into the feckless night.' She waved her hand through the air dismissively. 'Regardless, you simply need to provide the plans, I will organise the construction.'

'How long do I have to decide?'

'We will return to the front of the house. You have until then.'

If she said this to instil in me a sense of panic, and thereby turn the situation to her advantage, I admit she succeeded. My fears rose to the surface of my mind once more. I thought again of Carmichael's warnings, and those of the young fisherman – not to stay too long. Then I remembered Tobias Clarke, the old man in the Black

Lion who had suggested the house was being built for a reason so disturbing it had driven both Varano and Gosterwood mad.

'A question?' I asked.

She nodded.

'Why are you building this house?'

She inhaled from her cigarette and her eyes narrowed.

'Mr Etherstone, in the last fifty years, everyone I have encountered has wanted to ask that question – I've seen it in their minds as clearly as the nose on their faces – yet none of them have had the temerity to actually ask it. The last person who did was Clara here.' She gestured to Miss Thornwick. 'And that was before we even started building. Congratulations, you have endeared yourself to me further still. And you deserve an answer. But first, let me ask why *you* think I am building it?'

'I have heard rumours,' I said, deciding to continue with the policy of honesty that so seemed to please her.

'Oh? Which ones exactly? There are so many.'

'One, that your grief has peopled the world with ghosts and on the advice of a charlatan you built this house in the hopes it would protect you from them. But that the only demons you need worry about are the ones who feed off your purse-book.'

'Any others?'

'That, simply, you are mad.'

Mrs Chesterfield eyed me a moment, then that same eerie smile appeared once more on her lips.

'You are quite mistaken on both counts, Mr Etherstone. I am not building this house out of grief or out of madness. I am building it out of duty. Religious duty. As long as there are men in this world, there will be empires and war. The perpetual war our leaders promise will bring us perpetual peace. And I will supply the guns. Because it is my moral imperative to take on that sin, so as not to pass it on to the next soul and thus shirk the responsibility which divine providence has yoked to my shoulders. So I sell more guns than anyone else, and take on more sins than anyone else, and so I free other souls from bearing this burden, and bring them closer to God.'

I stared at her dumbfounded. She had created a whole theology with herself at the centre, a martyr taking on the sins of humanity, justifying industrial-scale death and violence with a saintliness that chilled me to the marrow.

'Believe it or not,' she added, as if sensing my feelings, 'we are doing God's work here.'

'And you would hire a non-believer to do God's work?' I asked, knowing even as I did so I might destroy the last chance I had of receiving the commission.

'I do not care for your opinions on God,' she said. 'You have been chosen to do this work and you will do it.'

'Chosen by whom?'

'The Almighty.'

I wondered if she meant God or herself, for it seemed that in her mind the two were the same.

'And if I refuse?'

'You will not.'

'You cannot force me to do your bidding.'

'It is not I who does the forcing, Mr Etherstone. I am simply the messenger. Do not fret, I have a feeling our collaboration will be a fruitful one. You are the first person in decades to be honest with me, and I respect you for it. Come.'

We turned and walked back through the same door, my mind in a tumult of indecision. I tried to weigh up the benefits of accepting the commission against the risks, but I could not. Partly because the risks were so intangible, partly because of my agitation, which had been heightened by the time limit she had imposed on me.

We followed another dizzying route through the house, made

a last turn, then arrived back at the Great Hall. We crossed its vastness, and approached the entrance in silence. We stopped at the ghost wall that stood in front of the doors and I thought I heard the noise of a carriage on the driveway outside. It reminded me of the accident I had witnessed back in London; the policeman appearing through the fog and shooting the Victoria's horse. Other images flooded my mind: Fitzpatrick's Boer warriors; Carmichael's skull's-head walking cane; my room in Whitechapel; Rose and Thomas's unmarked graves.

Mrs Chesterfield turned to me.

'Well, you've had time to consider. Your answer, please?'

The ticks of the clock she had set in motion boomed in my mind, unsettling my thoughts. I felt as if I was in a nightmare, drained of strength, moonstruck. I tried once more to use logic to make my decision, but the tide of emotions washing through me made it impossible. I thought about staying till the end of the year in this monstrous, desolate house. Then I thought about what awaited me back in London. Thus it seemed to become a choice between these two locations. If I refused the commission, I might escape the madness of Mrs Chesterfield's house, only to return to the madness of the slum, its poverty, its carceral despair. I was, in short, simply choosing between two forms of hell.

'Time is on the wing,' Mrs Chesterfield muttered.

She pinned me with her ghostly eyes and I felt the heavy, immortal march of the seconds. I wonder now if all her earlier talk about the power of destiny was a way of influencing me, diminishing my belief in my own free will. Or maybe it was the house tightening its grip over me already, beclouding me with fear and confusion.

An image of Rose's grave flashed once more before my eyes.

After that, all it took was a nod, and I had sealed my fate.

8

Ten minutes later Waylett was walking me to my room. He chatted to me amiably, commenting on the artwork we passed, but I barely listened, so thick were the thoughts in my head.

Eventually we arrived at an upper storey in the front part of the house where Waylett threw open a door and showed me my room. When I saw how pleasant it was, my anxiety lessened a touch. Sunlight bounded in from enormous windows along one side. The walls were hung with red damask and studded with ornate, bronze gas lamps. Persian rugs covered most of the floorboards. There was a bed and a cabinet and a wardrobe and a bureau, all of the finest quality. On the wall across from the bed was the fireplace, and in the corner, behind a folding screen, a hip bath and washstand.

As I looked around at all this, the fear of a few moments earlier lessened into near nothingness, and a sense of calm invaded me. I started to feel I had made the right decision after all, so much so that, when I thought back to my state of mind in the Great Hall, it almost seemed laughable that I could ever have considered refusing Mrs Chesterfield's offer for what awaited me in Whitechapel.

I crossed to the windows and saw we were on the house's inland side, looking out over the moors, with the coastline in the distance.

Only to the right of the view could I see the tumbledown wooden part of the house, disappearing over the closest hills.

'Your workroom, sir.'

I turned to see Waylett standing at a door, gesturing to the adjoining room. I walked over and we stepped inside. It was as large and bright as the bedroom. In its centre was a draughtsman's table and an easel. Next to them was a glass display cabinet filled with art materials; all of the highest quality by makers I could never normally afford.

'I'll leave you to settle yourself in, sir,' Waylett smiled. 'Your things are just to the side of the wardrobe. I'll be back in an hour to take you to the offices so you can sign the contracts.'

He nodded at me and exited.

I returned to the bedroom and walked over to my luggage – my valise, sketching box, the case with the cinematographic camera and rolls of film. Without my knowing it, they'd collected them from the Black Lion in the certainty that I'd stay. My portfolio, too, which I'd left in the waiting room downstairs. Was it so obvious to them I would accept their offer? Were they so sure people could be bought? Or was it, as Mrs Chesterfield said, simply fate?

I walked over to the bureau and opened its drawers. Inside I found some paper, a set of pens and a bottle of ink. Again, all were of the finest quality. I dashed off two letters: the first to my land-lady, explaining that I had accepted a commission and would not be back till January; the second to Carmichael, telling him that Mrs Chesterfield had commissioned me to design her mauso-leum, and the liberal terms offered. It was only when I was sealing the envelopes that I wondered how I could get them posted.

I still had time to kill before Waylett returned, so I crossed to the window and smoked and looked out over the shore, the hori-zon line of moorland and hill, the pale strings of smoke rising from the house's chimneys. Six months and I should leave here a rich man. All I had to do was draw up the plans for a mausoleum.

As I mulled it over, the image of Mrs Chesterfield standing in the field came back to me and I realised she hadn't actually answered my question of why she was building the house. She'd spoken only of her religious duty to fill the world with armaments, but not of why she was building the house. How had I not noticed it at the time? Thinking it over, I sensed she had deliberately evaded answering, smoothly, subtly, skilfully. It convinced me that the building of the house had nothing to do with the sins of war.

I thought once more of old Tobias Clarke in the pub, warning that Gosterwood and Varano had been driven mad by discovering the true reason for the house's construction. The ominous nature of his words seemed sharper now that I had agreed to stay. If my predecessors had lost their minds, had killed themselves, would I go the same way? Suddenly the mystery was not just a matter for idle conjecture, but linked intimately with my survival.

Waylett arrived some time later and we journeyed back through the house. With my thoughts calmer, I was able to take in something of our dizzying route: the corridors and stairs, the left and right turns.

'I fear it shall take me some time to learn my way around the house,' I said.

'If you'd like I can give you a tour. How about tomorrow morning? After breakfast?'

I smiled and nodded my agreement.

We continued on, passing through a long, straight passageway that lacked any windows or artworks on its bare, wood-panelled walls. Two mirrors had been placed at either end, which extended from floor to ceiling, from wall to wall, making the already lengthy and rectangular room appear to stretch on infinitely.

After a few more turns, we arrived at the Great Hall.

'Mrs Chesterfield's offices are on this side of the building,' Waylett said.

We crossed to the East Wing and passed into an open room filled with people working at desks, a scene so busy it reminded me of the magazine and newspaper offices I visited looking for illustration jobs. It sounds foolish to admit, but it was only then that I gained an inkling of the scale of the resources needed to run the house, the manpower, the supplies, the managerial and administrative tasks.

'We've a staff of over a hundred,' Waylett explained. 'We house and feed them all. The building work requires constant correspondence with merchants and manufacturers. But this is also where we manage Mrs Chesterfield's trust – we pay for all through the monies of the trust, and this entails a vast amount of legal and secretarial work.'

We crossed to the far wall, where a number of doors led into private offices. Waylett knocked at one of these and we stepped inside. It was a large room full of wooden filing cabinets, with a mahogany desk at the opposite end, behind which sat Mrs Chesterfield. Standing to her side were Miss Thornwick and two middle-aged men in suits.

'Mr Etherstone,' Mrs Chesterfield said. 'You found your rooms adequate?'

'More than adequate.'

One of the lawyers slid a paper folder over the desk towards me.

'Your employment contract,' Mrs Chesterfield said. 'It contains the terms we discussed previously and some additional stipulations restricting you from ever discussing the house in public once you have left it. Messrs Jones and Rhodes here are two of my solicitors; they'll be happy to explain the details. You can take the contract to the bureau over there to read, if you like.'

I walked over to the writing bureau she'd indicated and opened the folder. It contained three copies of an eight-page contract. I read through it carefully, trying to ignore the fact that I was keeping five people waiting, for I was sure this was yet another tactic designed to pressure me into signing.

The details were all as Mrs Chesterfield had mentioned, but also in there were stipulations about me staying on to oversee the completion of the mausoleum, and keeping to my room each night, and eating dinner each evening with the other residents. When Mrs Chesterfield had mentioned these conditions previously I had assumed they would be points of etiquette, not contractual obligations. I saw that failure to comply would lead to me forfeiting my payment, and I wondered how strictly the rules would be applied. What would happen if I was ill one night and could not attend dinner? Could this be used as a means of making me forfeit my entire payment? But I dismissed the fear – Mrs Chesterfield was burning through thousands of pounds a month, would she really stoop to such pettiness to avoid paying me? At the time it seemed ludicrous. Only later did I understand my mistake in brushing aside these peculiarities.

I returned to Mrs Chesterfield's desk with the contracts. She signed first, then so help me God I signed them too.

9

I whiled away the afternoon in my room, unpacking my things, reading the last of the magazine I had bought in King's Cross. Then I readied myself for dinner and a few minutes before seven there was a knock at the door. I opened it to see a maid standing in the corridor, a gaunt girl of sixteen or seventeen with a freckled face and brown hair tucked underneath her mobcap.

'Mr Etherstone, sir. I'm to guide you to the dining room.'

We made our way to the Great Hall following the same route Waylett had taken, passing through the same windowless passageway that looked as if it stretched on endlessly. I chatted with the girl and learned she was called Edith and had travelled from Scarborough just over a year ago to take up the job.

'And how are you finding it?' I asked.

'I'm very lucky to have my position,' she said in a flat, emotionless tone, as if she'd been instructed to repeat the phrase if anyone ever asked.

When we reached the Great Hall I noticed how it looked smaller in gaslight, with so much of its immensity shrouded in darkness.

We crossed to the side that led to the East Wing and Edith paused in front of one of the many doors there.

'I find it's easiest to remember the doorways by the statues, sir,' she said. 'This is the one for the dining rooms.'

She gestured to a sculpture standing on a plinth next to the door; a life-size granite carving of an Ancient Egyptian god, a tall, upright man with the head of a jackal, a staff in one hand, some kind of crucifix in the other.

Edith opened the door and we stepped down a passageway into a broad withdrawing room filled with sofas, armchairs and chaise longues. Edith bowed and slipped out and the people inside the room turned in my direction. There were five in total. The nearest to me was a slight, elderly man, wearing a vicar's collar and thin metal spectacles. He had a kindly face, a neatly trimmed moustache, and his hair was grey and closely cropped.

'Mr Etherstone?' he asked, holding out his hand. 'I'm Hartington. I'm the vicar at Heybridge, a few miles over the moor.'

He spoke in an educated voice. I approached and shook his hand.

'Let me introduce you to the others.' He gestured to a middle-aged couple standing behind him. 'Mr and Mrs Danby.'

Mr Danby was angular and bony-faced. A tall but unimposing man who would have left a fleeting impression were it not for his 'Piccadilly weepers' – side whiskers which extended from his hairline, down past his ears, all the way to his jaw. His wife was his opposite in many regards; small and round, with bulbous blue eyes and thin golden locks crimped and pulled back into a bun.

'And this is Alice, Mr and Mrs Danby's daughter. And her governess, Miss Pendle.'

Hartington gestured to the fireplace, in front of which was a girl of seven or eight years, and standing next to her, a young and attractive woman.

I said hello to them. The governess responded with a smile; the girl barely acknowledged my greeting. I wondered what they were doing there, having assumed the dinner would be formal, yet the presence of the girl and her governess suggested we would be dining *en famille*.

'I trust your journey from London was not too onerous?' Hartington asked.

'Not at all.'

'And how are you finding the house?'

'Overwhelming. But I'm getting used to it.'

'It is an overwhelming house, indeed,' said Mrs Danby. 'Not for the faint of heart.'

She had a strange, lilting accent, half-English, half-Australian, which made me wonder on her origins.

'A house of great spiritual power,' her husband added, in a nasal monotone that was unadulterated London. 'It takes much living here to become accustomed to its strength.'

'You live here?' I asked.

'We are Mrs Chesterfield's spiritual advisors.'

He swept a hand across the room, taking in himself, his wife, and the girl by the fireplace. I wondered then if since the disappearance of Gosterwood, Mrs Chesterfield's original psychic, there'd been a series of successors over the decades, of whom this mismatched couple were the latest.

'You commune with the spirits for Mrs Chesterfield?' I asked, trying not to let my disdain show.

'Not us,' Mr Danby replied. 'Our daughter, Alice. She is the one with the connection to the spirit world, and with a particular connection to Oliver Chesterfield, the babe that was so cruelly taken from Mrs Chesterfield in its infancy.'

I stared at the man, unsure how to respond, then I turned to look at his daughter again. She was a fine-looking girl, with her mother's blonde hair, but there was a sullenness in her bearing, a sadness, that made me feel sorry for her.

Just then the doors opened and Mrs Chesterfield and Miss Thornwick entered.

'Introductions have been made?' Mrs Chesterfield asked.

'They have,' Reverend Hartington replied.

'Very well, then. Let's proceed.'

The dining room was a long, rectangular space illuminated by candle-stands and a fireplace. We took our seats and my eye rested once more on the girl, and I thought how strange it was that we would be eating dinner with a child, her governess and Miss Thornwick, especially as the table appeared to be laid formally for *service à la russe*. Stranger still, I saw that even though a place had been set at the head of the table, Mrs Chesterfield sat instead on the next seat along on the right. I noticed then that two further empty places had been laid directly opposite her. I wondered if some guests were arriving late, and why one of them would be sitting at the head of the table.

The servants appeared and busied themselves at the sideboards before serving the hors d'oeuvres – a *galantine de faisan habillé* with cornichons, mustard and toasted bread – laying dishes down at all the place settings, including the three empty ones.

Mrs Chesterfield gave a nod and Hartington said grace. As he did so I studied the room once more: the stone vaulting above, the long table, the candles and shadows, the murmuring vicar – it all put me in mind of monks at a monastery, sitting down for their evening victuals. When Hartington had finished, everyone began to eat. I hesitated, wondering why no one was waiting for the missing guests to arrive.

I happened to catch Miss Pendle's eye, and sensing my confusion, she gestured for me to eat. I nodded at the empty places, and she shook her head. I smiled, feeling as if we had become co-conspirators, then I picked up my knife and cast a quick look back at the governess. She was in her middle twenties, fine-featured, with porcelain skin, bright blue eyes, and brown hair. I wondered how she had ended up in this desolate place, so distanced from the great world's movement.

'Mr Etherstone, your artwork is the most striking I have seen in many years,' Hartington said. I turned to see him smiling at me. 'When I saw it at the art market up in Leeds I knew instantly it would interest Mrs Chesterfield.'

'Then it is you I have to thank for my being here,' I said, giving the man the credit he was so clearly angling for.

'Oh, it was nothing. I'm just a lover of these things. It's my passion to browse the auctions and see what wends its way north from London and the Continent. As you can imagine, we are little served by art up here. I hoped that you might inform us of the latest developments in London's artistic circles.'

'I am, unfortunately, quite out of touch with London's artistic circles.'

'But you are a member of the aesthetic art movement, are you not? It said so in the auction catalogue I saw in Leeds.'

'I *was* a member. The movement is no more. Unfortunately.'

'Were the aesthetics not the people Oscar Wilde was involved with?' Mrs Danby asked.

'*Aesthetes*,' I corrected her. 'And yes, Oscar Wilde was part of our movement – at its head, I suppose.'

'Well, then I'm not surprised the movement is no more,' Mrs Danby said. 'How can you have a movement when its head is in prison?'

'Oscar's no longer in prison. He was released two years ago and fled to France.'

'And Britain is the better for it,' Mr Danby said. 'It's shocking that such a man could ever have occupied so prominent a place in public life.'

He made the comment blithely, as if discussing the weather, then leaned forward to shovel a forkful of food into his mouth.

I said nothing. In the years since Oscar's trial I had been subjected numerous times to similar sentiments and outrage.

'Well, it is no matter you are out of touch,' Hartington smiled sympathetically. 'We can make do with the many antiques dealers who pass through the house.'

I smiled back and took the opportunity Hartington had offered me to rejoin the discussion.

'Indeed,' I said, turning to Mrs Chesterfield, who was eating her toast in a joyless, mechanical way. 'You have quite the collection.'

'They have not been bought for their aesthetic value,' she replied, without taking her ice-pool eyes off her plate.

'You collect for some other reason?' I asked, remembering Carmichael saying she acquired religious artworks that were supposed to scare off evil spirits.

'I collect them for their spiritual power,' she said.

I nodded and wondered how she squared such beliefs with her Christianity.

'We, too, believe in the power of spiritual art,' Mrs Danby smiled.

'*Apotropaic* art,' Hartington corrected her. 'To use its formal title. Art with the magical power to ward away evil influences. Talismanic art.'

'Quite so,' Mrs Danby said. 'Artworks can and do indeed contain such power. Though I find it a shame such art is more common in the savage cultures of Africa and Asia than our own.'

'Oh, but it's not just the Africans and Asians who believe in such things,' Hartington replied. 'Gorgon heads were placed on temples in Ancient Greece and Rome for similar, protective reasons. And our own Christian churches were built with gargoyles and grotesques to scare off harmful spirits.'

'I do not recall seeing any such *grotesques* on the churches of England,' Mrs Danby said.

'We have our Protestant forebears to thank for that. The Reformation – when statues and adornments were stripped from holy buildings and destroyed. Leaving them without protection from evil, if the common wisdom is to be believed.'

'Well, perhaps there is something in *common* wisdom,' Mrs Danby replied pointedly. 'We have seen such power at work.' Here she turned and nodded at her husband, who nodded back in confirmation. 'And not just idols. All objects may possess spiritual power, for often spirits find themselves attached to the objects they had a connection to when they were alive. Many times when my daughter has held in her hand the beloved object of some passed person, the spirit finds its way to her.'

Mrs Danby gestured to the girl, who seemed not in the slightest affected by having become the topic of conversation; she continued to stare at her plate, eating the toast and galantine as unenthusiastically as Mrs Chesterfield.

'*Lacrimae rerum,*' I said.

Mrs Danby frowned.

'The tears of things,' Hartington smiled, translating the phrase for her. 'Mr Etherstone is quoting Virgil. *Sunt lacrimae rerum et mentem mortalia tangunt.* The tears of things and mortal burdens touch the mind.'

'I see,' Mrs Danby said, though she clearly didn't.

'A poetic way to express a well-known fact.' Mr Danby smiled, coming to his wife's rescue. 'For it is well known that objects contain some . . . *resonance.* Consider two knives, for example, identical in all respects, excepting that one of them was used in a murder. I can guarantee that most people, on holding the two knives and being told the sad history of one of them, would be able to deduce which one caused such a terrible event just through feeling. For the emotions of the crime persist in the object. I have seen the experiment conducted many times. Some, like my daughter, are more sensitive to these persistences than others. That is all there is to it.'

Mr Danby met his wife's eye and smiled again. Their daughter said nothing, nor moved an inch.

'Yes,' I replied. 'But the experiment is flawed. In such an instance a man through blind luck has a fifty per cent chance of picking the right knife. I wonder if the results would be the same if the deadly knife was placed in amongst ninety-nine other identical knives.'

'Indeed they would, sir,' Mr Danby said pompously. 'Indeed they would.'

'And what does your daughter have to say on the matter?' I asked.

We turned to look at the girl. Again she didn't move, her gaze staying fixed to her plate.

'My daughter finds it easier to commune with the spirits than with the living,' Mrs Danby sighed. 'You'll have to excuse her silence.'

'We take care of the earthly matters,' Mr Danby interjected. 'So Alice can concentrate on the spiritual ones. Each to their own, as it were. Each to their own.'

He chuckled and I could see that the speech was a well-worn one.

I nodded and wondered how Mrs Chesterfield had been taken in by these two haughty charlatans who had stooped so low as to coerce their own daughter into their schemes. How frequently did they force her to pretend she was one of Mrs Chesterfield's dead relatives in the seances they staged? How much did they train and practise her? I knew actors in the West End theatres where I worked who ended up exhausted after their performances, melancholy and listless. This sullen young girl had the same drained energy about her.

I looked to the head of the table and saw that Mrs Chesterfield was unmoved by the conversation, was instead staring at the empty place opposite her, as if it were occupied. A shiver ran through me as I finally realised for whom the places had been set:

her three dead relatives, whose deaths in quick succession had led to her madness.

As the revulsion ran through me, the doors opened and servants came in to whisk away the hors d'oeuvres. The three untouched plates were taken along with the rest. The soups arrived, and then all the other courses followed – fish, *relevé*, *entrée*, game, salad, sorbet, dessert, cheese, coffee. For every course the three empty places were set anew with food, and the food stayed uneaten, and then was taken away.

Eventually, the meal drew drearily to a close and at a nod from Mrs Chesterfield everyone rose.

'Well, it's time for our seance,' Mr Danby said, that self-satisfied grin on his face once more.

We bade each other goodnight and as we milled about the table, I noticed Alice, the Danbys' daughter, staring at me from across the room. I was surprised, for it was the first time I had seen her make eye contact with anyone over the course of the evening. She met my gaze forthrightly, opened her lips and mouthed a single word at me. I am no expert in such things, but it was clear what she had mimed.

Leave.

The blood in my veins ran cold. I stared at her, dumbfounded. Did she mean it as a command? A warning? A plea? It was not only the word that unsettled me, it was her manner, the look in her eye, how she'd waited till everyone else was engaged and so would not see the exchange.

She kept on staring at me until her father took her by the hand and her eyes darted to the carpet once more. They left the room, followed by Mrs Danby, Mrs Chesterfield and Miss Thornwick. Then Miss Pendle bade us goodnight so that just Reverend Hartington remained.

'It's still early,' he said. 'Shall we go to the smoking room for cigars?'

10

The smoking room was as warm and well appointed as any in a London gentlemen's club, with a roaring fire and comfortable chairs. Hartington poured us brandies and picked up a box of cigars from a sideboard. We took one each and settled in front of the fire. Away from the others, Hartington's manner was more relaxed, more assured.

'You find it a strange house, I suppose,' he said, staring into the flames. 'I've been visiting here for almost half a century and still I find it strange. I can only imagine what it must be like for someone coming to it fresh.'

'Indeed. A strange house built by a strange woman.'

He smiled without turning from the fire.

'What do you make of her?' he asked.

'Hard to say so early in our acquaintance. The only consistency I've noted is her inconsistency; sane in some respects, delusional in others; generous one moment, unyielding the next; a traditionalist somehow, but also a nonconformist.'

'A contradiction wrapped up in a paradox,' Hartington said. 'It's all done by design, I think, to shield herself. Did she commission some artwork from you?'

'She asked me to build her mausoleum.'

He turned to look at me in surprise.

'And you agreed?'

I nodded.

'You know she is dying?' I asked.

'Yes,' he replied. 'I've offered her my counsel. So far, she's rejected it.' He fell silent a moment. 'What do you have planned for the mausoleum?'

I paused at the question. In the events of the day, I had not even considered how I would actually execute the commission.

'I'm not sure.'

'One of your grotesqueries made real, perhaps? Some nightmare turned to stone?'

'I suppose.'

I wondered now if the man disapproved, if his Anglican sensibilities were offended by my artwork, by Mrs Chesterfield's house, by the Danbys and their spiritualism.

'She's paying you a pretty penny, no doubt?' he asked.

'Yes. And I feel quite the vampire for it.'

'Don't. You've seen what other flies buzz about the pot.' He gestured to wherever it was the Danbys were conducting their seance. 'At least you're providing something tangible. Something real. Something whose worth can be judged.'

'I hadn't thought of it in those terms. But when I think of all the money that's been lavished on this house. How it could have been better spent on charity for the poor, medicine, alleviating and elevating the plight of humanity. And to think I am now a part of this . . . diversion of means.'

'Mr Etherstone,' he smiled, 'if Greece had spent all its money on the needy, we would not have the Parthenon. If the Church had spent all of its money on the needy, we would not have St Peter's Basilica, St Paul's Cathedral, the Sistine Chapel ceiling. We would not have most of the world's great buildings, gardens, artworks, symphonies. You of all people should appreciate these things. They elevate every one of us. How much poorer would humanity be if we spent our spare money on the poor?'

He smiled at me again and I wondered if he'd spoken in jest. I was reminded of my uncle, also a vicar, who could twist both logic and theology to justify any cruelty.

'But is it really such a choice? Between great works and great charity?'

He shrugged. 'If artists are not to be paid for their work, then surely we're just adding them to the ranks of the poor? Do not feel guilty for having found the means to climb your way out.'

I supposed he was trying to reassure me, but all he had done was make me draw closer parallels between myself and the Danbys, who had likewise found a means to climb their way out.

'Do you believe all this spiritualism?' I asked. 'That she's building this place to protect herself from ghosts?'

'You mean that it's all been done to confuse dead soldiers?'

I nodded.

'I've heard the rumour,' he said. 'I can't say if it's true or not. Mrs Chesterfield has never revealed to me why she's building the house. And as far as I know, she's never revealed it to anyone else either. But it's a question that has often vexed me. I don't think I've ever believed she's doing it to ward off spirits; I've never got the sense that she was naive enough to actually believe in all that. But if this house is a folly, then so too is every church, monastery and cathedral in the world, for all are built on the presumption of an afterlife. And that's all this house really is, an expression of belief in life immortal, albeit a distorted one. No different in essence to those gargoyled churches I mentioned at dinner. Why should the grandeur of a cathedral be seen as normal, but not this house? Ultimately, they are no different, designed to assuage people's grief and fear of ghosts, which is really just a fear of death.'

74

I was surprised to hear such an argument from a vicar, and surprised further to hear myself make the counter-argument.

'But in these other places people can worship, rites of passage take place. There is a communal good. This place is built simply to help a single woman with her bereavement.'

'Are you so sure there is no communal good here? Are people not employed in the house? Are they not offered opportunity to put bread on their table? Does the house not cause goods and services and money to circulate through the economy, thus enriching us all?'

'I suppose in purely financial terms, you have a point,' I conceded weakly.

'Most often financial terms are the only ones that matter. Mrs Chesterfield used the very same argument to defend herself when she was brought before the madness courts.'

'She was brought before the madness courts?' I repeated, surprised.

'You didn't know? It was decades ago now; before your time, I suppose, but it was front-page news when it happened.'

I had seen reports in the press about the madness courts over the years, but never paid them much heed. Normally the cases involved some rich old man or woman whose offspring wanted to get at their wealth. By having two doctors declare the person insane, a lunacy order could be signed, the person moved to a madhouse, and their assets placed under supervision, most often the supervision of the same people who'd called in the doctors. Collusion between the doctors and the families was rife. Anyone declared mad could make an appeal to the lunacy commissioners, and an inquisition – a madness court – was held to determine if they really were insane, and if not, have their liberty, and wealth, restored.

'Her late husband's family fought tooth and nail to wrestle

back the company after it passed over to Mrs Chesterfield,' Hartington explained. 'As you can imagine, the line of inheritance didn't sit well with them. Particularly with the late husband's younger brother – a wastrel of the worst kind. He'd secured a marriage with lies about a guaranteed annuity and an interest in the business. When Mrs Chesterfield started spending the family fortune on this house, they used that as cause to have her declared insane so that the company could be put into their control. They could get no lunacy order signed, so instead they started a civil case and it was brought before the court in Chancery.'

'And they lost?'

'Indeed. Mrs Chesterfield addressed the court and gave an excellent account of herself and they found her sane.'

'She managed to convince a court she was sane despite all the evidence to the contrary?' I asked, gesturing to our surroundings.

'Oh, yes. She mounted a brilliant defence. When the brother's lawyers said building a house to honour the spirits of her dead was a sign of madness, she told them their logic would see every member of the Church locked up. When they said her project was a mad squandering of time and resources, she told them it was her hobby, and so no more meaningless and nonsensical than the knocking of golf balls across the countryside, or tennis balls back and forth across a court, or the shooting of clay pigeons, for these pastimes too serve no value except as entertainment. When the lawyers said the arms company was a concern of national interest, and its running could not be entrusted to a mere woman, she asked them if they had forgotten their very own Queen, who was running an empire and doing an excellent job of it, and if they had considered that their line of logic would see the Queen removed from her position too, and could thus be deemed treasonous. When they said her desire to constantly keep building and expanding the house was proof of insanity, she said this was no different to any business or corporation or empire, all of which for ever seek to secure themselves through constant expansion.

'For every argument the lawyers mounted to show that she was insane, she came up with a parallel, an analogy to some aspect of human activity which was just as ludicrous, but which no one ever questioned. Her defence was ultimately that *all* human activity can be considered mad and meaningless, and therefore she was no different to anyone else. The viewing gallery at the trial delighted in her, as did the journalists and columnists. She was quite the celebrity for a time.'

Hartington smiled and I smiled back awkwardly, for I had been disconcerted by his words, by the thought that all human activity could be considered mad. For ever since childhood I had been assailed by this very same fear, that we were all involved in a kind of collective madness, nothing more than a ship of fools set adrift through the universe, clinging to itself in the emptiness. And now I had come to the house of a woman who had publicly professed to believing the same.

'I supposed it helped her that she knows how to present herself as sane,' Hartington said. 'Ruthlessly sane. This building project of hers is one of the greatest feats of private engineering ever undertaken; look how successfully she's managed it, how, since the court case, she's suppressed any mention of her house in the press, stopped any photographs from circulating, how expertly she warded off decades of subsequent lawsuits from her dead husband's family. These aren't things that can be achieved by a lunatic.'

'Maybe she's simply suffering from monomania as the medical books define it; sane in all respects but one,' I suggested. 'Look at our dear old Queen. Completely rational except when it comes to the death of her husband, and there she acts with complete unreason and observes the strangest of ceremonies in his memory.'

'Possibly,' Hartington grunted. 'You know, before I took up my position here, in my distant youth, I was a missionary. Posted to Asia and then to Africa. It meant I encountered a lot of beliefs about madness. Beliefs which made more sense than our own Western views. I met tribes in Polynesia who believed madness was a predator, a hunter that stalked its prey in the dark, that set traps in out-of-the-way places. In Indochina there was a belief that madness was infectious and communicable like a physical disease. That it could pass from one person to the next till a whole village, a whole nation, could go mad. It may sound ridiculous but look at the hysteria that builds up in a country before a war. The fever of it, the way it spreads. Look at what happens in this very house. I have no doubt that if a sane man was put into an asylum for long enough, he would catch the madness of his fellow patients.

'But perhaps the beliefs that most made sense to me were those I encountered in Western Africa. There they treat madness as nothing more than an aspect of character. The mad are allowed to take their place in society and act in it as any other sane person so long as they cause no damage. They are not shunned, nor seg-regated, nor locked away, nor is any attempt made to cure them. Rather it is the society that must make room for them, and they all seem happy with the arrangement. If madness is simply what falls outside the social mind, then why not expand the social mind to encompass it? It certainly seems more pragmatic, and humane, than our own approach.'

He shrugged at me, then rose and refreshed our drinks.

We continued talking till long after our cigars were finished. At some point we checked the time and realised we should retire. Hartington rang the bell and asked for his carriage to be brought around.

'If you want to get out of the house,' he said, 'the walk to

78

Heybridge is a pleasant one. And if you need any diversions –
books or magazines – my library is well stocked, and the subjects
somewhat broader than those available here.'

'Thank you. I'm sure I'll take you up on that offer.'

We spoke some more till a servant came to let him know that
his carriage was waiting, and he bade me goodnight.

When he had gone there was a knock at the door and Edith
appeared.

'Mr Etherstone, sir. I'm here to take you back to your room,'
she said.

I noticed she looked worried, apprehensive.

'Is everything all right, Edith?'

'Yes, sir. It's just . . . It'd be best if you returned to your room
as soon as possible.'

'Why?'

She hesitated, taking time to formulate her response.

'It's . . . not best to be about the house at night, sir. Alone.'

'But, why ever not?'

Again she hesitated before replying.

'It's the house, sir. It doesn't like people being about at night.'

11

I was so surprised by Edith's words, I merely nodded and let her lead me back to my room, which she did with a quick, purposeful stride. It took me a few seconds to fully take in what she'd said, and then to question her on it.

'Edith, what did you mean about the house not wanting people about at night?'

Her demeanour stiffened.

'It was nothing, sir. Please.'

'You're scared of the house, aren't you?'

She paused, turned to look at me and nodded.

'Yes, sir,' she admitted.

'And you only work here because you must.'

She nodded again.

'I know your plight,' I said. 'I, too, am only here because I cannot find other work.'

She frowned at me, not quite believing this.

'Sir, it's just . . . please do just stay in your room at night.'

'I might find that difficult. I sleepwalk.'

Her breath caught and she grew pale to her lips. She stopped and turned to stare at me.

'Please, sir,' she implored. 'Lock your door before you go to bed. Please.'

I studied her and thought that she might be trembling.

'I'll be certain to.'

She continued to stare at me for a few more seconds, then nodded and we carried on with our journey.

When I entered my room I locked the door as she had bidden me. I turned up the gas lamps and wondered what I should do with the rest of the evening. I picked up my cigarettes and crossed to the window seat, sat and smoked, watching a storm approach over the moors. My mind was awhirl with the day's events. I thought of Mrs Chesterfield seated at the dining table, the coterie of queer characters she'd surrounded herself with. She reminded me of Oscar holding court back in London, who likewise surrounded himself with peculiar types. The parallel highlighted Mrs Chesterfield's decadence, and I wondered if she was not, in her own way, the ultimate aesthete.

As I mulled it over, the wind across the moor picked up, heralding the approaching storm, making the house groan and strain, as if it were a great wooden beast stretching from a sleep. Soon rain was clattering down and lightning flashed and for an instant I thought I saw something moving in its illumination, something out there, on the moor.

But when the lightning's blaze faded from my vision, all was as it should have been – the landscape was empty, the beach deserted, the house lay still. The only movement was the rain and the trees shaking in the wind. A few seconds later I heard booms of thunder rolling down the moor.

Then a second round of lightning filled the heavens and in its momentary flash I had the sense of shadows moving, of something approaching with the storm, a presence.

But before I could make anything out, the lightning faded again and the landscape was empty once more. As quiet as a tomb.

Had I imagined it? Had my eyes been fooled by the alternating light and dark? Or was there really something out there, writhing in the storm light?

I waited for further lightning, but none came, and eventually the storm swept itself out to sea and the skies cleared. The moon shone through a film of cloud. The ground gleamed wet with the rain. Sheep on distant hill farms bleated.

Whatever had moved out there, moved no more.

12

I awoke the next morning with a stinging headache, the muscles in my face clenched, my jaw aching from what must have been the grinding of my teeth. Memories of a dream flickered through my mind, fading as soon as I became aware of them; visions of a horde, a hellish army, a trauma that filled me with panic.

Here I was, not twenty-four hours since I had arrived in the house and I was already waking up pained and dazed and agitated. I realised how careful I would have to be if I was to survive the next few months, complete my commission, and leave with my fortune and my wits intact.

I crossed to the washstand and splashed cold water on my face then went over to the window. All was serene. The morning sunshine gleamed across fields of dew and there was barely a whisper of wind, leaving undisturbed the lines of smoke rising from the house's chimneys.

There was a knock at the door and I opened it to see Edith standing outside.

'Sorry to bother you, sir. It's past nine and we were wondering if you would still want breakfast.'

I had to make the unfortunate girl wait as I readied myself, then we journeyed to the breakfast room.

'Did you get back to your room in good time last night?' I asked.

'Yes, sir. Thank you. And yourself, sir, did you manage to get some sleep?'

'A little.'

'I'm glad to hear it, sir. Many guests find their first night in the house fraught.'

We turned into the East Wing and went through into the breakfast room, which was empty, presumably because the other residents had already eaten.

'I'll leave you alone to have your breakfast, sir. But Mr Waylett said I should take you to him when you are done.'

I remembered the major-domo had promised to give me a tour of the house. I thanked the girl and she left, then I walked over to the buffet laid out on a long sideboard and heaped a plate with scrambled eggs and kippers and poured myself a pot of tea from a samovar. I sat by the windows, which looked out over the cliffs, and as I ate, I watched the blue sheet of the sea, its thin white embroidery. In the distance packet boats and fishing trawlers traversed the pale horizon, their sails shimmering, their passage smooth.

Losing myself in the view, I pondered my commission; how would I go about designing a mausoleum? How would I do it in such a brief space of time? The speculation was rimmed with anxiety that I might fail, that I might be asked to leave the house, that I'd return to London as poor as I had been when I left.

I needed some inspiration to come up with a design, and I wondered, looking out over the calming sea, if it would most likely come from the local topography, the natural environment in which the house was situated. I decided therefore to go for a walk around the surrounding countryside as soon as I could, hoping something might enthuse me, stir my imagination, spark an idea.

*

After a quarter of an hour Edith returned and led me to Waylett's office. I knocked and he bade me enter.

'Mr Etherstone, sir,' he smiled, rising from his seat. 'Good morning.'

'Good morning, Mr Waylett.'

I took a seat at his desk and looked around. His office had the air of an overworked lawyer's chambers in Lincoln's Inn – cramped and messy, the filing cabinets bloated, piled high with ribbon-bound sheaves of paper, every surface dusted with disorderliness.

He gestured to some architectural drawings laid out on his desk.

'Now, before our tour, I'd like to show you these. Plans of the house. The early part, at least. We stopped trying to keep schematics years ago as the house is constantly changing, with new sections being added and others falling into disrepair, and others still being renovated. To keep a map of the current state would be as much work as actually building the thing, so at some point we let the house be its own map. But this is how it looked many years ago. The front sections are the same.'

The plans were excellently drawn and clearly the work of a master architect.

'Who made these?' I asked.

'Signor Varano. Francisco Varano. He was the Italian gentleman who first built the house. He's responsible for the main section: the two wings, the Great Hall, all the stone parts at the front.'

I nodded. The architect who had lost his mind and killed himself. But the drawings were not the work of a madman. Far from it, they displayed a precision and elegance that was anything but.

I studied them more closely and saw the house – even the old version – was larger than I'd imagined. I had originally thought it was five or six storeys high, but when I flicked through the sheets, I saw that there were elevations of at least seven different storeys, not including the various basement levels. I wondered how it was possible for the house to have sturdy foundations when there was so much emptiness beneath it. I remembered Tobias Clarke mentioning caves under the moor. Did the house burrow into them? Were its vaults part of some ancient, natural formation in the rock?

'The key to finding your way around is the Great Hall,' Waylett said, tapping the plan where a giant empty rectangle indicated the hall's location. 'All the corridors in all the wings lead back to the Great Hall eventually. To get from one wing to the other, from the front of the house to the back, from the sea-front to the moor-front, slice your journey in half by returning to the Great Hall. Here, I took the liberty.'

He passed me a stack of cards.

'These are walking instructions,' he said. 'There's one to get you from your bedroom to the Great Hall. Then there are others to get you from the Great Hall to the dining rooms, to the offices, and lastly, to the clearing at the centre of the house where you'll be building the mausoleum.'

I looked at the cards and saw the instructions had been written in a clear, strong hand:

Bedroom to Great Hall

Turn L. out of bedroom door, in corridor turn 3rd R, at 2nd stairs go down 2 flights, at bottom turn L.

'If you turn the card over you can see the journey in reverse,' he said.

I flipped the card over and saw a journey titled *Great Hall to Bedroom*.

'I find orientation is best from the Great Hall,' Waylett said.

86

'Perhaps you could use the cards on our walk there, see if you can navigate yourself?'

'That's an excellent idea.'

I flicked through them till I found the one for *Offices to Great Hall*, and we set off.

It was easy to follow the instructions and I guessed this means of introducing newcomers to the house was an old one, refined over many years.

'You have worked in the house long?' I asked.

'Decades, sir.'

'Are you local?'

'Aye. From Heybridge originally. I've always lived in these parts save for my time in the navy. That's where I picked this up,' he gestured to his wooden leg. 'Nothing so interesting as a shark attack or a battle with pirates, before you ask. Just a mundane accident in Barbados. A piece of cargo not rigged right fell from a height and crushed it.'

'So you made your way back home and took a job at the house?'

He nodded. 'In all those years of travelling around the world I've never seen a place as beautiful as the moors. Have you been here before?'

'It's my first time in Yorkshire.'

'Ah, then you've only seen them in these summer months. But it's a landscape that takes time to know, for its beauty is in seeing it change. In winter it's laid over in white like it's been covered in a great altar-cloth, and in autumn it flushes with colour and warmth like the cheek of a maiden. In spring there's a rainbow of plants everywhere you look and every stream murmurs with the trickle of snowmelt. And the skies – their colours shift with the weather, blues, pinks, oranges, purples, like an artist mixing his paints.'

I was surprised by his keen wit and feeling for the landscape

87

and found his passion so infectious I couldn't help but feel a growing fondness for the man.

When we reached the Great Hall Waylett led me to its centre. We turned so that the entrance and its ghost wall were at our back, and the interior of the house was in front of us.

'To our left is the West Wing,' Waylett said. 'Where the bedrooms are. To our right is the East Wing, where the offices are, as well as the dining rooms, library, observatory and the seance room. Straight ahead is the rear section of the house, the centre, the clearing for the mausoleum. The passages that lead there are many and they cross one another, thereby multiplying the routes. I'm not sure how many miles of corridor we have. Shall we continue on with the East Wing?'

I nodded and he led me through it, explaining the layout with the ease of a practised tour guide, giving me the sense once more that this was a well-worn process. As we passed from room to room I noticed how every one of them seemed to be singular and disconnected from the whole, provoking a state of constant flux and unfamiliarity. This was added to by the disjointed nature of the rooms themselves; if one drew a line from the floor, it made the angle of the ceiling seem off. If one drew a line from the ceiling, the floor seemed off. The same was true when trying to square one wall against its counterparts; the angles were all ever so minutely askew, the elements misaligned, so that the rooms seemed to get taller then shorter, wider then narrower, the odd geometry causing a sort of dizziness. The angled mirrors placed everywhere added to this sense of disorientation, of the house not being quite solid, of being ever so slightly *wrong*.

I am well aware how vague a term that is, but there's no other way to describe it. At least not in English. The Germans have a word, *unheimlich*, often mistranslated as 'uncanny', whose idiomatic meaning is perhaps more expressive – *un-homely*. Maybe this

88

is the best way to describe the house – the opposite of what a home should be, the opposite feeling of warmth and comfort and ease that a home provides. There was something malign to it.

After the East Wing, we toured the West Wing, and then returned to the Great Hall so as to go from there to the site reserved for the mausoleum. As we journeyed we passed a constant stream of people: maids, labourers and clerks; and yet still I got a sense of emptiness, of *perverse* emptiness. The endless passageways and chambers had not been built for any family to live in, nor for any business to be conducted, except the business of maintaining the house itself. The place had been built simply to be, to exist. A house constructed for its own sake. Looking back I wonder now if this was why the house seemed to have a presence, a personality, a malevolence to it.

We journeyed on, moving ever onwards into the heart of the house. As we did so I noticed how the section we were in was badly decaying; the floorboards warped, the plaster falling off the walls in chunks. The beams which held up the roof were bending and straining under its weight. In some sections extra supports had been installed to buttress them, but still I felt that all it would take was some heavy snowfall and the whole edifice might give way.

Waylett must have sensed the concern with which I was studying the surroundings, for when he next spoke it was to explain the dilapidation.

'Our focus is on adding to the house. Constantly adding. This means that entire sections are disregarded as soon as they're finished. We do our best to maintain them, but inevitably, large portions fall into disrepair. The east side of the house, that which overlooks the sea, is the worst for damage.'

We arrived at a door next to which was a cabinet filled with means of illumination. I could not be sure if it was the same spot

I had been taken to the previous day, but Waylett did as Miss Thornwick had done, availing himself of an oil lamp and lighting it before we stepped through into the sheer and utter darkness beyond.

This cavernous part of the journey seemed much shorter this time, and I wondered if Waylett had taken me on a quicker route, perhaps along the house's seaward side. My suspicion was confirmed as we travelled, for while the passages I had walked through the day before had seemed dry, here they seemed damp, cloying and mouldy; with a ceaseless dripping from the roof, and a stagnant smell so strong it was as if the place had been under-water for centuries.

Eventually Waylett threw open a door and we stepped out into the field where the mausoleum would be built. After the close-ness of the passageways, the sky seemed even more majestic and bright.

I stopped and studied the emptiness around us, then looked into the distance, at the hills all smothered by the house's carpet of tangled roofs. I wondered again *why* it had been built. Because of one woman's madness? As a fortress against ghosts? I felt sure that such a huge, complex structure could not have arisen from something so base as a fear of ghosts. Was it simply that Mrs Chesterfield had turned grief into a shape? Into a wasteland of corridors? I thought once more of Tobias Clarke telling me the house had been built for a reason so diabolical it drove its own architect mad.

What could it possibly be?

13

We returned to the Great Hall shortly thereafter and parted company. I used the cards to navigate back to my room, where I gathered together my sketching book, pencils, brushes, bottle of water and a travelling box of watercolours, and put them in my knapsack. Then, using the cards once more, I went back to the Great Hall.

When I rounded the ghost wall and stepped outside I saw the sun was high and there was a light breeze in the air. I took a northward route from the house, up a hill which afforded me a wonderful view of the scenery beyond. The long expanse of moor stretched from the sea in the east to the horizon in the west. The land itself was a rolling patchwork of heath, marsh and pastures speckled with sheep. Elsewhere escarpments gouged their way through meadows of gorse and bracken, speckling them with chalk whites and shale greys. Drystone walls wove over hills, and in the lower valleys, blackbirds and robins flitted around birches, ashes and oaks.

In short, everywhere I looked there was a work of art, a landscape worthy of painting, for to capture even a fraction of the beauty would have been beauty enough. I stopped every quarter of an hour or so to sketch some aspect of the scenery – from the pale hills, to the drystone walls, to the minutiae of the flora which lined my path.

Thankfully there was no cold in the air to numb my fingers, nor was there rain to blot my paper, nor a strong wind blowing insects, pollen and leaves onto the freshly laid paint. For being able to sketch well *en plein air* requires all these conditions to be met, and more. Perhaps one reason why the practice has a much longer history in southern France than it does in Britain.

A couple of hours into my explorations I spotted a hill a quarter-mile or so off from the path. Atop it was a ring of standing stones in a formation similar to that at Stonehenge, though only a handful of them were still upright; the rest had fallen onto the grass, one on top of the other, like a circle of toppled dominos, or steps rising and going back down to their start. Similar in their way to an impossible staircase motif I had used in a number of my paintings. I wondered if this might be the inspiration I had been looking for, if I could use the conceit as the basis for my mausoleum design.

Since it was not too great a detour, I decided to get closer so as to make sketches. Wary of the warnings I had heard about sticking mud, I didn't leave the main path till I found a small trail that wended its way towards the hill.

It was only after I had traversed most of the trail that I saw it ended some distance before the foot of the hill, and that the gap between the two was taken up by a broad, marshy depression ringed with towering fen-sedge and bog asphodels, and filled, surely, with sticking mud, too. As I rued my luck the wind picked up, rustling the grasses. Then another sound rose and fell with the wind that utterly entranced me. It was a mournful sound, somewhere between a moan, a wail and a whistle, rendered in that eerie borderland between a human voice and the vibration of an object.

I looked around for the source and realised it was coming from the foot of the hill. On the other side of the marshy expanse was a small opening, half hidden behind large rocks, that looked like the entrance to a cave or a long-abandoned mine. The wind, passing by this aperture, made a vibration which was causing the sound to rise up.

I stood for a few moments, listening to it as if to a hymn being sung by somebody inside the cave, calling me in. I realised then that the standing stones on the hill above could not be a coincidence, and I wondered if the ancient people who raised the stones did so because of the sound, to worship it somehow.

Minutes passed by in the soft, rich contemplation of the music, until I had the thought to sketch this place, for there was a melancholy beauty to the spot – the marsh water, the cave, the swaying grasses, all pale greens and greys, speckled with the bold yellow flowers of the bog asphodels.

I reached behind me to take my knapsack from my back and it was only then that I realised with a shock that I was no longer standing at the end of the path, but some ten yards further forward, well into the marshy ground. While I had been listening to the whistle of the wind, I must have walked forwards without realising it.

I looked down and saw one of my feet was sinking into the mire. I felt the chill of mud and water soaking through the leather of my shoe, the suction of the bog pulling me into the depths below. In a panic I prayed my other leg was still on firm ground and put my weight on it, pushing myself backwards.

But even as I succeeded in freeing my half-sunken leg, the one I had pivoted on plunged further into the morass, unbalancing me, causing me to fall. I reached out a hand as I hit the ground and the cold mud soaked me along one flank. The hand I had put out to arrest my fall disappeared into the mud, too, and a terror filled me as I realised I was being sucked in. It felt as if something was drawing me down into the black earth, dragging me to its bosom.

I rolled onto my front, and pulled my leg and arm from the mud, and with no extremity protruding into the marsh, I somehow managed to stay stationary on its surface without sinking further. Looking behind me, I saw a patch of what seemed like firmer ground. I reached out a hand and grabbed hold of a clump of mossy earth there. I hoisted myself upwards, praying it would hold firm.

It did. I pulled myself over to it, rose, and stumbled backwards.

I collapsed onto the path and breathed a sigh of relief, even as my heart thumped. When the palpitations subsided I sat up and looked around as if having woken from a dream. Were it not for the urge I'd had to sketch the surroundings, I might not have noticed the danger before it was too late. I looked again at the marsh and could no longer see in it the melancholy beauty that had previously been in evidence. Now the sight of it inspired nothing but a depression of spirits; a drab, mean anxiety.

I rose, eager to get away from the place. Agitated, cold and half soaked, I turned and began the long journey to the house, brooding not just over the incident, but also over my failure to find any inspiration for the mausoleum.

Eventually I climbed the last of the hills and the house came into view to the south, its spider's web of timber and stone like an empty, decaying town tumbling into the sea. I thought of Coleridge and the opening lines of 'Kubla Khan' and once more the whole thing seemed like the mad folly of some ancient despot. I continued on, walking around the house, making for its front.

As I reached the avenue of elms, the stone section loomed ever larger, and I noticed once again the sculptures running along its top, depicting an army of snapping, snarling demons. I marvelled once more at the artistry, at the dark and grotesque sensibility that seemed so in tune with my own. I felt then that I had seen the images somewhere before, in a dream or a long-forgotten book. I turned back the pages of my memory, trying to recall where – in Doré's engravings of *Paradise Lost*? In Goya's *The Disasters of War*? In one of Bosch or Bruegel's hellscapes? Perhaps even in one of the fire-and-brimstone religious pamphlets my uncle used to show me when I was a child?

I passed by underneath the sculptures with a pressing sense of failure; worried that I might never find a spark of inspiration for the mausoleum and that I would fail at this very first hurdle.

I stopped in the Great Hall and pulled Waylett's cards from my pocket, searching for the one that would lead me back to my room. As I flipped through them I came to one marked *Great Hall to Library*. I paused and stared at the card and a flimsy hope arose in me that after my failure this morning, I might find some inspiration in the library instead.

14

I used Waylett's cards to return to my room, where I changed into dry clothes and shoes, then used the cards again to navigate my way to the library. When I stepped inside I saw it was as well furnished and welcoming as the smoking room. In amongst the bookcases and cabinets were sofas and reading chairs and a pair of writing desks. A fire had been lit and its glow lent the place further warmth.

I browsed the bookcases and was surprised to see it was indeed a well-stocked library, with books and bound volumes of newspapers and magazines on the most varied of subjects: history, politics, philosophy, natural history, theology, art. There were also plenty of tomes on spiritual and psychic topics: *There Is No Death*, *The Spirit World*, *Materialised Apparitions*, *The Night Side of Nature*. Even the bound magazine anthologies were full of similar titles: *Borderland*, *Spiritual Notes*, *Daybreak*, *The Medium*.

Did Mrs Chesterfield actually read these anthologies? Or were they here for another reason?

When I sifted through the art books I found a collection of Doré's prints, another of Goya's, a copy of Fuseli's lectures to the Royal Academy, the most beautiful collected edition of Blake's illuminated books. I put them in a pile on a side table and wondered what else I might avail myself of.

Further along I happened upon a collection of travel journals, some from recent decades, others from the previous century. I flicked through them and saw they contained detailed descriptions of religious buildings the various authors had encountered in Africa, Arabia and Asia, buildings constructed so as to ward off evil spirits. Along with the descriptions were topographical pictures, plans, elevations, details of the buildings' supposed geomantic effects. In a few of the books were drawings of ancient Chinese temples in Chang'an that employed the same ghost wall behind their entrances as I'd seen here.

I put together a small selection of them, thinking that I might employ some of their motifs in the mausoleum, then I took them to one of the armchairs by the fire, sank into it, and began studying them in more detail. As I did so, the door opened and Miss Pendle, the governess, entered. Not noticing me, she strode over to one of the bookcases, returned a book she had in hand and took another from the shelf.

When she turned to approach the sofas, she saw me for the first time and seemed taken aback.

'Mr Etherstone,' she said.

'Miss Pendle. I'm sorry to have startled you.'

'No, please. I'm normally quite alone in the library so I . . . It's my own terrible nerves. Please,' she smiled.

She had said so little at dinner the previous evening it was only now that I noticed her Scottish accent, softened by some education, but not entirely erased.

'I just came in looking for some art books,' I explained. 'Please, feel free.'

I gestured to the sofa that she had been making for before she saw me.

She smiled again and sat and we looked each other over. In those warm surroundings she seemed even more attractive than she had the night before. Slender and pale, with brown hair and sparkling blue eyes.

'I come here each afternoon,' she said. 'I always have a couple of hours free as it's when Mr and Mrs Danby instruct Alice on their own.'

I nodded, wondering if they used the time to train and rehearse the girl for their seances.

'What are you reading?' I asked.

'Ruskin,' she said. 'It's not my usual fare but I've already made my way through all the library's fiction. It's a well-stocked library, but not for novels, and those it does have are all sensation novels from thirty years ago.'

'And you don't enjoy them?'

'Not very. They all seem to be based around the idea that readers enjoy heroines being tortured. It's quite sad that many of the same books are written by women.'

'I agree. A friend of mine once said that in modern literature, women are either angels or monsters.'

She frowned. 'That was Oscar Wilde, was it not?'

I nodded, surprised that she had placed the quote.

'It was mentioned at dinner last night that you were in the aesthetic art movement together,' she said.

I had all but forgotten that we had discussed it the previous evening. I nodded again and Miss Pendle smiled at me.

'I must be honest,' she said. 'I expected an aesthete from London to be a little more outlandish.'

'Outlandish how?' I smiled back.

'I'm not sure. Long hair like Oscar Wilde, Middle Eastern robes like Holman Hunt, maybe a velvet jacket like Swinburne. A green carnation?'

I thought of the odd flowers Oscar and a few of the others had worn, dipped in malachite to give them their colour. I assumed she did not know what they signified, so made no comment on them.

'Well, I'm sorry to disappoint you with my normality,' I said.

'Not at all. It's something of a relief in this house.'

She said it light-heartedly but something more meaningful underpinned her remark.

'How long have you been here?' I asked.

'A little over a year.'

'And you worked for the Danbys before they arrived?'

'Oh, no. They came here a year and a half ago, with a German governess. She left after six months, complaining of her health. I was hired via an agency in Leeds to be her replacement.'

I nodded and wondered if the German governess had succumbed to the house's influence.

'You enjoy it here?' I asked.

'It's as good a place as any. Though rather lonely. There's not much chance of meeting people one can talk to.'

'And yet you stay on?'

She hesitated before replying.

'Yes,' she said eventually. 'I stay on.'

She said it in such a mournful way I got the sense there was something keeping her in the house, some bitter reason she didn't want to reveal.

'And where are you from originally?' I asked.

'Edinburgh. Although I was born in Elgin. My father died before my birth and my mother moved me south to stay with relatives. From there I came to Leeds through a long series of mundane events too dreary to bore you with.'

'My father died before I was born, too.'

'Oh, I'm sorry,' she said, studying me with a compassionate look.

'That's quite all right. You don't miss what you've never had,' I lied.

Our conversation returned to the book she was reading, then moved on to Ruskin himself, then to Shaw and Morris and other freethinkers and nonconformists. She was well versed in current affairs and progressive politics, and it took me by surprise, not only because of her gender and station, but also on account of how far removed she was from the world in this godforsaken, wild corner of the country. I wondered if she'd had a liberal upbringing in Edinburgh which had guided her in such matters.

We spoke of all the organisations working to dismantle one part or other of the established order: the National Secular Society, the Rational Dress Society, the Birth Control and Free Union Movements. We spoke of how the 'new' had been promoted in so many different ways – the 'New Unionism', the 'New Woman', the 'New Journalism', the 'New Hedonism', the 'New Aestheticism'. We moved on to socialism and the various types that jostled with one another – Libertarian, Fabian, Christian, Darwinian.

'Let's not talk of Darwin,' she said. 'It's been forty years since he published his book and still all one hears are arguments that pit science against religion. I wonder when people will ever grow tired of it.'

We talked instead about Bradlaugh, the *National Reformer*, the *Freethinker*.

The conversation rolled on and we soon dispensed with formalities and called each other by our Christian names.

At one point she asked the hour and I checked my watch and realised we had not left ourselves much time to get ready for dinner. The thought of returning to my room made me think of the walk back with Edith the night before. I mentioned the girl's fearful warnings, expecting Sarah to make light of them, but was surprised to see her demeanour turn solemn.

'Many of the staff think it's dangerous to be about the house at night,' she said. 'When I first arrived, three different servants warned me about it.'

'What did they say?'

'That strange things happen at night.'

'Such as?'

She paused before replying, as if temporarily overcome by some irresolution.

'They say that the house changes in the darkness. Reveals itself. Doors which open onto walls in the daytime, open to reveal hidden rooms at night. You know that some parts in the middle of the house have no means of entry or exit? They used to have doors until some annexe or extension was built next to them which cut them off and so they became dead spaces. Empty and lifeless. Well, the staff say that at night, the house shifts so those rooms become accessible. But if you wander into them, you might be trapped there for ever. It's a strong belief that's taken hold. When the maids are tasked with cleaning those dark, inner sections, they take coils of rope with them so they can retrace their steps, like Theseus in the Labyrinth.'

'And you believe all this?'

'No. But the staff do. They say bodies have been found. In the mornings people have been discovered in the middle of vast rooms, as if they fell to their death from a staircase or balcony that's no longer there. As if they walked out into thin air. Apparently the most dangerous time of all is on stormy nights, when there's lightning in the sky. They say that's when the dead soldiers who seek Mrs Chesterfield can be most easily seen, rattling the doors, trying to get in. And were it not for the strange nature of the house, they would succeed.'

A wave of apprehension rushed through me as I remembered the lightning storm the previous night, when I thought I sensed something crossing the moor.

'They're just maids' stories,' Sarah said. 'Silly little ghost stories. But for all that they're superstitions, it's hard not to believe when everybody around one does.'

'I've read somewhere that ghost stories serve two opposite purposes at once,' I replied, trying to recover myself. 'They scare us with the supernatural, and they reassure us with the promise of life after death.'

She considered this a moment before speaking.

'In that case, the real horror is not the ghost story, it's why we tell the story in the first place.'

15

Dinner passed even more interminably than the night before as Hartington didn't join us. I tried to strike up a conversation with Sarah, but she seemed constrained by the presence of the others – whether the Danbys or Mrs Chesterfield, I could not say.

When the meal was over I retired to my room, and flicked through the stack of books I'd brought back with me from the library. But I was feeling too weary, so soon went to bed. I fell asleep quickly, into a slumber disturbed by dreams of the future mausoleum, seen in fragments, in glimpses; sculptures of a race of mythical creatures, war-like and abyssal, adorning some foreign, devilish temple, which itself was constructed like an impossible object, only making sense as one moved around it, as parts of it flickered in and out of existence.

When I awoke the next morning I rushed into the studio adjoining my room to try to sketch these images. But as soon as I had a pencil in hand, they receded from my mind, scurrying away as I tried to shine the light of my consciousness on them.

It was only then, as I stared at the blank paper, that I realised whence the dreams had come – the sculptures adorning the front of the house, merged with the barbarous, geomantic temples in the travel journals, merged again with Sarah's maids' tales of rooms drifting in and out of reality. All had combined into a single great pool of darkness which had filled my mind while I slept.

Suddenly I was assailed by a flash of inspiration – the sculptures could form the basis for the mausoleum. By adorning it with similar sculptures, it could echo the house's exterior, so that the house would contain a smaller, mausolean version of itself. Thus the two could reference and reflect each other, like Russian matryoshka dolls, like infinite mirrors. It would make the house into a kind of loop, its own impossible object. The more I thought about it, the more my heart filled with excitement.

I threw on some clothes, and using Waylett's cards, ran out onto the gravel in front of the house.

The sculptures were pink now with the rising sun, but no less ghoulish. I was struck once more by how familiar they felt, and also how they seemed to contain something of my own art, and with this rare affinity in mind I knew that this was the inspiration I needed for the mausoleum.

After breakfast I gathered together a sketching kit then sought out Waylett in his office.

'Good morning, Mr Etherstone. What can I do for you?'

'I wanted to talk to you about the sculptures that run along the outside of the house. I think they might be good inspiration for the mausoleum. I was wondering who was responsible for making them, and where I might find the sketches and elevations that were drawn up before they were built.'

'Those sculptures were made by Signor Varano. He was a sculptor as well as an architect. But the *signore* made them alone. If he ever created preparatory sketches, I never saw them.'

'I don't understand. A work of such scale and complexity.

He can't have done it by himself, and certainly not without preparation.'

Waylett shrugged. 'The *signore* laboured on those sculptures for years. All through his madness, but as I said, in all that time I never saw him make any plans for them. We had a workshop built on the grounds for the stonemasons and he used to go in there and sculpt. I think as a way to take his mind off the madness that was consuming him. As he completed each section, the engineers raised them to the roof. He only finished the last pieces just a few days before his death.'

I couldn't quite believe it, yet what reason did Waylett have to lie? Could Varano really have sculpted them in the midst of madness? Without even planning them out first? How did the engineers know where to place them?

'Perhaps I should make my own sketches,' I said. 'Is there a way for me to get onto the roof so that I can look at them more closely?'

'You can get onto the roof, but you won't have a good view of them from there.' He drummed his fingers on his desktop a moment then smiled. 'I think there might be a way.'

He crossed to the back wall and opened a shallow cabinet that was filled with bunches of keys hanging from hooks. He picked out a set and turned to me.

'Follow me,' he smiled.

We left his office and ascended an interminable series of staircases till we reached the top floor of the building, then we traversed a few corridors and stepped through into a long-abandoned attic room. It was small, dusty and empty, the floorboards bare. The only decoration was a mirror hanging above the fireplace.

Waylett led me to the windows and I realised why he had brought me here. The room was at the same height as the frieze, in the part of the East Wing that projected outwards. By standing at the window, and looking back at the central section, the sculptures that adorned it could be easily studied. Up close I could see that the figures were almost twice life-size, and even more ghastly, their proportions amplifying their grotesqueness, their blood-curdling ferocity.

'Monstrous things,' Waylett said.

'But made with much skill.'

He turned to me and nodded.

'This was Signor Varano's room,' he said. 'In his last days, when the madness had taken hold. A sickroom, I suppose. Strange to think while he was going insane he could look out of his window and see his own mad works.'

'What was Signor Varano like?' I asked.

Waylett smiled.

'He was a good man. A little aloof, maybe, but he had gentle ways about him. Even in the midst of his madness.'

'And why do you think it was that he went mad?'

Waylett frowned as he considered the question.

'I suppose,' he sighed, 'coming here, so far from his home, made him lonely and isolated and his foreign mind succumbed more easily to despondency. To the hardships he faced, the misunderstandings. But I think what really caused his decline was what happened with the Marsden girls. You're familiar with the story?'

'When I was staying in the Black Lion, an old man told me some girls disappeared when the house was first being built.'

'Sisters from Lunham,' Waylett nodded. 'They went missing at the time we were laying the foundations. People connected the two events and thought Signor Varano was responsible, no doubt because he was the only foreigner many of them had ever seen. He tried to clear his name, but failed, withdrew into himself, and slowly went mad, which just further convinced the locals of his guilt.'

'And there's a superstition surrounding the girls? That they sing at night across the moors to lure men to their deaths?'

Waylett shook his head disapprovingly.

'Ever since they disappeared it's been said that they haunt the moors. Homer had his Sirens and the folk here have their Marsden girls. But it's all just fool's talk. The men receive their pay from Mrs Chesterfield at the house, they spend it all in the pub the very same night, then they get lost on the walk back in their drunkards' haze and stumble into the marsh waters and drown or freeze to death. It's drink that kills those men, not the ghosts of three long-dead village girls.'

'And how did Varano die?'

A pained look crossed Waylett's features; a look of remorse, or perhaps even guilt.

'No one knows. But he suffered from sleepwalking, which got worse as he grew madder. He took to sleepwalking out on the moor. He'd labour away on the sculptures in the workshop from dawn till dark, then return here, where he'd be locked in for his own safety. And yet, now and again, he'd find some way to escape and a search party would be sent out and he'd be found shivering in his nightshirt some great distance from the house, babbling. He'd catch a fever. He'd recuperate. And then he would be back at his sculptures once more and the cycle would begin all over again. Until one morning he went missing and the search parties couldn't find him and we never saw him again. We assumed he'd got out onto the moors and was sucked into the bogs. Winter has rolled over this land nearly fifty times since he disappeared, but even now I recall him often.'

A chill ran through me at the parallels between Varano and me; both of us suffering from somnambulism, both of us with foreign minds, affected by the environment. I thought of my fall into the sticking mud the day before and how I might have gone

107

the same way as the poor man. It all reinforced the sense I'd had that Varano's fate was in some way connected to mine, a precursor, a warning of what might happen to me. Again I felt that to solve the mystery of what happened all those years ago might help me escape my present danger.

'I know it was his madness that killed him,' Waylett said. 'But we all played our part by not helping him more. We pressed Mrs Chesterfield to have him sent to an asylum, or back to Venice, but she just smiled whenever the topic was raised and would always reply, "His place is with the house."'

His words surprised me, for it was the first time he had said anything even slightly critical of his employer.

We lapsed into silence and looked over the sculptures once more, the clanging sound of building works in some distant part of the house penetrating the room.

After a few seconds Waylett turned his gaze to the low clouds scudding across the sky.

'Looks like rain,' he said. 'Do you remember how to get back?'

'I'm at a loss.'

He gestured towards my art materials. I gave him a pencil and my sketching book and he jotted down instructions. Then he left me and I got to work copying the figures closest to me. Despite their fantastical nature, there was an incredible naturalism to their anatomy, their bodies writhing and rippling with dark energy. Their faces sneering and howling and grinning. I was certain on seeing his work up close that Varano was a true master artist, and had his circumstances been different he would have gone down in the annals of art history, instead of dying in complete obscurity. What black scandal had made him flee Italy and come here? Where his work was destined to be forgotten?

I carried on working up my sketches through most of the morning. Time passed. The wind sang its song, swooping over the house and making timpani of the rafters. Eventually the heavens proved Waylett right; the sky turned grey with low clouds and rain began to fall in specks, and then in great sheets. Thunder echoed down the valley from Heybridge, booming like quarry explosions. When I had copied as many of the sculptures as I could, I went through my sketches and was surprised to see that they contained something of the sculptures' monstrous energy in their rapidity, the hatch-like swathes of charcoal I'd used to depict them.

I tied them all up in my portfolio and was just about to leave the room when I saw four wagons approaching the house along the avenue below. I paused to watch them nearing through the worsening rain. When the wagons reached the head of the driveway, they turned parallel to the house so the sides of their canvas covers came into view, which were elaborately painted in bright, gaudy colours, like the wagons of a circus troupe. Amongst the designs were the words *John Thurlby Esq. Antiques and Curiosities, Cheapside, London.*

When the wagons stopped, men jumped down from each of them, and I was shocked to see that they were dark-skinned and their faces were covered in tattoos. Among them was a lone white man who I guessed was John Thurlby. He was in his fifties, ruddy-faced, chubby, dressed in a longcoat and stovepipe hat of the type that had not been in fashion for decades. Even from this distance I could tell there was something shabby about him.

He walked across the gravel and shook hands with Waylett, who'd come out to greet him. They said a few words to each other then Thurlby shouted hoarsely at his men, and they pulled back the canvas covers of the wagons to reveal, in their beds, man-sized shapes covered in cloths and tarpaulins, fixed into place with ropes. More demonic statues were arriving, as if an army of them was being assembled.

The thought filled me with apprehension and I turned away from the window and looked about the empty room. It really did feel like a sickroom, a cell in a madhouse. I studied the fireplace, then the mirror above it, and my reflection seemed odd in the looking glass. There I stood in my suit and tie, with my portfolio under my arm, a tin of charcoals in my pocket. My thin face, my black hair, my sallow skin. But it all felt wrong. As though I was the wrong person. As though I was in the wrong time.

As I studied the mirror, I saw in the reflection of the empty room behind me a veiled figure, eyes the colour of fog.

I shrieked and spun about.

But the room was empty.

Had I imagined it?

I turned to look at the mirror once more, to see what I might have misperceived as a figure.

When I did so, however, the mirror no longer reflected the room behind me, but somewhere else entirely – a ballroom. A vast Italianate ballroom, gilded and frescoed and mirrored and lit by a thousand candles. Empty except for my own reflection.

No sooner had my eye landed on this vision, and my mind begun to comprehend it, than the mirror exploded, showering the room with shards of glass. I raised an arm to shield my eyes, barely able to breathe.

When all was quiet, I moved my arm away and looked once more.

Everything was as it had been but for the broken mirror. Its frame still hung above the mantelpiece, but it was empty now, its wooden back exposed. Below it, scattered across the floorboards, was a carpet of shattered glass. All the pieces were tiny, except for one; a single large shard, in the rough shape of a long triangle. It had fallen and embedded itself like a dagger, upright, in the floorboard just by my feet.

16

I followed the instructions Waylett had scribbled down in my sketchbook, using them to return to the Great Hall. It had been my plan to go from there straight to my room, where I could steady my thoughts, but when I entered the Great Hall it was bustling with people, among them Waylett, who gestured me over.

As I approached I saw the scene was somewhat reminiscent of an art gallery or museum, for the antiques man and his attendants had unloaded their cargo near the ghost wall and several of the house's residents were looking them over. There were perhaps two dozen sculptures on display, ranging from foot-high wooden idols to temple statues made of stone and rising to eight or nine feet.

'Mr Etherstone. Allow me to introduce Mr Thurlby,' Waylett said, gesturing to the red-faced man in the stovepipe hat I had seen on the driveway.

Thurlby turned to me and grinned. Up close I could see that there was some winter in his auburn hair, and that his brow protruded markedly, casting his eyes into shadow, giving him a lurking, mischievous look, as if his gaze was loitering somehow, waiting for something to pounce on.

'Marcus Thurlby,' the man said. 'Dealer in curiosities and procurer of *objets d'art* from the four corners of the globe.'

He had an east London accent, overlaid with an odd twanging

drawl. I couldn't be sure if this was an affectation designed to hide his origins, or if years of overseas travel had altered his manner of speech. He pulled a business card from an inside pocket with a flourish and passed it to me.

'Glad to make your acquaintance, Mr Thurlby,' I said, shaking the man's hand.

'Mr Etherstone has been employed by Mrs Chesterfield to build her mausoleum,' Waylett explained.

As soon as Thurlby heard this, I sensed a change in his manner, as if I was now of greater importance to him.

'Mr Thurlby is freshly returned from a tour of the Orient and is about to show us his latest finds,' Waylett said, gesturing to the row of sculptures. 'Why don't you join us?'

'I would be glad to,' I said. Though in truth I wanted nothing more than to return to my room as soon as possible.

We turned to look at the statues, but my eyes were drawn to Thurlby's attendants, who were standing in a line behind them. I realised at this closer distance that they were probably Polynesians, for they resembled those members of their race I had seen around the docks in London. Close up, they looked even more fearsome than they had from afar, for I could see more clearly now how large and muscular they were, and I could make out the details of the tattoos on their faces – whirling blue curlicues of the most elaborate design over their cheeks and foreheads. It was almost as if they were wearing masks, or were a second row of statues placed behind the first.

'These are just the sculptures, of course,' Thurlby said. 'We have also brought paintings, scrolls and other, smaller items of interest, but these are still packed away in trunks, safe from the rain.'

There was a noise behind us and we turned to see Mrs Chesterfield and Miss Thornwick approaching, arm in arm. Thurlby trotted over to greet them, bowing obsequiously.

'Your latest acquisitions, Mrs Chesterfield,' he said. 'I have scoured the globe personally. And along with my agents have secured the following for your delectation.' He waved a hand over the row of statues like the ringmaster at a circus. The gesture reminded me of Fitzpatrick, the film producer whose cinematographic camera I had brought with me; both had the air of showmen – imposing, attention-grabbing, a hint of something disreputable.

Mrs Chesterfield gave the man a look, annoyed by his chatter, though Thurlby didn't seem to notice.

They approached the first of the sculptures, a wooden statue, almost life-size, depicting a demonic-looking man wearing a robe, with a noose in one hand and a sword in the other, around which a dragon coiled. His expression was wrathful and scowling. His hair was knotted short. Behind him was a stylised back panel made to resemble a wall of flames, so that he seemed to have just stepped out of a portal that joined our world to a realm of fire.

'*Fudō Myō-ō*,' Thurlby said, 'one of the Japanese Kings of Brightness. One of the five Wise Kings. Protector of the Buddhist Law, direct emanation of the Buddha Dainichi Nyorai. The work is some eight hundred years old, by my guess. Made of Japanese boxwood with metal supports and was at one time covered in lacquer. I bought this one myself from a trusted dealer in Yokohama.'

Thurlby grinned. Mrs Chesterfield nodded. She stepped forward and ran her hand over the statue, as if judging its worth from its texture; an action which seemed to panic Thurlby.

'*Fudō-sama* protects the living by burning away all illusions and impurities,' he said. 'And thus helps believers towards enlightenment.'

'Mr Thurlby,' Mrs Chesterfield said, 'in the last decade you have brought me over a dozen *Fudō Myō-ō*s, both statues and paintings. I am familiar with the deity and his various depictions and this is not a great example of the motif. And it is certainly not eight hundred years old.'

Thurlby paused, and I caught a flash of anger in his dark, darting eyes. But it passed quickly.

'Waylett,' Mrs Chesterfield said.

'Yes, ma'am.'

'This one is for the section to the east of the mausoleum,' she said, gesturing towards the statue. 'At the junction of the third corridor and the staircase which ascends to the fourth floor.'

Waylett nodded, took a notebook from his pocket and jotted down her instructions.

'Let's move along,' she said to Thurlby.

They walked a few steps to the next object in the row – a Chinese sculpture of some other deity, equally as fiery as the first. Again Thurlby detailed a little of its history and provenance. Again Mrs Chesterfield contradicted his comments and explained to which part of the house it should be taken, Waylett scribbling down her instructions.

And so they continued, making their way along the row of Oriental gods and demons. As I watched them I thought how odd they looked, both as people – for they were a peculiar assortment – but also in their actions, which were almost ritualistic, as if they were taking part in an archaic ceremony. At every sculpture Mrs Chesterfield remained unimpressed, undercutting Thurlby's enthusiasm, so that by the end of their progress, he appeared drained and listless. I wondered if this was Mrs Chesterfield's intention, if beneath her solemnity she was delighting in playing with the antiques man thus. It was certainly so for Miss Thornwick, who grinned broadly at each slight and haughty remark her employer sent Thurlby's way.

'That is all for the sculptures,' Thurlby said. 'The paintings, scrolls and other *objets d'art* are still under canvas in the wagon.'

'When the rain clears have them brought through to my office,' Mrs Chesterfield said.

Thurlby bowed and Mrs Chesterfield and Miss Thornwick made their way back to their offices. Thurlby turned to his Polynesians and barked at them in their own tongue.

I returned to my rooms forthwith, feeling nervous and tired. I lay down on the bed to try to think through what had happened in Varano's room, to find a rational explanation. Maybe I had hallucinated the figure and the ballroom. Maybe the mirror had shattered for some logical reason – the room had been unoccupied for years and my movement in it had caused hairline cracks in the glass to finally break? Or maybe the vibration of the storm?

But no matter how many theories I came up with, none of them satisfied me. My thoughts returned to the same two worrying possibilities – either the house was trying to tell me something, or it was trying to kill me.

17

~~~

I must have fallen asleep as I mulled it all over, for the next thing I knew I was waking up from a nightmare, snatches of which remained with me: a bonfire on a wintry moor, shards of glass falling through fog, a girl in a veil, a deer's skull with antlers made of yew tree branches, a godly majestic sky. I had a sense that these images were connected by some important narrative which had been lost with the dream. I tried to recover its thread from my quickly dissolving memories, but could not.

I looked around and saw it had darkened and checked my watch in a panic; it was almost time for dinner. As I readied myself I noticed the sound of the rain and wind outside; the earlier showers had picked up while I'd been asleep and were now a torrential storm.

I descended to the East Wing, and entered the withdrawing room, where I saw that Reverend Hartington and Mr Thurlby were present and would be joining us for dinner. We chatted amiably until Mrs Chesterfield and Miss Thornwick arrived, then we all walked together to the dining room.

'Excellent food as always, Mrs Chesterfield,' Thurlby said, as we were making our way through the hors d'oeuvres. 'Your cook is to be congratulated.' He turned to address the rest of us. 'After all these months in foreign lands it is good to be back in England, with good, honest, English food.'

'I believe the *gratiné* is French,' Mrs Chesterfield said, without taking her eyes off her plate. 'As is my chef.'

Miss Thornwick grinned.

Thurlby cast them both a look before smiling. 'Still an improvement, ma'am. Still an improvement.'

I looked again at Mrs Chesterfield. She was being as cold and dismissive to Thurlby as she had been in the Great Hall. Did she have a particular dislike of the man? Or was she just displaying the same iciness that characterised most of her interactions?

'How long were you in the Orient?' Mrs Danby asked in her strange, lilting accent.

'Nine months, not including the voyages there and back. Nine months collecting what treasures I could.'

'I imagine it must be hard work?'

'It is, indeed.'

'And where did your latest travels take you?' Hartington asked.

'We sailed from Portsmouth around the Cape to Hong Kong. From there we journeyed inland, through the Chinese interior, then across to Shanghai. Then we crossed the East China Sea to Nagasaki. We travelled up Japan to the northern regions, then back to Osaka. And finally we sailed home, and mightily glad am I to be safely back in England, and gladder still to be staying in Yorkshire.'

'You will be staying with us a while?' Mrs Danby asked.

'For a few months, at least. All our purchases could not fit in the ship we returned in. There are still a few treasures making their way here on a number of different vessels, arriving in dribs and drabs over the next few months, via Rotterdam and Scarborough. Mrs Chesterfield has kindly allowed us to stay here while we oversee their receipt.'

'And in these places you visited, were there any signs of

Christianity?' Hartington asked. 'Or are the natives still practising their own local religions?'

'Few signs, sir,' Thurlby said in a tone of disappointment. 'In the larger port cities – Hong Kong, Shanghai, even Nagasaki – there were missions, and fine work they were doing. But travel inland and the people are still under the sway of their old superstitions. Ancestor worship, nature worship, reincarnation are the order of the day.'

'I must confess,' Mrs Danby said, 'I have never understood how these people make do with religions that believe one is endlessly reborn, with no prospect of ever arriving at a heaven or a hell. How can there be no ultimate destination?'

'But there *is* an ultimate destination,' Hartington smiled. 'I have studied the teachings of many religions, including the Oriental ones. They believe that after many reincarnations one may attain a sort of heaven, a pure land populated by enlightened beings.'

'And what of hell?' Mrs Danby asked.

'To be reborn eternally is hell.'

'Then that would make this Earth we live on hell.'

'And the millions around the world who are trapped in misery would agree.' Hartington smiled again.

'When I was travelling through the mountains of Akaishi,' Thurlby said, 'I stopped at a Buddhist monastery where I saw some illustrated scrolls which I tried to buy, though the monks would not sell them. I asked my man to translate what the scrolls said and he told me they depicted an old religious folk tale designed to explain to the lay people the concept of reincarnation. If you'd like I could relate it to you, though it is rather ghoulish.'

He looked around the table. Some of us nodded, but we all knew that the decision rested ultimately with Mrs Chesterfield, so all eyes turned to her.

'You can speak freely here, Mr Thurlby,' she said.

Thurlby nodded.

'The tale concerned a local brigand,' he began, 'the leader of a gang who robbed and killed those passing through the bamboo forests that lay across the mountains in that part of Japan. At one point his band attacked a convoy of monks returning to the monastery from a pilgrimage. They tied up the monks while they rifled through their packs and luggage. As they did so, one of the convoy, a senior abbot at the monastery, a very holy and devout man, tried to reason with the brigand. He tried to convince him to give up his evil ways and make amends for all the sins that would cause him to be reborn for thousands of years to come.

'The brigand quipped that he quite liked the idea of thousands more years of life, which caused all his men to laugh.

'When they'd been through the convoy's packs, they slit the throats of all their prisoners, including the abbot's. Then the gang took their purloined goods to a local town and sold them through the criminals who deal in such things. They spent the night at a tavern, drinking and enjoying the company of the women who worked there. When they had finished their revelries, they fell into sleep, and the brigand dreamt he was wandering about in a nightmarish, barren landscape; a plain that had no features to it except a giant mountain in the distance. The brigand spent days approaching it, thinking that if he could climb to its peak he could get the lie of the land. But when he was closing in on it, he saw that it was made of skulls and bones, an infinite number of them, both human and animal. With no other option, he set about climbing it.

'As you can imagine, it was hard work, for this was not a sturdy mountain of rock and stone. The brigand stumbled, tripped, slid downwards on avalanches of bones and so was constantly set back in his progress. Eventually, however, after days of effort, he finally reached the summit, but when he got there he was dismayed to

119

see that even from this elevated vantage point, there was nothing in the plain below – no towns, villages, houses, no signs whatsoever of another living being in all the world. In total despair, he considered throwing himself from the top of the mountain, but knew somehow in his heart that this would not actually kill him and end his misery.

'Contemplating the bleakness of his own immortality, he scrambled around the mountain's peak until he noticed a cave further along. He went inside and saw the abbot he had murdered, sitting there unharmed, smiling at him. The abbot revealed himself to be a *bodhisattva*, something like the Buddhist version of a saint – an enlightened being who has forsaken his place in heaven to stay among the unenlightened and help them with their own enlightenment.

'The brigand asked him what hellish place this was, and how the mountain of skulls had come to be there. The abbot smiled again, and informed the brigand that the mountain was made up of the brigand's own skeletons, one for each of the millions of past lives he had lived, human and animal. And with that, the brigand recoiled in horror, and realised the futility of his situation, the pointlessness of being endlessly reborn.'

Thurlby paused and looked around the table with a grin, enjoying the hush that had descended upon us, and I thought once more how he was a consummate showman.

The Reverend Hartington cleared his throat.

'What happened to the brigand?'

'No doubt,' Mr Danby chimed in, 'he awoke in a panic and fled to the monastery, where he repented of his sins and lived an exemplary life till the end of his days.'

Thurlby smiled wryly.

'Perhaps if this was an English tale, Mr Danby, but this is an Oriental tale. The brigand awoke in the tavern and did indeed wish to ride to the monastery and atone for his sins. For in a panic he had realised that each transgression, each wasted life, just made the mountain of bones even taller, the journey out of the nothingness even harder. With his new-found knowledge, the bandit could begin to put his soul on the path to liberation. But before he could do so, he was apprehended by the authorities, and executed, right there in the tavern grounds. And so he was condemned to be reborn once more, just another skull on the mountain, with all the knowledge he had gained from his encounter with the *bodhisattva* lost. So you see,' he turned to Mrs Danby, 'the eternal life offered us by reincarnation may indeed be a despairing kind of hell.'

He took a sip of his wine.

Mrs Danby's eyes narrowed, piqued by Thurlby's condescending manner.

At this point the servants arrived to take away our plates and there was a lull in the conversation until Mrs Danby turned to Thurlby and spoke to him in an oddly sweet and bright tone.

'These savages whose temples you visit to buy your wares,' she began. 'I had the impression they were very attached to their idols, and would part with them for nothing.'

'Oh, yes,' Thurlby replied. 'But in these instances it is best to go straight to the chief. Pay the chief and he'll tell the rest of the tribe what to think. New idols can be carved to replace the old. They don't mind when you show them money, or more often than not, trinkets. Many's the time I've outwitted a savage by swapping some priceless idol for a compass or some other ephemera, convincing them it is precious back in our civilised world. Occasionally we have a deranged old priest or shaman telling us the idol will curse us and we are sailing back to our doom, but we have no time for such superstitions.'

'Have any of these curses ever come true?' Mrs Danby asked. 'Any ships ever sunk?'

'Some have, yes, of course, but never nearly so many as have been cursed.'

'So you don't think these idols contain any . . . supernatural power?'

As Thurlby went to answer, he paused, and whatever he had planned to say stuck in his throat, for he realised Mrs Danby had quite expertly backed him into a corner – he couldn't admit to the idols having no supernatural power without making a fool of Mrs Chesterfield for buying them. Neither could he admit to selling her items that were cursed.

I looked closely at Mrs Danby and saw a vicious little smile playing on her lips. She was getting her revenge on Thurlby for the way he'd used his story about the mountain of skulls to belittle her. Both she and the antiques man made their living exploiting Mrs Chesterfield's madness, and I supposed beyond any personal animadversion, they both considered each other a threat, like rival cousins fighting for the affections of a rich old aunt. God knew why they should spar so; Mrs Chesterfield had enough money to waste on everyone, but still they sniped at each other, jostled for position and favour. Perhaps it was the house at work, setting them against each other, like the tale Tobias Clarke told in the pub, of his school friends, the one killing the other and going to the gallows claiming the house had made him do it.

'I believe,' Thurlby replied, 'that the power of curses lies in their being believed.'

He grinned at Mrs Danby.

Mrs Chesterfield turned to look at her as well, which made me wonder again if, despite those cataracts in her eyes, some of her vision still lingered on. For why else would she turn to the woman in such an instance but to take in her discomfiture?

Mrs Danby wilted under her employer's gaze, shifted in her seat, then looked around the table, flustered, until her eye landed on me.

'Mr Etherstone has previously expressed doubts about the spiritual power of objects,' she said desperately.

Everyone turned to me and I struggled not to send a glare in the woman's direction.

'No, I do not believe in such things,' I said flatly.

'What about other aspects of spirituality?' she pressed on. 'Do you not believe in ghosts, for example?'

'No, Mrs Danby. There are enough horrors in this world without us inventing more.'

'Do you not believe in any life after death?'

'No.'

'You reject *all* belief in an afterlife? Even the Church's teachings?' she asked, with a flick of her eyes to the Reverend Hartington, trying to recruit him to her cause.

'I'm an orphan, and was raised by an uncle who was a minister in the Church,' I replied. 'He was sadistic and cruel, and so I rejected both his and all religious beliefs in general.'

Mrs Danby pretended to be shocked, but she couldn't keep that vicious smile from her face.

'So when we die, Mr Etherstone, you believe that is it?'

'Quite.'

'Nothing happens at all?'

'Exactly. We will return to a realm of nothingness after we die, as it was before we were born.'

'A needlessly melancholic view to have on this world.'

'Melancholic but liberating.'

'A person is not just their body,' Mr Danby said, weighing in on his wife's side. 'No, Mr Etherstone. We are soul, too. We are spirits clothed in flesh. When the clothing falls away does the wearer die too?'

'Our bodies are not clothes. If an arm is severed from the body it cannot be sewn on again like a sleeve.'

'And what of all the evidence which proves the existence of spirits?' Mrs Danby asked.

'I have yet to see any.'

'And all the eminent people who believe in spirits?'

'Duped.'

'Indeed?' she said, genuine shock discernible in her voice for the first time. 'So, John Ruskin is a dupe, is he? Conan Doyle, A. R. Wallace, the Prime Minister, the Queen? Are all these people wrong in their belief of congress with the hereafter?'

She didn't add Mrs Chesterfield to her list, but there was no need – everyone knew what she was insinuating. I paused, feeling the attention of the entire table on me, including that of my employer.

'I believe they have all been duped, yes,' I said eventually. 'There is no hereafter for anyone to have congress *with*. These people are no doubt intelligent, but they were probably fooled by some trick or other, subjected to some pantomime which made them suggestible to manipulation.'

'Pantomime?' Mr Danby said. 'You mean seances?'

I nodded, unsure if he was genuinely outraged or just playing the part along with his wife.

The Danbys shared a scandalised look. The husband puffed out his chest and his face reddened. A heavy silence descended on the table and I realised I had overstepped the mark, made enemies of the Danbys.

'Perhaps,' Thurlby said, 'Mr Etherstone could join you for your seance tonight. He can see first-hand the evidence he has so unhappily missed his entire life, and then judge afterwards if the spirits do in fact exist. Begging Mrs Chesterfield's approval, of course.'

The Danbys' faces dropped at the suggestion, for surely having an observer at their seance – and a confirmed sceptic – might well cause their charlatanry to go awry, and Thurlby knew it. I turned to him and saw once more a gleam in his dark eyes, for undoubtedly now he had bested Mrs Danby in their spiteful game.

'Having a disbeliever at a seance would put the whole enterprise in jeopardy,' Mr Danby protested.

'Like casting pearls before swine,' his wife added.

As the pair waited for Mrs Chesterfield's decision, I saw how scared they both were, for if their seances were exposed as fraudulent, they might well be turned out from their lucrative perch.

'Why don't we all attend?' Mrs Chesterfield finally said, making a sweeping gesture which took in everyone at the table.

We all looked at each other in surprise and a wave of claustrophobia came over me, a sense of having been ambushed.

'I do not wish to attend such a . . . charade,' I said.

I must have laced my words with too much derision, for Mrs Chesterfield turned to look at me in a most cutting manner, putting those unsettling eyes of hers to full use.

'You will attend. You will *all* attend,' she said softly, before turning back to her food.

18

The storm had grown even fiercer while we had been eating and now, as we stepped inside the seance room, the rain and wind pounded against its windows. It was a smaller room than most in the house, but no less well appointed. While the Danbys made their preparations, I crossed to the drinks cabinet in the corner and poured myself a tumbler of whisky. Hartington and Thurlby joined me, both of them as reluctant as I was to be there.

Mrs Danby circumambulated the room, covering all the mirrors with black shrouds – lest the spirits be trapped in them.

'If this is their seance room, why not just do away with the mirrors altogether,' Thurlby muttered.

'It's all part of the ritual,' Hartington muttered back.

As Mrs Danby fixed the mirrors, her husband lit a few candles on the green baize table in the centre of the room, then turned the gas lamps down till their flames were nothing but blue flickers.

'For the spirits do not like bright lights,' he told us. 'Their unworldly shapes are most comfortable in the darkness, and come to us most easily at night, when we're all pulled closer to a realm of death.'

In the time it took them to prepare the room, Mrs Chesterfield smoked two cigarettes, so the air was soon thick with tobacco and opium smoke. Perhaps due to the warmth in the room, or the whisky, or the opium, or all of these combined, I felt woozy and feared I might pass out, and was glad when eventually we sat.

Alice took her place at the table with the same unnerving stillness with which she did everything. Her parents sat either side of her, and next to them Miss Thornwick and Mrs Chesterfield, with Sarah, Thurlby, Hartington and me forming the other half of the circle.

'If everyone is settled?' Mr Danby asked.

He looked around at us, then shared a conspiratorial glance with his wife. I noticed that there was a thin seam of anxiety in both their manners.

Next Mr Danby blew out the flames from all the candles but one, and the room was plunged into a thick, syrupy darkness. He moved the last lit candle to the centre of the table, then spoke in hushed, solemn tones.

'Please place your hands on the table so that your little fingers touch the little fingers of the person next to you. Now we will wait in silence while Alice prepares for the spirits' transmissions. This may take a few minutes – it may take upwards of an hour. I encourage you to be patient, stay silent, and above all, to keep your minds at ease.'

I looked through the gloom at the girl, and saw she had closed her eyes, a slight frown disturbing her brow. Once more I found it hard to reconcile her age with her sullen manner and lineaments, and again felt pity for her. I turned my gaze from the girl to her parents and wondered what tricks and sleights of hand they would perform in their attempt to dupe us.

We waited some long moments in the murk, the storm outside the only noise rising up out of the silence. As time passed, however, I noticed the sound of our breathing; it seemed to fall into unison, each person's individual rhythm coming into alignment, becoming almost like a chant, so it was as if there was just a single person in that room, breathing a single breath.

I could not say how long we stayed like that – if it were two minutes, twenty minutes, or an hour. Time seemed to lose its forward momentum, seemed to swirl about itself, to clot in the heat and darkness and opium smoke.

Then, out of nowhere, the candle flame guttered and leapt, as if a breeze had passed through the room, and I heard a low moaning sound. I realised with a shock that it was coming from Alice. As the noise continued, it thickened, as if its source was moving further to the back of Alice's throat, further into the pit of her being.

She started shuddering, as if in the grip of a fit, writhing about on her seat, her breathing short and violent. Wilder and wilder she shuddered. Then her eyes rolled into the back of her head and everything reached a climax; with a fierce jolt she lurched forward, her hair whipping down and covering her face.

Then all was still, the fit having subsided as quickly as it had begun.

She stayed hunched over for a few more seconds then she raised her head slowly and resumed her earlier posture, but her face was completely changed: her skin was bloodless, her nostrils flared, the edges of her mouth pulled back, her eyes narrow and gleaming cruelly in the dark.

'Is someone there?' Mr Danby asked. He phrased the words strangely, interspersing them with unnaturally long pauses, elongating a couple of syllables just as unnaturally. Even in my drowsy state, I could tell there was something deliberately peculiar about the way he spoke, and I wondered if he was sending his daughter secret messages with this queer enunciation, a code that was directing her performance.

Alice stayed as she was, breathing heavily, her face a rictus of straining muscles.

'Is someone there?' Mr Danby repeated, phrasing the words in the exact same manner.

Again Alice didn't respond, but continued to breathe heavily, animalistically. I turned to Mr Danby and saw how worried he was. Things were not going to plan. Perhaps Alice was not complying with his directions.

I turned back to the girl and saw her hands gripping the edge of the table tightly, fingers turning white, as if she was trying to stave off another convulsion.

Mr Danby repeated his question a third time, changing the phrasing now.

Finally, Alice spoke. It was in a wholly unnatural voice; deep and gravelly, that of a grown woman, not a child.

'I am here,' she said.

'Is that Mr Chesterfield?' Mr Danby asked, his voice quavering. Again I noticed the odd phrasing, the code of silences and slurs.

'No.'

Danby shot a concerned look at his wife, who met his gaze with equal concern.

'Then to whom are we speaking?' he asked, turning back to his daughter.

'I am surrounded by the dead.'

'To whom are we speaking?'

'I called to you from the mirror.'

'To which spirit are we speaking?'

Alice turned her head slowly and her gaze bore into me. Any drowsiness that still remained about my mind evaporated in an instant.

'Time's mirror,' she said. 'In every created thing resides death. You didn't recognised me, Sam.'

A wave of revulsion rushed through me, fast and stinging as a slap, for I knew the voice.

'Rose?' I mumbled.

'Leave this house, Sam. Leave at once.'

129

My shock and revulsion turned into a stock of anger too great to countenance.

'No!' I shouted. 'How dare you?'

I jumped up and ran towards the gas lamps.

'Stop! What are you doing?' Mr Danby shouted.

He rose and wheeled around to follow me.

'You'll bring her out of her trance prematurely!' Mrs Danby screamed.

I paid her no heed. I reached the lamps and turned them full flare. As light flooded the room Alice unleashed a volley of shrieks worthy of hell and exploded into a fit of convulsions.

'You fool!' Mr Danby screamed.

Mrs Danby turned to restrain her daughter but there was a flash of movement and the woman was knocked from her seat and went sprawling onto the carpet, her chair tumbling after her. Everyone else jumped up and the room erupted in a tempest of gesticulations and shouts.

Mr Danby turned to me with the Devil in his eyes.

'What have you done?' he yelled.

He balled his fists and was about to stalk towards me when Alice's convulsions ceased abruptly and she sat upright.

We turned to look at her and there were a few seconds of hushed silence.

Then she gently leaned her head back, paused, and with great, sickening force, launched her head forwards again, pummelling it into the edge of the table with a heavy thud that chilled my bones.

The girl raised her face slowly, blood dripping from her forehead.

'Alice?' her mother screamed, seeing the blood dripping into her daughter's eyes now.

Again Alice leaned her head back.

'NO!' her mother yelled, realising what was about to happen.

She launched herself at her daughter but it was too late. The girl slammed her head into the edge of the table again, causing an even greater quantity of blood to spatter.

In a paroxysm of shock Mrs Danby froze, and so did we all, staring at the girl in a bewilderment so deep it kept us from coming to her aid.

Once more Alice launched her head towards the edge of the table before Thurlby and Hartington, who were the closest to her, snapped out of their trance and grabbed the girl's shoulders to stop her. Even as they held her in their arms, she resisted and it took all their strength to subdue her.

The rest of us continued to look on in shocked horror, as the girl twisted about and Mrs Danby tried to soothe her. Then Mr Danby glared at me and charged in my direction, and Thurlby detached himself from the melee to pull the man back.

'Look what you've done!' Mr Danby screamed.

'You dared bring my dead wife into this charade of yours!' I shouted back.

'I did nothing of the sort. I have no control over what the girl says.'

'You were passing her messages.'

'I did no such thing.'

'Gentlemen,' Mrs Chesterfield said calmly and we both turned to her.

'You have disturbed the child enough. Clara, call the servants. Send a coach to Heybridge for the doctor and have the girl taken to her room. The rest of you, calm yourselves.'

I turned to Alice and saw that a gruesome gash had opened up on her forehead and her entire face was covered in blood, her mouth rimed with spittle. She was still convulsing, but not as wildly as before. I looked from her to the others and saw they were all staring at me, as if this were entirely my fault. I knew not what to do, so I turned and left the room.

19

Two glasses of brandy later and I had still not calmed down. I paced the smoking room and drank and smoked cigarettes even though my throat was already raw from them. The child had spoken in Rose's voice, I was sure of it. But how had she managed it? Whether by the most sophisticated deception, or by genuine psychic ability, I had been warned to leave the house by my own dead wife. And heed the warning I would. Mrs Chesterfield and her cathedral full of ghouls could go to hell. I would leave on the morrow.

I was just pouring my third drink when the door opened and Sarah entered.

'I thought I might find you here,' she said.

'How is she?'

'Well enough. We took her to her room and cleaned up the blood. There are bruises. Swelling. But she's lucid. The doctor from Heybridge should be here soon. Would you pour me a glass, too?'

I nodded and crossed to the drinks cabinet, made up a brandy and soda and handed it to her. We both sat and stared into the fire silently for some time.

'I am sorry for the way I acted,' I said eventually. 'I thought if I turned the lights on suddenly . . . Well, I'm not sure why I did it.'

'To catch them at it?'

'Yes, maybe. Foolish, of course.'

'Not at all. I was wondering how they were doing it. Mr Danby was sending her coded messages, perhaps in how he was talking to her, or maybe through touch underneath the table. They were both either side of her. But why did they anger you so? You mentioned your wife?'

'I thought . . . I thought the girl had spoken with the voice of my wife. She died eight years ago, shortly after the birth of our child. I lost both of them in such a brief span of time . . .'

I tried to continue but found I could not. I raised a hand to my eyes to stop the tears from coming.

'Alice spoke in her voice,' I muttered. 'In Rose's voice.'

I wiped my eyes and took my hand from my face. Sarah was looking at me with a woe-begotten expression.

'How could she?' I asked. 'How?'

Sarah seemed to be on the brink of telling me something. But instead she seemed to change her mind and took a large gulp of her brandy and soda.

'What is it?' I asked.

She shook her head.

'It's nothing.'

I frowned at her, confused. If she had information that she could bring to bear on the situation, why keep it from me? What possible reason could she have?

We fell into silence and I finished my brandy and rose to pour myself another, steeling myself for what I was about to say. I returned and sat opposite her once more, studying the beauty I would be leaving behind.

'I've decided to return to London,' I said.

Though it is vain to admit, I thought I saw some disappointment in her face.

'I see,' she replied.

I felt I needed to explain my decision, to show my reasons were understandable, for I desperately wanted to keep myself in her good regard.

'I have had a bad history with matters of illness and insanity,' I said. 'And I am worried that being here, in this insane house, might cause me to relapse. Maybe the episode tonight was just the beginning of something. You see, a sort of madness is the reason I became an artist. When I was eight years old I contracted an illness, a brain fever that affected me sporadically for the rest of my childhood. It induced hallucinations. It's these same visions I have spent my life trying to emulate in my art. My life's endeavour has been to capture the madness of these visions, to make them real. Perhaps that is the best summation of art there is. I'm worried now that my being here might cause them to return. I was warned before I came here, but I dismissed the warning. And now I wonder if I did so in error.'

'But your childhood illness was just that,' she said, 'a *childhood* illness. From decades ago. There's no reason to believe it is still inside you, just waiting to come out.'

I shook my head.

'I wish I shared your view,' I said. 'But I don't think it's the case. I really do believe there's something inside me. And not just me, but many of the other artists in my circle, my old friends and loved ones. I've seen it happen over and again.' I paused, trying to think how I might explain it to her, the long history of instability through which we'd all crawled. 'Have you heard of Nordau?' I asked.

'The philosopher? Yes, though I've not read any of his works.'

'I have, unfortunately. He believes Western society is on the point of collapse. If species can evolve, why can't they *de*-volve? If we can generate, why can't we *de*-generate? And if that's true for species why can't it also be true for civilisations? It's all based on a misreading of Darwin, of course, but that's what Nordau and his followers believe is happening now: our society is degenerating, regressing to a bestial state. And they cite people like me – aesthetic artists, symbolists, decadents – as an example of it. We're the rot at the heart of Europe, the malaise, dogged by scandal and ennui.

'When we first read Nordau's book we did so in horror and amusement. But the more distance I have, the more I wonder if he wasn't right. All the aesthetes and symbolists and decadents I ever knew had some kind of self-destructive streak. Now four years on from the trial, Oscar's rotting away in an attic in Paris; Beardsley died before his twenty-sixth birthday; Pigot Johnson's an alcoholic recluse; Francis Thompson's an opium addict, living by the Charing Cross riverbank; Ernest Dowson is likewise homeless; Verlaine died of his addictions; Arthur Machen has had a breakdown and can get none of his novels published, and Simeon Solomon was convicted of sodomy and has for years lived in the St Giles Workhouse. Our whole movement has been lost, gone mad or died young, and now I think that maybe Nordau is right. Maybe we do have something in us. Maybe we do carry around the seeds of our own destruction, and maybe that is where our need to create comes from. Maybe the two are the same thing.'

I looked up at her.

'You feel you may succumb, like so many of your friends,' she said, her tone plaintive, understanding. 'Then I think you are right to leave the house. But it's a shame we never got to know each other better.'

'Perhaps we can maintain a correspondence.'

'Yes, I'd like that.'

We smiled.

'When shall you leave?'

'I shall let Mrs Chesterfield know tomorrow.'

When I returned to my room I lay down on my bed and a thought came to me which reframed everything that had happened; that it was the house behind it all. It was the house that had caused Mrs Danby and Thurlby to goad each other, to send us shuffling into the seance room. It was the house that made Alice speak as Rose, that made me turn on the lights, that grabbed Alice's hair and smashed her head into the table. It was the house that had done such injury to a mere helpless child. The house was capable of doing such things, and as long as I stayed inside it, I was in mortal peril.

20

I dreamt not of Rose that night, but of the house. That I was running through it, trying to escape, fear flashing through me like a blade. As I ran I became ever more lost in its countless corridors. Passageways receded infinitely into the darkness, staircases extended as I traversed them. Some rooms I crossed were so vast I lost sight of the walls. Whichever way I turned, the floorboards stretched unbroken to a dark horizon.

At some point I stumbled into a ballroom, the same one I had seen reflected in Varano's mirror; lavish, Italianate, gilded, candled. Now I could see how exquisite were the frescoes on the walls, how intricate the chandeliers, how delicate the mouldings and friezes. But everything was begrimed and suffused with an air of decay, as if no one had entered the room for centuries. When I crossed to a door on its opposite wall, I stepped through into an identical ballroom, and again into another, and another. All windowless, with the dust of ages coating their floors.

I cannot tell for how long I stumbled through this endless railroad of rooms, each just another stage in a recursive sequence that had no end. In the despair this induced I felt the house was revealing its true nature to me, the full force of its cruelty. For surely the house *was* cruel, its energy malign. Whatever wandered its corridors at night, shifting the arrangement of its reality, it did so with malicious intent. It drew lost souls to it, people who had roamed the dark passageways of life. It called them to its own dark corridors, so it could trap them for all eternity, and feast.

When my desperation eventually overwhelmed me, I crouched down into a ball and screamed, knowing that the house had succeeded in driving me mad.

21

I awoke the next morning with a headache and a sore throat from all the alcohol and cigarettes I had partaken of the night before. I stared at the moulded ceiling above my bed and with a heavy, mournful sobriety thought of Alice and the injuries she had sustained, wondering now if maybe I was to blame after all. In a fit of remorse I decided to visit the girl before I left the house, to beg her forgiveness, and that of her parents. Then I would hand in my resignation letter to Mrs Chesterfield and arrange my departure, for I was convinced more than ever that I was in danger.

I swung my legs out of the bed and my bare feet landed not on the rug, but on paper. I frowned and looked around the room and was shocked at what I saw, for the floor was carpeted with drawings. Charcoal sketches on loose sheets scattered about so thickly that not an inch of floor was visible. I picked one up to examine it and was surprised to see my hands were covered with charcoal.

When I studied the sketch I saw it was an architectural study of what looked like a section of a mausoleum. I groped for a memory of the night before – for surely I had made these drawings in some feverish fit of sleeplessness, and yet I remembered nothing. Had I made them whilst sleepwalking? Was such a thing possible?

I collected up the sheets and went through them. They were

haphazard, dashed-off sketches that would need refinement, but it was all there. Scattered across the drawings was the detailing and structure of a mausoleum in its entirety. Every aspect of the design.

The sketches depicted a pyramid made up of tiered platforms rising mountain-like to a pinnacle, similar to those I had seen in Mrs Chesterfield's geomantic books of Asian architecture.

Arrayed around the pyramid's base were gateways in the form of impossible triangles. These seemed to be nothing more than random angles and lines when viewed from most vantage points, but as an observer walked around the mausoleum, and reached a certain point of perspective, the angles and lines would come together to form themselves into the illusion of a geometrically impossible triangle. As the observer continued to walk, and the perspective changed again, the angles and lines would collapse once more into a seemingly random collection, only for the next gateway along to form itself into the next illusion, and so on. Thus the unreality cascaded around the mausoleum like a wave, rotating with the viewer, accommodating itself to every step.

These were not, however, the main decorative feature, for on each platform were the other motifs I had been using in my art for years – impossible stairways, columns of air, floors that seemed to float with no means of support, and covering every inch and corner of these were intricate stone tableaux, a mixture of high-relief and actual sculpture, depicting the same creatures that adorned Varano's friezes at the front of the house. Demons and half-evolved human forms, screaming mouths, disfigured skulls. An army of nightmarish, unimaginable things.

There was such an abundance of adornment it reminded me of an Indian temple – the Meenakshi in Madurai, the Kailasa in Ellora – line upon line of mythical beings rising into the sky, frieze after frieze, into a mountain of monstrous imagery. It made

140

me think of Thurlby's mountain of skulls. A *visio malefica*. It was like the house itself in miniature, as if its essence had been distilled into a smaller, more potent form.

A disturbing mix of emotions filled me – exhilaration, excitement, fear. For this night-powered art encapsulated perfectly the sheer terror of dreams, the feverish, nightmarish, bewitching quality I had searched for my entire life. These sketches were unequivocally the best work I had ever done, because for all their grotesqueness, I could not take my eyes off these figures; the arrangement was so rhythmical, it made my gaze leap across the drawings, cascading from one point to the next and back again.

As my eye darted about in what felt like a perpetual loop, I remembered my dream. Running through that shifting, endless house that was also a kind of loop. It seemed somehow that the mausoleum depicted in these sketches had come from that same horrifying realm. I was sure of it.

I wondered then if Varano too had made his designs in like fashion. From sleep and nightmares. Were we both simply conduits for the same dark creative force that resided here? If that were so, then it was not Mrs Chesterfield's mad soul that haunted the house, but Varano's. It was *his* nightmare made real.

I rose and took the drawings to the easel next door to begin working them up. In my excitement I did not stop to question their appearance on my bedroom floor the very morning after I had decided to quit the house. I did not think that this might have been the house bending me to its will. Looking back now it seems so strange that I could have been beguiled thus; but in the moment, I did not think again of my previous decision to leave; it had dissolved from my mind as surely as my dreams.

22

For three days and nights I stayed in my rooms working up the drawings into something coherent enough to present to Mrs Chesterfield. I spoke to Edith and told her I would have breakfast and lunch served to me in my room. I arrived at dinner late and left as soon as I could to return to my room, except for the first night, when I told Sarah I had changed my plans and would be busy over the next few days executing a design for the mausoleum. If she was perturbed by my abrupt change of heart she did not show it. Or if she did, I was in too great a fever of artistic creation to notice.

I slept little, spurred on by that strange, delirious energy that comes sometimes from sleeplessness. The only break I took from my routine was to visit Alice in her sickbed. It pained me to see her bedridden, her head still heavily bandaged. Luckily there had been no internal bleeding, no swelling of the brain. But there had been concussion, contusions, most likely a mild fracture to the skull, meaning the doctor could not rule out permanent damage, or so Alice's parents informed me. The girl herself said nothing when I visited, but simply sat upright in her bed, pale as death, as sullen and speechless as she had been before the seance. I gave the Danbys my apologies and they accepted them begrudgingly.

This visit and the dinners aside, I stayed in my rooms and at eight clock in the morning, almost exactly three days to the

hour after I had awoken to find the sketches on the floor, I had a
design for the mausoleum that could be shown to Mrs Chesterfield. I ate breakfast in my room, washed and dressed, and with
a sense of excitement, went to present them to her, my portfolio
under my arm.

As I walked to the Great Hall I fell into the morning tide of
workers: the maids setting off on cleaning expeditions, the clerks
heading to their offices, the workmen trudging to and from the
areas that were under construction. I turned at the far end of the
hall and entered the East Wing, then the main office, where I
approached the secretary whose desk was closest to the door.

'Good morning. I'm here to meet with Mrs Chesterfield. I sent
her a note earlier.'

'Mrs Chesterfield is busy at present. Please take a seat.' He
motioned towards one of the chairs along the wall. I sat and
noted how reminiscent the scene was of my experiences in
London, arriving at magazine and newspaper offices, portfolio
in hand, trying to secure employment. And yet this also felt like
being a court artist taking his work to a king for approval. Once
more I got the sense of Mrs Chesterfield as a potentate, an Empress. Certainly the term fitted her better than any other.

As I mulled this over I heard raised voices coming from Mrs
Chesterfield's office. I frowned and looked over to the office door,
noticing that the secretary had stopped his work to listen in too.
The voices grew steadily louder until I recognised one as Mrs
Chesterfield's, the other an unknown male voice. After a few
more minutes the argument reached a crescendo and the door
to the office flew open and a tall, suited man in his seventies
stormed out.

'You shall not hear the end of this!' he screamed, his face fixed
into an iron scowl.

The man rushed past me without so much as a look, then Mrs

143

Chesterfield and Miss Thornwick exited the office on his heels. When the man reached the main office door, he flung it open and slammed it after him. The two women stopped and a look passed between them. Then they walked over to the windows opposite me and watched as the man descended the front steps of the house and hopped into a carriage that was waiting for him in the driveway. The carriage's driver whipped the horses, and in a sweep of gravel they turned round the fountain and off down the avenue.

Mrs Chesterfield and Miss Thornwick watched the man's departure with amused expressions. Then Mrs Chesterfield noticed me and smiled.

'Mr Etherstone. We have a meeting, I believe?'

She didn't wait for any reply, but turned back the way she'd come. I rose and followed her.

When we entered her office Mrs Chesterfield sat at her desk and gestured for me to sit opposite. Miss Thornwick took up her perennial position at her employer's shoulder.

'Since you are no doubt wondering,' Mrs Chesterfield said, 'the man you just saw is a relative of my husband's. He represents the interests of a party of my in-laws who believe I am squandering their legacy. They have heard about my ill health and want to assure themselves of their position once I die. They would have feasted on my late husband like a clot of maggots, and now they wish to do the same to me before I am even dead. Clara, a cigarette.'

Miss Thornwick passed over a cigarette then lit it.

'Aristocrats,' Mrs Chesterfield said, blowing opium smoke into the air. 'They look down on people who work for a living, but find no shame or vulgarity in begging. I am not of gentle blood and they see it as a travesty of fate that I should have ended up in control of their family business. The man you saw, a number of years ago took me to the courts to have me declared insane, and yet still he comes pleading.'

'Why do you allow him to visit?' I asked, surprised that she would entertain one who had done her such wrong.

'It's my sport to watch their indignation. And truthfully, I had fun in the madness court. I knew I would be proved sane, because I had money. They paid the judge handsomely and sat in court smugly expecting him to rule in their favour. But they did not know that I paid the judge's superiors far more.'

She smiled and drew a mouthful of smoke from her cigarette and I was surprised at the levity of her manner; had the conflict with her in-law buoyed her spirits? Did she draw amusement from baiting the man? I thought of how she'd needled Thurlby when she was inspecting the sculptures, and again at the dinner table. Had this too been done purely for her entertainment?

'We have seen little of you since the incident in the seance room,' she said.

'I've been working up my plans.'

'And now you are here to show them to me? Lay them out on the desk. Waylett will be here momentarily and we can discuss your work. As per the terms of our contract, if I am unhappy with it, you go back to the drawing board. Or leave without pay.'

I nodded, rose and untied the ribbons of my portfolio. I took out my sketches and laid them on the desktop. Just as I was finishing, Waylett entered.

'The matter has been dealt with, ma'am,' he said to Mrs Chesterfield with a nod.

She nodded back and gestured to the desk.

'Mr Etherstone has brought us his plans,' she said.

Waylett smiled and approached us.

I cleared my throat.

'It's a pyramidal design,' I began, pointing to the first of the sketches, a realistic rendering of the mausoleum in three dimensions, as it would be seen by someone entering the clearing from one of the doors on its northern side. 'The form is inspired by images I came across in the geomantic books in the library, illustrations of a Tibetan Buddhist temple called the Stupa of a Thousand Doors. The mausoleum likewise has multiple gates leading into it, though obviously not quite a thousand. You'll see the gateways are in the shapes of impossible triangles. These are illusions, of course. As someone walks around the building, the lines and angles of one gateway will move with their perspective until the viewer reaches a point where everything comes together and the illusion forms. As they walk on, and their perspective changes, the illusion will come apart again. But at this point, the next gateway illusion will form, and so on, all around the building, making it so that there will always be one gateway held within an illusion.'

I turned over to the next sheet to reveal elevations and floor plans of the mausoleum's interior.

'From all these gateways, however, only one path leads to the central burial chamber, much like the design of the Egyptian pyramids. Each path is crossed with blocks of stone set at right angles, as in Chinese temples, and our own Great Hall.' I flicked through more pages, coming to detailed renderings of the sculptures on the outside of the mausoleum. 'The exterior decoration is, as you can probably already see, based on Signor Varano's sculptures on the front of the main house. I think using the same motifs makes the mausoleum an echo of the house's exterior, contained within the heart of the house itself.'

I turned over to the last set of sketches, and spread them out across the desktop: renderings of the sculptures that displayed in detail how the figurative pieces mixed with the elements of impossible architecture I had designed.

All three members of my audience leaned forward, their eyes fixed to the images, scouring them, entranced by them, just as I had been when I first saw them. I wondered at that moment, as I had previously, on the extent of Mrs Chesterfield's blindness.

Just then she reached over and put her hands on the papers, running her fingertips over them as if she were reading Braille. Was this how she would 'see' my designs? By searching the paper for the grooves embedded into it by my ink pen?

I knew it was my best work and had been confident in it before its unveiling. But now, under the scrutiny of others, all my confidence evaporated and a knot of nerves tightened in my chest. The more she ran her fingers over the sheets, the surer I was that she would reject the designs, and ask me to leave the house.

I studied her face, looking for any signs, but could find none; her features were as cold and emotionless as they always were.

I continued to wait for her judgement in an agony of uncertainty.

'Yes,' she muttered, eventually. 'Yes. Just as I dreamt they would be.'

She turned to me and nodded.

'The plan is approved,' she said. 'Speak to Waylett about having the designs sent to the engineers.'

In an instant my confidence returned, cascading through me with a dizzy, joyful warmth.

23

The next few weeks passed by in a fever of work. Never in my life had I been so productive, so creative, so focused. It was as if a spirit had entered me. I worked on the plans along with three men Mrs Chesterfield had hired and brought down from York: two architects and a master stonemason, all of whom had much experience in building funerary architecture. At first they each remarked on the impossibility of getting the mausoleum completed by New Year, but as the work ran its course, we saw that with enough money and manpower, anything could be conjured into being.

Perhaps it was because of this that the days passed so quickly. I began to feel at home in the house and all my earlier anxieties receded. I looked on my fellow residents as colleagues in a great endeavour, in the building of a cathedral. I even learned to traverse the house's passageways with ease, moving through its cold emptiness with a warm glow.

I visited Alice frequently in her schoolroom, Sarah letting me in when the Danbys were absent. Over the course of a few weeks her head healed almost completely, and any lingering worries about permanent damage disappeared entirely. During my visits I took paper and watercolours with me and sketched for her fairies and animals and characters from nursery books, all of which delighted her. On these occasions she spoke to me a few times and we even laughed together. But when she was at the dinner table she never turned her eyes to me.

'Would you show me, please?' she asked one day when I was painting a watercolour of some birds for her.

'Show you what?'

She paused, then looked at the floorboards.

'How to draw and paint.'

She spoke in such a low, uncertain voice it took me a few seconds to understand what she had said. She looked up at me with a fearful expression and I realised it was the first time she'd ever asked something of me. Judging by how worried she was, I wondered if it was the first time she'd ever asked anything of anybody. Had her parents inculcated in her such a sense of her own worthlessness that she thought it was wrong to make any requests for herself?

'Of course I can teach you how to draw and paint,' I said. I smiled at her, and a few seconds later she smiled back hopefully.

And so I taught her the basics of how to draw, to sketch, to paint. I taught her how to look at things so that she could copy them accurately. I taught her how to choose colours, how to breathe life into lines. And so she became my student, something I had never had up till that point in my life, something which rewarded us both.

In the afternoons I spent time with Sarah in the library and we grew ever closer, which further increased my happiness, so that a virtuous circle formed. I went for walks when I could, along the moors and coast, sketching the views. I visited Hartington and found the village of Heybridge was the kind of picturesque Yorkshire hamlet one saw on railway postcards, with rolling cobbled streets and stone walls, and a pretty Gothic church, and green hills as a backdrop to every view.

As the summer waned, and the nights drew in, Sarah and I decided it would be good to take Alice on a trip out of the house, while the fine weather lasted, just the three of us, to one of the sandy bays near the house for a seaside picnic. We suggested it to Alice and the girl was most excited, but when Sarah asked her parents, they refused permission.

'I'll find a way,' was all that Sarah said when she relayed their decision to me.

A few other dark spots blotted this otherwise buoyant time. The first was that I failed to keep up a correspondence with my friends back in London. I had sent off an initial round of letters via the house's office post, and my friends had replied to them, but I had posted nothing further. I kept promising myself I would write when a natural break occurred in my work, but it never did.

The second happened on a walk I'd taken one afternoon down the coast. I'd been meaning to skirt around Lunham, but as I passed by on the land above it, I saw that a funeral was taking place so I descended into its lanes. Having spent weeks in the house, I found the village looked entirely different to how I'd remembered it. The biggest change of all was the villagers themselves; they appeared healthy and animated, despite their mourning. I wondered if this was because I had become so used to the sickly pallor of the house's residents.

When I asked who it was being interred into the church's graveyard that day, I was informed it was Tobias Clarke, the old man from the Black Lion who'd told me so much about the house and its mysteries.

'Died out on the moor,' was all the villagers would tell me. 'Missing for weeks before we found his body.'

I could gather no further details from them, even though I was eager to know more, for the timing suggested he'd disappeared not long after I'd spoken to him on the night of my arrival and this worried me greatly. Though when I returned to the house and immersed myself once more in my work, the worry of it faded away.

At one point my cigarettes ran out and I was supplied with some of the same type Mrs Chesterfield smoked. The visions and delirium they induced, rather than derailing my work, only made me more focused and intensely involved in it. As I worked on the plans, Waylett took charge of operations, clearing the field, levelling it, building a passageway from the house's outer walls directly to the field so that equipment and materials could be moved to the site with greater speed and ease. Workers were hired and laboured away, setting up machinery, so that they could see the project through to Mrs Chesterfield's New Year's completion date.

When I went on my walks now I stopped on the heights overlooking the house and stared down at the field in its centre where the mausoleum would be. Even from a great distance I could see men and machines there, the shimmer of movement, the smoke from their fires and engines rising into the air, where the clouds formed a vault over the house's many roofs. As I studied this hotchpotch of rooftops I came to see that they possessed the flawed, jagged texture of organic structures – rocks, crystals, tree bark, beehives, hares' burrows, the homes of other insensate creatures – built with no logic, no plan, with nothing organising it except an expedient blindness. This quality made the house look as natural as the landscape that surrounded it, more so than any regularly ordered architecture might. It made it feel as if it belonged.

And yet when I had first seen the house, just a few weeks before, it seemed monstrous, absurd. Why did it now seem so perfectly suited to its environs? Had my notions of beauty and order already been redefined?

By September my plans were completed, and work was well underway. With all this in place, I had nothing more to do but oversee construction to make sure there were no deviations from the plans. I enjoyed this new phase; with fewer duties, and the house now my home, I could relax, work on my own art, go for long walks, sketch, read, spend more time with Alice and Sarah. It was at this point Sarah told me she'd found a way to get Alice out of the house for our seaside picnic.

'The Danbys are going up to Scarborough next Wednesday on a matter of business,' she explained. 'Alice is supposed to stay with me all day. The only question is how to get together a hamper of food to take with us without anyone knowing.'

I spoke to Edith about it, for the two of us had fallen into an easy friendship over the weeks.

'I'd be glad to put something together,' she said. 'And the chef would, too. The way they treat that poor girl is awful.'

When the day came around, we were all in good spirits, for, of course, we did not know what was to happen.

24

The morning the Danbys left for Scarborough I met Edith at the kitchen door, where she and the chef passed me over the hamper they'd prepared.

'There's also something else,' Edith said, giving me a canvas bag.

I looked inside it and saw a bucket and spade and a ball, along with other toys for the beach.

'For the girl,' Edith smiled.

I thanked them and left the house. When I stepped outside I saw it was a bright, warm day. I went to the place in the gardens where I'd arranged to meet Sarah and Alice and after a few minutes they arrived. I was shocked at how different Alice looked. Outside of the house, eager to get to the beach, she was grinning broadly, excited and animated. Even her pallor seemed to have gone, replaced by a healthy pink flush. Was this marked transformation simply because of the anticipated excursion? Or because the girl was finally free of the house's malign influence? And that of her parents?

We left the grounds, and turned south and walked a few minutes up the coast, to a bay I had earmarked a few weeks earlier. When we got to the sand we spread out the blankets Sarah had brought, weighing them down with a few rocks. We spent the entire morning on the beach and the change in Alice was even more marked here. She ran about gleefully. We played with the ball. We built sandcastles. We looked in rock pools and made sketches of what we saw – spindly brown-shelled crabs; deep red anemones; swaying, bumpy tendrils of kelp. We tried to draw the gulls, terns and gannets that alighted on the rocks. Alice was already displaying a strong talent for art, her drawings showing she had a knack for capturing the world around her in all its vibrancy. The girl was as excitable and full of life as any child of her age should be.

After spending some time playing and exploring the beach, we sat down to have our lunch. We opened up the hamper and saw it was stuffed with food: cold roast beef, tongue, cheese-and-cress sandwiches, pork pies, scones, jam, clotted cream, blancmanges, even a pear upside-down cake wrapped up with cloth and ribbon. There was elderberry cordial for Alice, and gin and beer for Sarah and me.

We sat and ate and then Sarah and I stayed on the blankets while Alice went to the water's edge, took off her shoes and stockings and paddled about in the water.

'The change in her is remarkable,' I said.

'It is. I think perhaps this is the first time I've ever seen her in the fresh air.'

'You think it's the house that's responsible for her normal demeanour?'

Sarah paused, considering her response.

'No,' she said eventually, not taking her eyes off Alice, who was splashing about in the waves, kicking her feet forwards so arcs of water pearled and tumbled before her.

Sarah turned to look at me, her expression completely transformed, deadly solemn now.

'I've never spoken to anyone of this, for I never had anyone to speak to about it,' she said. 'Those hours I spend in the library every afternoon, when they take her away to give her instruction

in spiritual matters. When she returns, she is at her most sullen.
I have found bruises on her.'

'They beat her?'

'All over her body, but never on her hands or face, so that
anyone would notice.' She paused, then sighed. 'So I think it is the
malignancy of her parents, rather than the house, that is mostly
responsible for how she is.'

'Have you spoken to her about it?' I asked.

'I have. She tells me the bruises come from the dead people.
From dead soldiers.'

'Her parents have trained her to explain them away in such a
manner.'

'Yes,' Sarah replied, her tone implying that she had come to a
similar conclusion. 'This is why I stay here,' she added, looking at
me with a resolute expression. 'I stay here to protect the girl, to
alleviate the cruelties she suffers with kindness and compassion.
I could not leave her to another who might not care for her as I
do. I also try to find some way of freeing her from the evil under
which she lives. But in all these months I have yet to come up
with a scheme that has any hope of working. And so I stay on in
the house, tied to it by a bond of love to a child who has experienced no such love from her own parents.'

I realised now the bind she was in. She clearly did not want to
stay, and yet she could not leave without abandoning Alice, so she
gave up her own chance of happiness to look after the girl.

'The manner in which they treat the child,' I said. 'As nothing
more than an instrument for enriching themselves. I wouldn't
be surprised if they'd bought her as a baby, the way a magician
might buy a rabbit or a dove. Are we sure the Danbys are her
actual parents?'

'I've wondered the same myself. But I have no means to make

155

enquiries about their history. Neither the girl nor her parents ever provide substantive replies when I question them about where they came from, their families, social circles. Nothing. What they did before they arrived here, I do not know. Whenever I ask Alice, she says she doesn't remember. There is, however, some physical similarity between Alice and her mother. But who knows? Perhaps she is an orphan.'

'I know something of Alice's plight from my own upbringing,' I said. 'I, too, was raised by people who didn't love me. I, too, suffered cruelties, though not anywhere near as bad.'

Sarah turned to me and as I looked at her I knew I could trust her more than anyone else in the world, so I decided to tell her about my own painful origins, to unburden myself of the scandal that had surrounded my birth.

'My father was a missionary,' I began. 'Posted to a city somewhere along the coast of China. He met my mother there, the daughter of a local landowner. One of the people Thurlby and Mrs Danby refer to as savages at our dinner table. My father and mother fell in love, I suppose. She was soon with child and so the affair became common knowledge and a scandal ensued. My father was defrocked and shortly after took his own life. My mother's family disapproved of the relationship as much as the Church had, for when my mother came to term, I was left as a babe on the mission-house steps. I suppose they reasoned that a half-white child was the white man's problem. The missionary society sent me back to England and I lost all contact with my mother; I don't even know her name or the place where she lived.

'Eventually I was taken in by my father's brother, also a vicar. I was raised by him and his wife in their vicarage in Haslemere, in Surrey. It was an unhappy childhood. My uncle raised me out of a sense of duty, not of love. I suffered many cruelties at their hands. I'm not sure if it was because he blamed me for his brother's death or that I was a blot of sin and shame on the family. Some of it was no doubt because of my Chinese blood, my "barbarian blood", as he liked to say.

'I spent much of my childhood being forced to study the religious pamphlets my uncle delighted in, all luridly illustrated with the fire-and-brimstone hellscapes sinners would inhabit if they didn't follow the word of the Lord. I suppose, in some way, their nightmarish quality informed my own art – perhaps, too, my own need to be an artist. As soon as I was old enough, I fled to London, to the Slade, where I met Rose. We fell in love and married, but she passed away not a year after the wedding. I tell people she died in childbirth, but it's not true. The child died a few days after he was born and Rose was deeply affected by it. She killed herself shortly thereafter with poison.'

'Sam, I'm so sorry,' Sarah said, tears welling in her eyes.

'Don't be. I didn't say all this for you to pity me or see me as some tragic figure. I've just told you so that you may know me better.'

We smiled at each other then her gaze turned downwards, to the tartan blanket we were sitting on, to the archipelagos of sand drifting across it.

'Sam, please don't think ill of me, but I, too, need to tell you something. I should have told you long ago, but I didn't want you to think badly of me, and I could never find the right time.'

'What is it? I doubt I could ever think badly of you.'

She inhaled, steeling herself, then looked up at me.

'I, too, have a dead marriage in my past,' she said. 'I had a husband. Six years ago now. He died not long after we married. It's how I ended up a governess.'

'Why would I think badly of you for that?' I asked.

'Well, maybe not for that, but for keeping it from you. Like I said, I could never find the right time to tell you.'

I shook my head, letting her know it didn't affect my opinion of her.

'We married young, back in Edinburgh,' she continued. 'He had prospects with the civil service and secured a position out in Calcutta. He took what meagre savings we had with him, to help set up a home, so that I might join him some months later. But within a few weeks of him being there he died of malaria. All the money was lost, for I could never find out what happened to it. And because his service was of such short duration, I was not entitled to a widow's pension. So I became a governess, for what other options are there for young widows with no means and too much education? I signed up to a work agency and they sent me here. So, here I am. And he's still out there, in the Calcutta British Cemetery, so far from home.'

She smiled and I leaned over and squeezed her hand, and she rested her head on my shoulder. We settled into silence and watched the beach. The waves were coming in more strongly now, the wind having picked up. I looked into the distance and saw clouds forming on the horizon.

'How did you not say anything during all those dinners?' she asked.

'What do you mean?'

'When Thurlby and the Danbys were talking about savage races and barbarians, you never challenged them. But you're half Chinese.'

I stopped then to wonder why, for I'd never contemplated my own muted responses before. I knew that they'd only spoken thus because they couldn't tell from my appearance that I had a Chinese parent, and by raising this with them I would have been making an uncomfortable situation worse; but I also knew there were other, more significant reasons too.

'I suppose I'm just used to it,' I said. 'I've grown up with it.

It's not something I think or worry about. They've been taught to view the world in that way. I doubt it's something they ever consider either.'

'But that's exactly why it's important. *Why have* they been taught to look at things that way? Because these same countries we say are populated by savages are the same countries we're subjugating. If we admitted they're human beings just like us, then it would make *us* the invading barbarians.'

'We paint others as monsters to stop ourselves from being the monsters,' I said.

She considered this before replying.

'Then this is the tragedy of empire – it makes monsters of us all.'

I nodded and we said no more and fell into our own thoughts. I considered then how much Mrs Chesterfield's house was like our own empire – its facade of stateliness and grandeur hiding its true reality of shanty towns behind.

I finished the bottle of beer I'd been drinking. Sarah ran her fingers through the sand, raking it into lines. We both watched Alice play, all of us feeling at ease, contemplative, happy.

As the afternoon wore on, the weather worsened, so that eventually we gathered up our things and headed back to the house. We reached the headland and were approaching the driveway when Alice turned to us with a worried look.

'The ball,' she said. 'We've forgotten Edith's ball on the beach. She'll be angry.'

I frowned, surprised at how agitated she was.

'No one will be angry,' I said. 'And certainly not at you. I'll run back for it. You two go on ahead and get inside before any rain comes. I'll see you both at dinner. Here.'

I passed Sarah the hamper, which was light enough now for her to carry back, and then I returned alone to the beach.

25

When I reached the beach I spotted the ball at its far end. But as I made my way over to it, a gust of wind sent it bouncing over the wall of rocks that separated the bay from the next one along.

I rushed across the sand, clambered over the rocks and dropped down onto the adjacent beach. I looked around and realised that I was actually standing in a tiny, secluded cove. The cliffs behind loomed over it, cutting out the light. At their top I could see the edge of the house, teetering far above. At their foot, a series of cave mouths led back into the rock. Due to the way the coast curved, this cove was more exposed to the wind and incoming waves, and was already filling with the tide.

I saw the ball further on, in a gap at the bottom of a mound of rocks. I crossed to it and picked it up, then turned to head back. But as I did so I spotted something on the sand further on, floating at the water's edge.

A blade of shock stabbed through me as I realised it was a naked body. Either somebody had fallen from the cliffs above, or they had washed in with the tide. I continued staring, as if frozen in a dream. And then the body turned, jerking onto its side and back again. Had it been moved by the waves? Or was the person still alive and in need of help?

I burst into a run, sprinting over the wet sand. As I neared, I saw it was a woman, red-haired, young, floating face up in the water.

Eventually I reached the shallow pool where she lay, gently rocking in the swell, and I saw undoubtably that she was dead; her chest unmoving, her eyes open, the seawater rolling over them as if they were tide pools. And yet, all across her nakedness, she had not a single mark on her body, nor was she bloated. If she had fallen from the cliffs, or washed in from the sea, surely there would be marks of passage on her?

I studied her and it was only then that I noticed how well she resembled my dead wife Rose – beautiful and pale-skinned, with lips both full and delicate, a rhythm of freckles sweeping across her face. Her hair was a burning orange that rippled and gleamed in the greenish water. The sharp and ancient rocks that encompassed her made her seem even more fragile and otherworldly.

As I stood there a raging anger filled me at the injustice of Rose's passing, the same larmoyant fury that had afflicted me in the years immediately after her death. I looked up at the cliff, where the very edges of the house were tumbling down, and for some reason I directed my anger at the house, as if Rose's death was its fault. And as I directed this anger at the house, I felt it was reflecting it back at me, the same malevolent energy. A shiver of fear ran through me.

I looked at the pool once more and was shocked to see that it was empty. There was no dead woman. There were just the waves foaming as they broke, and further on, the gulls and the immensity of the fathomless, devouring sea. Had she been dragged out into the water once more? Or had I simply imagined her?

A woozy sense of disorientation pulsed through me like poison. I stared at the empty pool, trying to make sense of what had happened, but my panic only increased, my bewilderment made worse by the shriek of the gulls, the boom and crash of the waves reverberating through the deathly stillness.

I turned to leave, but jumped back in shock, horrified to see the girl was standing behind me. Worse still, she was a girl no more. Her skin was green and rotting, her hair matted and drenched and falling off in clumps, her yellow bones showing through her corrupted flesh, her hollow carcass of a face.

A woozy nausea blazed through me with such force I felt as if I might collapse. And yet, as revolted as I was by the apparition, I could not turn my gaze away. As my thoughts continued to swirl, she raised an arm into the air, and I saw she had something gripped in her fist – a shard of broken mirror, long and triangular. The exact same shard of mirror that had broken off when I was in Varano's room, which had embedded itself, point first, into the floorboard.

The apparition stared at me a moment longer, then she opened her fingers. The shard dropped to the beach and embedded itself, point first, into the sand, just as it had done in the house. I realised now the message she had come to deliver to me.

26

I ran to the end of the cove and clambered over its rocks. Before I dropped down into the bay I turned and looked once more at the beach. All was empty. No sea waif in her saltwater cradle. No Venus. No Ophelia. No Rose.

Just spume and spray and waves leaping onto rocks in a shattering clatter of white.

I rushed back to my room, where I rifled through my sketchbooks, looking for the one I had taken with me to Varano's room, whereupon Waylett had written directions on how to get back to the Great Hall. Eventually I found it. By reversing the directions I could navigate from the Great Hall to Varano's room, and this is exactly what I did.

It was unchanged from my previous visit. The fragments of broken glass were still scattered across the floor, and the same shard of mirror was still sticking into the same floorboard. I knelt and saw that there were scratches around its edges, where an instrument had been used to remove it. I had brought with me a sturdy metal ruler from my studio, and wedged it now into the space between the floorboards. I levered it back and the board came loose easily.

I removed it and peered into the cavity beneath, where I could see a dust-covered wooden box. I hauled it out of its resting place and inspected it. There was a series of curlicues engraved into its wood, which must at one time have been finished to a high shine before years of neglect had left it cracked and half rotten.

I turned the latch and looked inside, where I found a set of three musty old books. I wiped away the dust and spots of mould from the cover of the first, but there were no markings on it. I opened it and on the inside page there was a name written in ink – Francisco Varano.

I flicked through more pages and realised it was a journal, written in Italian. Like all art students I had studied the language, along with French and German, at art school, but it had been years since I'd had cause to read anything written in it, so I struggled to make out the words. I saw that the journal covered the second half of 1848, and the first half of 1849. I looked at the other two and they detailed the following years. All the books were mouldy, damp and fragile. They would need much care to be read without damaging them further.

Why had Varano hidden his journals thus? And why had the apparition on the beach led me to them? Was it the same apparition that I had seen in the mirror before it had smashed? Had it attempted to lead me here twice?

I took the journals back to my room so that I could study them more closely. The text was not easy to read: the tiny, cramped handwriting; the considerable damage the books had suffered over the years; the use of Italian. I would certainly need a dictionary to help me with the translation, and even then it would be painstaking work.

In amongst the entries were pen-and-ink sketches of the house. In the earlier journals they were lifelike, precise, elegant, but as I flicked through the pages, and the years passed, an erratic quality entered them, till those at the end of the last journal were little more than crazed, expressive scribbles. Here I came across a packet of letters, wedged into the back cover. The letters looked just as fragile and damaged as the journals themselves so I did not want to untie the string which held them together, but I could see that the uppermost envelope was addressed to someone called Emily.

I put the packet on the floorboards in front of the fire, along with the journals, so that they could dry and be easier to handle. Then I went to the library and was relieved to find an Italian dictionary on its shelves. I took it back to my room and set it down on the desk, eager to find out what the journals would reveal – perhaps they would tell me why Mrs Chesterfield was building the house, why Gosterwood and Varano went mad, why I felt that Varano's and my own fate were somehow intertwined, and why the apparition had led me to these journals, for I was convinced now that that was what she'd done.

At the time I thought reading them would set my mind at ease, explain away all the mysteries which had been agitating me.

But what I discovered in the journals did the exact opposite – their horror chilled me to the core. Indeed, I came to understand exactly why Varano and Gosterwood went mad, and how it was all tied in with the deaths of the Marsden girls. Worst of all, I realised the danger I was in, that the same dark mysteries might also see me killed.

Rather than give a summary of these documents, I present them here in their entirety, so that their authors, Varano and Gosterwood, may speak for themselves, for they are the protagonists of their own stories, as I am of mine.

PART TWO
The Journal of Francisco Varano

1848

15 December

Everything is arranged; in three days' time we leave for Yorkshire.

Thank the Lord!

I will go north, build Mrs C—'s house and return a rich man.

I cannot wait to be rid of miserable London.

Of counting the pennies.

Of choosing between a loaf of bread or a scuttle of coal.

I welcome the journey into the unknown, even though it will pull me further from my family.

Lux ex tenebris.

16 December

Last night I dreamt of the war again.

Gun smoke. Bullets. Blood. Screaming.

How many months since I fled Italy, and still I dream of the traumas of battle?

I pray I will recover one day.

I pray I will see my family again.

17 December

Thank the Lord I only have a day left in London, which must be the gloomiest city on Earth.

Grey buildings and streets and skies and faces.

Grey torrents of grey rain.

In the afternoons the city has the aspect of a graveyard; its buildings like so many tombstones, its citizens like so many mourners.

Did I really survive the war?

Or did I die and enter a necropolis?

18 December

King's Cross.

At the hotel I met Mrs C— and her retinue, of which I suppose I am now a part.

We boarded our train.

London to Yorkshire on the Great Northern Railway.

The train is a thing of dreams, the country it passes through, nightmares; lands filled with so many factories and smoke stacks blasting black clouds into the sky that a great hellish smog lies across the Earth, as if the place has been ravaged and burned by a dragon.

Even sitting in my carriage, its sulphurous smell stung my nostrils and chest.

At each station there were ragged beggars.

It was dark by the time we alighted in Yorkshire and the group split up; while Mrs C— and her closest companions caught a cab to a hotel just by the railway station, I and a few others were driven to a fishing village nearer the land she has purchased, where rooms have been rented for us.

19 December

I washed and changed and descended to the inn's main parlour.

I expected the place to be empty but there was a man there I recognised from the previous day's journey.

'Hello, I'm Gosterwood,' he said. 'I'm one of Mrs Chesterfield's advisors.'

He's a tall, thin man with a haunted look to him and a shock of grey hair, even though he must only be a little older than me. He wore a purple cravat, moustaches pointed to tips in the Continental style, and most oddly: a walking cane topped with a silver skull's head.

'Mrs Chesterfield apologises,' he explained. 'She and her secretaries have an appointment this morning with the owner of Bastwick Hall, a manor house a few miles from here; they're hoping to take a lease on it while the building works are undertaken.'

He gestured for me to sit at his table. I sat and poured myself some coffee and cut a slice of bread from the breakfast tray that had been laid out.

'Mrs Chesterfield suggested that I should take you to the site,' he said. 'It's a pleasant walk over the hills. Or if you'd prefer, we can arrange for a villager to take us in a cart?'

'A walk would be good,' I said.

As we ate, Gosterwood questioned me amiably on my history.

I told him about my upbringing in Venice and my work as an architect and sculptor.

'So you're a stonemason as well as an architect.' He smiled. 'Like the grand master Palladio. I visited many of his buildings on my tours of Italy. Some of the greatest in the world.'

'You've been to Italy?'

'Several times,' he said breezily. 'I know Venice well. So how did you end up in England?'

'The war,' I sighed. 'I joined the revolution when independence was declared. We all did. But I had the misfortune of being drafted into the Italian army that was defeated by the Austrians in the Battle of Custoza in July. My unit was cut off from the main fighting force, and fearing capture, we fled.'

I didn't go into the details of how I fled – in the dead of night, with a bullet in my leg, leaving behind my family and friends and everything I had ever known or loved.

I didn't tell him about the terror of it all, or of the ruthlessness of Field Marshal Radetzky; of trekking, injured, over the Alps into France.

I didn't tell him any of this because I didn't want to relive the horrors, but still they resurrected themselves.

'I've been living in London ever since,' I said.

'And how did you find our fair capital?'

Images of the city flashed through my mind: arriving in the dead of night – penniless, homeless, friendless, the thin months of living as a pauper until I managed to secure work sculpting gravestones at the great West Norwood Cemetery.

I told him all in a precis, leaving out the hardships, the continuing trauma.

'And where did you cross paths with Mrs Chesterfield?' he asked.

'At the cemetery. Her family are buried there and she visited frequently. She saw some of my funerary sculptures and enquired after me, and then when she learned I was an architect she suggested I apply for the commission to build her house.'

'And out of all the applicants she chose you,' Gosterwood smiled.

I wanted to ask him of his own history, the exact nature of his relationship with Mrs C—, but the conversation kept getting away from me, with Gosterwood asking constant questions about my background, my art, Italy, my impressions of England.

When I had finished eating I went up to my room and changed before meeting him again on the steps outside the inn.

'Good Lord, man, you can't wear that,' he said when he saw my frock coat. 'You'll freeze to death. Do you have nothing thicker?'

'I could put on an extra vest.'

172

He smiled and ran his eye over my figure, like a tailor appraising a customer.

'Come,' he said, stepping back inside.

We went to his room and he rummaged about in a luggage trunk and took out a long, thick watchcoat in grey wool.

'It'll be big for you but it should do the trick,' he said.

I thanked him and put it on.

There was no doubting how much warmer it was, but the sleeves came past my fingertips, something that caused Gosterwood to boom out a laugh and slap me on the back.

We set off from the inn and headed up the hill.

Soon we were on the headland, where the wind was high and bitterly cold, and I was glad of both my companion's coat and his thoughtfulness.

When the moor came into view I finally got a first look at the place that will be my home for the next few months.

For all its harshness, this is a beautiful land.

So different to the Mammon-ravaged industrial areas the train had passed through; rolling hills, russet flora, moss and heather that capture moisture which captures sunlight, so everything shines and glitters and glows as if lit by a holy illumination.

Even though it was grey, the sky felt as magnificent as it does in Venice.

After a walk of about an hour, we arrived at a great wide plain, many acres across, nestled amongst the otherwise hilly terrain.

On one side it sloped down to the sea-cliffs, on the other it rose to reach the high ground inland.

We approached a depression in its centre where there was a rocky outcrop and a few mounds.

As we neared, I realised the mounds were actually great slabs of fallen stone, half reclaimed by the flora.

'Standing stones,' Gosterwood said. 'Though they stand no

more. The ancient people here would set them up in sites they considered holy. All long before your Roman forebears came to these lands.'

I wondered why these ancients had undertaken the Herculean task of bringing standing stones to such a desolate spot.

And this made me wonder what had led Mrs C— to want to build here, too.

Did she have family close by?

Did she want to shut herself away from the world?

I regretted not having brought my papers and pencils to sketch the site, its topography and features.

I knelt and pressed my fingers into the earth; the soil was springy, waterlogged, yielding.

I wondered if it would be possible even to build a house on such ground.

Would I have to use the same engineering techniques for laying stable foundations as I did when building in the Venice lagoon?

'Do you know the make-up of the ground here?' I asked.

'You mean for laying foundations? I think you'll have to speak to an engineer, but there's decent rock underlying all of this if the caves are anything to go by.'

'The caves?'

He pointed to the rocky outcrops in the centre of the mound of fallen standing stones.

'This is why the place was considered sacred,' he said.

He gestured for me to follow him and we walked over to the rocks.

I saw amongst them, in the middle of the depression, a cave mouth, as large as the entrance to a mineshaft, descending steeply into the earth.

'Natural caves,' he said.

'But what's special about them?'

'Nothing special; all caves were considered sacred. Pagans valued any place where two worlds met. Lakesides, beaches, bogs, hills, caves; all borderlands where earth meets water or sky or underworld. If you can travel between physical worlds in these places, then why not spiritual ones, too? Hence their religious significance.'

'You know a lot about this.'

'I've devoted most of my life to studying Britain's ancient religions. I'm currently writing a book on the topic, *A Psychic History of the British Isles*. I hope it to be the most comprehensive study yet undertaken.'

I nodded and turned to examine the cave and its surroundings once more.

In the silence the wind picked up and something strange happened – as it blew past the mouth of the cave, a low, mournful moan rose into the air.

'The moor whistle,' Gosterwood explained. 'Maybe another reason the ancients worshipped this place.'

We listened to the sound for a few seconds; it had an unsettling restlessness to it, as if a Siren somewhere was calling for help, for an end to some blissful sadness.

I turned to the cave's entrance and approached, wanting to see the type of rock inside, if we could actually build here without risk of collapse.

I stepped into the shadows at the mouth, walked a few yards in and inspected its walls, which seemed to be composed of limestone.

I looked into the depths, wondering how far the cave stretched, when I suddenly felt a presence in the darkness, and a chill fear ran through me.

I turned to the entrance to see if it was Gosterwood who was watching me, but I was startled to see that I'd travelled much further into the cave than I'd assumed – I thought I'd just taken a few steps inside, but I was a good thirty or forty yards from the sunlight blurring about at the mouth.

How could this be possible?

Before I could dwell on it, I felt the presence once more.

I turned and stared again into the darkness that twisted down into the depths of the earth.

I definitely felt something in there, as if the darkness was in possession of some ancient, malignant intelligence.

It left me with a sharp feeling that I was in imminent peril.

A notion came upon me that Gosterwood was in league with whatever lived down there, that he had brought me to it as prey, as a sacrifice to those archaic gods he was so enamoured with.

It seemed that the most sensible course of action was to arm myself and come out of the cave and attack Gosterwood before he should attack me.

Looking back on it now, I don't know what came over me, but in the moment, my fear was so great that this scheme seemed the product of clear and compelling logic.

I found an appropriate-sized rock, gripped it tightly, then made my way back.

When I stepped out onto the moor, I saw Gosterwood in the distance, sitting on one of the fallen standing stones, smoking a cigarette.

All the fear and dark energy dropped away from me and I looked at the rock in my hand and wondered with a wave of revulsion what had come over me.

I dropped the rock, ashamed of myself, walked over to my companion and sat next to him.

He offered me his cigarette case and we smoked in silence, surveying the plain, the moors, the sea in the distance.

Gradually, through the contemplation of the surroundings, my heart quietened and my nerves stilled.

'How much of this land has Mrs Chesterfield bought?' I asked.

'As far as the eye can see. And then that much again. After the Queen and the Church, she's now the largest landowner in the county.'

We finished our cigarettes, then rose, and I turned to look at the cave once more.

Again I sensed the presence of some evil in the landscape.

Some cruelty, watching us, hating us.

Suddenly Homer came to mind, his description of the Cimmerians, who live to the north of Europe, in a land of fog and darkness, by the entrance to Hades.

On the walk back to the inn, I considered how this desolate spot had come to be my place of work, the turns of fate and history that had brought me here.

I asked Gosterwood about Mrs C——, why she would want to build a house in such a locale.

'What do you know of the woman's past?' he asked.

'Next to nothing. I am a foreigner here and only recently arrived. All I know is the stonemasons' gossip from the cemetery.'

He told me about the deaths in her family, a great inheritance, then how she communed with the spirit of her dead husband, on whose instructions she had decided to build the house.

'Spirits?' I said, incredulously. 'She is building all this on the say-so of some—' I tried to think of the English word for a trickster, but could not, so Gosterwood finished my sentence for me.

'Charlatan?' he suggested.

'Yes,' I smiled. 'Thank you.'

'I would hardly call the medium a charlatan,' he said.

'Why not?'

'Because I am the medium.'

He turned to me and grinned, seemingly not bothered in the slightest by my unintentional insult.

In Venice, such an affront would be cause for the severing of ties, but Gosterwood almost looked pleased.

I wondered if this odd reaction was particular to the man, or if all Englishmen would have reacted thus, for I am still finding their customs and manners hard to gauge.

'When Mrs Chesterfield decided to move out of London, she tasked me with travelling the country to find somewhere suitable to build,' he explained. 'Somewhere secluded, isolated, secure, but most importantly, somewhere that had a strong spiritual resonance. I spent over a year trawling these isles, visiting different sites, consulting the occult histories of Britain. Ever since ancient times this land has been venerated as holy, so this is where we settled.'

I looked at him in dismay, for my brief experience of the place had been anything but holy.

'You do not believe in the supernatural?' he asked.

'The only greater power I believe in is God Almighty. But you believe that there are such things as ghosts?'

'It's not such an outlandish proposition,' he said. 'If we come to an accepted definition of them. Are they energies that live on after we die? The last splinters of a life? Are they emotions trapped in time? Warnings we should take heed of? Or are they simply a lingering memory?'

'A memory of what?'

'Of themselves.'

I looked at him in confusion and he smiled.

'Imagine for a moment that the universe is not as we have been taught,' he began. 'Not something that was created aeons ago, and that will go on existing until the end of days. Imagine instead that it is constantly being reborn, moment by moment, that each new instant a new incarnation of our world comes into being which extinguishes the one that existed before. Some things are lost with each rebirth, others appear for the first time. Thus change doesn't happen *within* the universe, but *to* it. Our reality is a flickering carousel, a cascade of incremental changes too fast and vast for us ever to comprehend, leaving us constantly clinging to a world that has already fallen into the past by the time our plodding minds have had the opportunity to perceive it. Is it any great leap then to imagine there are ghosts, too, clinging on to this ever-changing world? Ghosts who, just like us, are merely the memory of themselves?'

He turned to look at me with a smile.

I could tell the speech had been rehearsed, perfected, memorised, that it sought to add a sheen of logic to the irrational; and yet, despite knowing all this, I felt there was some truth in it: that one's identity, one's sense of self, is mostly constructed from one's memories of oneself.

But I did not agree that this could be used to justify the existence of ghosts.

We continued on in silence as I mulled over the notion, and my strange companion.

He seems a gentleman – educated, intelligent and cultured – and yet he is a swindler, feeding Mrs C— lies so that he may feed on her purse-book.

I suppose a prerequisite of being a successful swindler is not having the manner and appearance of one, but still I wondered about the variance between his fine bearing and his occupation.

All in all, the experience is unnerving.

20 December

This morning Mrs C— and her retinue returned to London, having secured their rental of the manor house.

She called me in for a meeting to confirm our plans – I will stay on to survey the land and work up my designs, then after Christmas a surveyor will join me from Leeds, and all being well, clearing of the site is to commence once we are through the worst of the winter.

We concluded our conversation and I returned to my room, where Gosterwood found me a few minutes later.

'Pleased to be returning to London?' I asked.

'Ever so. Though sad to be leaving my new Venetian friend, and worried that you may go out of your mind up here alone. So I brought you these to pass the time.' He took his hands from behind his back to reveal a case containing a number of books. 'You can return them to me when we come back in the New Year.'

I thanked him and looked through the titles eagerly, but was disappointed to see they were all books on the occult and paganism.

'And you can keep my coat, too,' he smiled. 'It'll give me an excuse to visit my tailor for a new one.'

We spoke some more as I readied myself, then we descended to the inn's parlour for our breakfast.

As we ate, there was an odd scene:

The front door opened and a peasant girl entered.

On seeing the girl, the landlord of the inn became angry and marched across to her, clearly intending to throw her out.

'She's here to see me,' Mrs C— said.

The landlord paused and turned to frown at Mrs C—.

'Very well,' he grunted, returning to the bar.

The girl flashed a triumphant smile at the landlord, then she was taken by Mrs C— into a side chamber.

'The new lady's maid,' Gosterwood explained.

It was only then that I realised Mrs C— had been without her lady's maid on the trip.

'The old one refused to come north,' Gosterwood continued. 'They had a falling-out and no one's seen her since.'

'And the new one?'

'An unusual choice, but then that's Mrs Chesterfield's nature. The girl goes by the name of Thornwick. A local outcast. Mrs Chesterfield took pity on her. She's to leave with us for London and return in the New Year. I suppose Mrs Chesterfield wants to train her in proper comportment.'

A few minutes later Mrs C— and the girl stepped back into the parlour.

Mrs C— returned to her place and room was made at the table for the girl.

I cast my eye over her as she waited to be seated; she is about thirteen or fourteen years old and exceptionally handsome for a low sort, with dark hair and eyes, and delicate, frosty features.

Even though her beauty is of a cold and sinister type, she would not look out of place in the finest ballroom in Venice.

And yet here she is, at the end of the world, in a dirty smock, with mud under her cracked fingernails.

I wonder what she has done to turn the locals against her.

23 December

During the daytime I work on my plans.

In the evenings I read Gosterwood's books and study to improve my English, although now I am in Yorkshire, I find I have to relearn much of the language as the dialect here is thick and quite different from that spoken in London.

When I have free time I go for walks across the moors.

I take my sketching materials with me to make studies of the locality, but I know not why – as soon as my hands are out of my pockets my fingers freeze, and if I actually open my sketchbook the paper is drenched in rain before I have the chance to make a single mark.

25 December

Christmas Day.

In the morning the landlord knocked and asked if I would be attending church.

When I explained I am a follower of the True Faith he seemed put out, but said nothing.

After he had gone I read from some of Gosterwood's books and listened to the church bells tolling, the pleasant chatter of the villagers as they returned to their houses.

The locals are friendly enough, but look on me with suspicion – the foreigner in their midst.

Does my absence from their Protestant church make this worse?

Should I begin attending Sunday services?

Would they even allow a Catholic to enter?

In the afternoon I went downstairs to eat my dinner.

The food here is somehow even more foul than that in London – meat and vegetables all overcooked to the point where the meat is tough and the vegetables are mush, with no sauce or seasoning or spices or oils or juices or herbs to make them more flavourful.

Not wishing to insult the landlord's cooking I ate as much as I could stomach, then returned to my room.

This was my Christmas Day.

31 December

Another day on the moors.

A snap chill in the air, the frost crackling underfoot.

Another evening in my room.

The bar below filled with villagers seeing in the New Year, the revelry lasting well into the night.

The crowd spilled out onto the street and a bonfire was lit.

The noise kept me up and jangled my nerves, and all the while I thought of the New Year's balls we used to have in Venice, at Father's, or the Palazzo G—, or R—'s country estate.

Will we ever enjoy such balls again?

How many who attended them have been killed in the war?

How many have fled to the furthest corners of the globe?

Will we ever return?

1849

1 January

God prosper the New Year to those I love.

Wherever they may be.

I resolve myself to aims:

1) Complete my commission and return to London a rich man

2) Wait out the war in Italy and return to my family

3) Recover my spirits and put the traumas of war behind me

2 January

The surveyor and his men arrived from Leeds and I thank the Lord.

We journeyed to the site together and started making our way through all the tasks that lie before us.

The surveyor – George Fernhurst – is brusque and humourless, but seems capable and knowledgeable, with a good understanding of the local topography.

He and his men seem of a type – solidly built and suited to the land, all of them dressed in scarves of bog wool and flat caps.

183

There are some difficulties of language – particularly the technical language of the engineering trade – but we navigate these with the help of my dictionary, and occasionally, by the use of Latin, in which we are both well versed.

5 January

Days on the moor with Fernhurst and his men.

Out in the frost and wind from first light till last.

I feel for ever penetrated by the cold.

I cannot even think for it.

7 January

I dream of my family back in Venice.

Perhaps by some miracle I might receive news from them.

But even if they could get a letter out of the city, through the blockade, how long would it take for it to cross Europe, to reach London, to wend its way up here?

9 January

The survey is complete.

Fernhurst has confirmed the work of the surveyors who assessed the land during Mrs C—'s purchase; it is good to be built on, it can be cleared and the foundations laid.

I relay all to Mrs C— and she instructs me to hire men to clear the land.

16 January

The promise of work has ingratiated me with the locals.

I have spoken to the landlord and he has gathered together a team of men happy to have some extra money during the lean months.

Shrubs and heather, trees and their stumps, are all cleared from the few acres where the first section of the house will be built.

20 January

We finished clearing the ground today.

The collected material, which we've been rolling into great bales, was set on fire.

Black smoke blighted the sky.

30 January

I spend my days among the moor's solitudes.

This land of crows and gorges, of mausolean light.

This land where the world dies in winter.

2 February

The sound of carriages in the mud lanes outside the inn signalled Mrs C——'s return.

I went down to greet her and was glad to see familiar faces.

Gosterwood, smiling as always, shook my hand warmly, and asked after my health.

It is good to have him back; I have missed his riant nature and mordant humour.

The party came into the inn and sat down to eat before moving on to Bastwick Hall, the manor house they have leased for the year that the initial building works will take to complete.

At the table was Mrs C——'s new lady's maid, the local girl, Miss T——.

She was much changed after her time in the capital; cleaned up and well attired in a rose travelling dress trimmed in mauve, with a moss-agate brooch at her breast and her hair pinned up into one of the styles I saw sported by the wealthy women in London.

In her fine new clothes, she has the wintry perfection of an enchantress.

I noticed again that the landlord seemed much irritated by her presence.

At one point she asked him to fetch her more ale, holding her jar aloft in a display of insolence clearly designed to provoke the man, who did a poor job of hiding his annoyance.

When he took the jar from her I noticed her eyes stay with him as he crossed the room, a sly little smile on her pink lips.

After dinner I returned to my room and there was a knock at the door: Gosterwood, holding a stack of books tied together with a leather strap.

'For you, old man,' he said. 'I brought two crates of them up with me to take to the manor house. I thought perhaps you'd like a few.'

'Thank you.'

'I also brought these.'

He took his other hand from behind his back to reveal a bottle of brandy and two cigars.

We drank and smoked and passed a merry evening.

4 February

Today Fernhurst and I gave Mrs C— a tour of the site.

It was odd seeing her there on the moor, wearing her widow's weeds of total black; a full-length dress over a crinoline, a bonnet, and a weeping veil of crêpe, some six feet long, which covers her face, and gives off a caustic chemical smell, as if the dyes used to stain it have not properly set.

All her other accoutrements are likewise coloured – black gloves and studs and cuff-buttons and a brooch made of jet pinned to her dress's quilted bodice.

It all seems so strangely suited to the desolation of the moor.

PALACE OF SHADOWS

10 February

With the land cleared there is nothing to do now but wait for the bitter months to pass and the ground to soften enough for the levelling to begin.

I go for walks, I sketch, I work on the plans for the house.

30 March

Fernhurst and his men suggest the last of the cold weather is behind us and the hardness has left the earth.

Work can finally commence.

2 April

The mechanics have arrived with their great steam-powered levelling machines and after a day of orientation and preparation – for the machines had to be reassembled after their journey – the levelling of the plain has begun.

20 April

The levelling machines are unearthing artefacts as they dig into the moor: arrowheads, helmets, pieces of armour, broken shards of swords and pikes and other instruments of death.

Gosterwood claims they date to the 1640s, the period of the English Civil War, when a battle took place in the locality.

23 April

As the great machines continue their work, more layers of history are revealed; the artefacts now being dug up are from the Anglo-Saxon period.

There are even some Roman coins.

This morning I held in my hand a silver denarius from the reign of the Emperor Vespasian in the first century *anno domini.*

Strange to think that over one and a half thousand years ago, people from my homeland marched through here, conquered, lived.

How did they find this land?

As peculiar and unsettling as I now do?

24 April

Today a gruesome discovery.

A cart transporting soil tipped over, and in pulling it out of the marsh, the men somehow dislodged a body which floated to the surface.

It had been so well preserved by the peat waters that at first we thought it the body of one of our own labourers, but it soon became apparent it was hundreds of years old.

The poor soul appeared to be an elderly man, with his hands tied behind his back, and his throat slit.

'A sacrifice,' Fernhurst suggested.

Most gruesome of all, however, were two holes in the top of his skull, spread a few inches apart; extending from each hole was a stout tree branch, snapped off so only a stub remained protruding.

But under the body we found two yew tree branches which matched the stubs in the man's skull.

We all came to the same assumption – that the branches had been smashed into the man's head so that they resembled antlers.

As we did on previous occasions, we called for Gosterwood, who, on seeing the body, confirmed it had probably been the human sacrifice in a religious ritual.

We studied the poor victim, so rudely pulled from his icy, black water tomb, staring endlessly upwards now at the godly mass of light and space that was fixed above the moor.

'Shall we move the body to the cemetery?' I asked. 'Give it a good Christian burial?'

The men considered this, but Gosterwood shook his head.

'That's the last thing this pagan would want,' he said. 'Though I don't suppose there's anywhere else for him to go.'

When I returned to my room I could not think for the grim discovery, so I sat at the bureau and flicked through Gosterwood's books on paganism.

Marshes are listed in them as sites sacred to the ancients, for they are a bridge between the realms of water and earth, so were often chosen as the sites of human sacrifice.

Deer, too, were seen as sacred animals for similar reasons – their feet on the earth, their antlers in the sky.

Did this explain why the victim's skull had been punctured?

So that he resembled a deer, with antlers made of yew?

Further on I found descriptions of the ceremonies the pagans conducted for their sacrifices: bonfires, drinking, the consumption of noxious brews and mushrooms.

I copy down here the relevant extracts:

> *Human sacrifice was long practised among the people who inhabited these lands before the coming of the gospel, and there are many suggestions that it continued for centuries afterwards . . .*
>
> *Sacrifices were closely associated with the building of religious structures . . .*
>
> *A victim was sacrificed at the start of construction to consecrate the ground, and the building would be anointed at the end of construction with another victim . . .*
>
> *The calendar also played a part; sacrifices were thought to be more powerful if they occurred on dates of astronomical or calendrical significance: the equinoxes, the solstices, the night of the New Year . . .*

The sacrifice is unnerving, of course; as, too, is the fact that the victim lay hidden in the earth for so many centuries: interred in the freezing marsh waters, while fog and frost came and went above him.

It made me think of the inscription that it was customary to leave on tombstones in ancient times: *Sit tibi terra levis.*

May the earth rest lightly upon you.

25 April

The plain is levelled, the retaining walls are up, the mechanics have left, and building work finally begins.

In the afternoon labourers arrived from York with dray horses, heavy-lifting equipment and great drilling machines to lay the foundations.

Seeing all this activity has given me renewed hope that I can survive out here.

The days are getting longer and I feel the sting of the interminable winter no more.

With the improved weather we have agreed upon plans to build huts for us to stay in on the site, so we do not have to journey to and from the village each day.

I am looking forward to it as Lunham feels ever more oppressive.

26 April

Proper work at last.

We started early, digging shafts into the ground that will hold the foundations.

The men are in good cheer.

They have mostly been recruited from Lunham and Heybridge, the two villages either side of Mrs C—'s land.

For the most part they are like Fernhurst and his team: hard, taciturn, inscrutable.

When Mrs C— and Miss T— visited the site to see the shafts being dug, the men hushed up.

I couldn't help but feel it was on account of Miss T—, who always seems to bring the cold with her.

28 April

To celebrate the laying of the first foundations tomorrow, Mrs C— arranged a gathering in what passes for the village square.

Food and beer was served, all paid for by Mrs C—, who is eager to maintain good relations with the locals.

Musicians played and there was much singing and dancing.

It seemed the whole of Lunham and Heybridge was there, all in good cheer.

And as the people drank, the atmosphere became more raucous.

When the sun was setting, a great bonfire was lit and the locals danced around it.

The celebrations reached a peak when a man made of straw and yew tree branches was placed on the fire and burned for good luck, a tradition in these parts dating back to pagan times.

As the man burned, yew tree branches were passed around the crowd, some of whom lit them on the bonfire and danced, the glowing tips making shapes in the night.

One group of children began using them as make-believe swords, while others pulled off the leaves and put them in their hair.

I watched as three girls – twins and a younger child – took a pair of stout branches each, and gripped them tightly in both hands, as if they were holding clubs.

They looked up, and I caught their gazes, eyes gleaming at me through the flames.

My mind jumped back to the body in the marsh, the yew tree branches pummelled into its skull, and I suddenly had the chilling notion that these three girls might likewise commit some act of ritual violence.

But almost as soon as the thought had arrived, the girls smiled, and ran off to play with their friends.

As I looked around I was reminded once more of Homer and the Cimmerians, the mysterious and barbarous race who live at the mouth of Hades.

I decided to return to my room for I had tired already of this poor, provincial imitation of a carnival.

As I crossed back to the inn I noticed figures lurking in the shadows of doorways, behind trees, writhing on the ground.

I was shocked not at the licentiousness of the acts I witnessed – I have seen much worse in the slums of Venice – but at the people involved in them, for the men and women of the locality have a sullenness about them, a paleness, a bloodlessness, a puritanism.

It was strange to see them that night so wholly transformed simply by an excess of alcohol.

Then as I passed by the village's tiny church, I spotted Miss T— striding at great speed through the shadows towards the beach.

I was surprised by her presence there for Mrs C— and the rest of her retinue had returned to Bastwick Hall directly after the festivities had started.

When I reached my room, I could not sleep for the noise of the revelry, so I picked up one of Gosterwood's books to read, and it was only then that I realised I hadn't seen my friend all that night, and wondered where he had been.

29 April

In the afternoon, a commotion.

The village priest and two constables, locals charged with enforcing the law, arrived on site, trailing behind them a gang of villagers.

They approached Carberry, the foreman, who called the works to a halt and gathered everyone together.

'These men have important news,' he said.

The priest stepped forward: a young man with dark hair, a thin moustache and a scholarly air.

'Last night three girls from the village disappeared,' he said. 'John Marsden's daughters. The locals shall know them. They have not been seen since the start of the celebrations. The older two are twins aged thirteen, the younger is aged ten. We want to know if any of you have seen them.'

He scanned the crowd of workmen, but they just stared back at him blankly.

My thoughts turned to the three girls I had seen the night before, the ones holding the yew tree branches like clubs, for surely it was these same girls who'd gone missing.

'Their parents,' the priest continued, 'and others in the village, are worried that perhaps they came up here out of curiosity to see the works, and perhaps some . . . *accident* befell them. I understand you are laying foundations, digging shafts. Is there any chance that perhaps . . .'

He trailed off, too embarrassed to say what he meant, but we all understood.

The priest waited patiently for someone to respond, and might have waited the entire day were it not for Carberry breaking the silence.

'If anyone knows anything,' he said, 'or saw anything unusual, say something now. These girls' parents want to know what happened to them.'

Again, there was nothing but the sound of the wind over the moor.

Carberry looked at the priest and shrugged, then a voice called out from amongst the men.

'Perhaps we should stop the works and conduct a search. Here and across the moors.'

Murmurs of assent greeted the suggestion.

'It's for Mrs Chesterfield to decide that,' Carberry said. 'I'll send her a note at the manor. In the meantime, back to your jobs.'

The crowd dispersed, grumbling, but an hour later word came from Mrs C— to stop work and search for the girls.

We downed tools and were divided into groups, with a local in each who knew the terrain.

We were each assigned a different section of the moor and spent the rest of the afternoon searching.

As the light began to fail, we came back to the site for torches and lamps and continued throughout the evening.

It was not till past ten we gave it up and returned to the inn.

We could find no trace of the girls.

30 April

My worst day yet, and I am contemplating returning to London.

We were searching for the girls once more.

In my group there were whispers that they must have wandered into sticking mud and shall never be seen again.

It was not till almost eleven that I came back to my room.

As I was changing my clothes, there was a knock at the door: Gosterwood standing there with the two constables I had seen the previous day.

'Sorry to bother you, old man,' he said. 'These two gentlemen are constables, policemen. They wanted you to answer some questions and they asked me to act as intermediary.'

'I speak good enough English, I don't need an intermediary.'

'Well, it was more as a matter of politeness. To help keep things cordial. May we come in?'

I let them into the room.

'It's about the missing girls, sir,' said the first of the two constables.

'Have they been found?' I asked.

'No, sir. That's the thing. Well, it was noticed that on the night they went missing, you left the celebrations early. Almost everyone else in the village was there or close by. We'd like to know where you were.'

'I was here.'

'All night?'

'Yes. After the straw man was burned I came back here and read.'

'You have someone who witnessed this?'

'Of course not, I was alone in my room. Everyone else was at the bonfire, or . . . in the streets.'

The two constables shared a look, then one of them nodded at Gosterwood, prompting him.

'They also wanted to know something else,' Gosterwood said. 'Why you've not attended church since you've been here.'

I looked at them, astounded.

'I am a Catholic. It would be against my religion to visit a Protestant church.'

'I see,' the first constable said flatly. 'Well, I'll leave you to it. Thank you for your time.'

When the three of them had gone, I collapsed onto the bed.

How low have I sunk to be accused of murdering children?

As I lay there stewing in my anger there was a knock at the door.

Gosterwood.

'I saw them back outside,' he said. 'Shall we talk?'

I rose and bade him take a seat on the bed.

'Ghastly business,' he said, lighting a cigarette. 'It's been two

195

days now and the girls are nowhere to be seen and the local authorities are looking like fools.'

'That doesn't mean they should accuse me. Just because I am a foreigner and a Catholic doesn't mean I am a child killer.'

'Of course not. But look at it from their point of view. These are not people used to having outsiders in their midst. For them, even York and Leeds are foreign places.'

'What do you think happened to the girls?' I asked.

'Could be anything. Maybe they used the distraction of the celebration to run away. Most likely they got drunk on Mrs Chesterfield's free beer and fell into the marsh and drowned.'

'That was the view of the men I was with in the search party today. Although this isn't what those policemen believed.'

'I spoke with them as I was letting them out. They are of a similar opinion, but they felt they had to question you as some of the locals are certain the girls ran out to see the building works and fell into one of the shafts.'

'And they think I had something to do with that?'

Gosterwood paused.

'Again, look at it from their point of view, dear boy. If the girls did go to the work site that night, and everyone else was accounted for at the fete, except you, then they have to come and ask you what you were doing.'

'But I wasn't the only one missing from the fete,' I said. 'On my walk home I saw half the villagers strewn about the lanes and alleys fondling one another. Why am I to be singled out thus?'

It was then I remembered that Miss T—, and also Gosterwood himself, had not been there at the bonfire.

'Why *did* you leave the revelries?' he asked.

'I just wanted to come back. I was tired and I had to get up early and I was excited for the work that was to commence the next day.'

'So you spent the rest of the night in here? Alone?'

'As I have done every night since I arrived here four months ago.'

He smiled at me.

'I believe you, dear boy. And I'll do my best to make the rest of them believe you, too.'

He smiled again and I broached the subject of his own whereabouts.

'Oh, I didn't stay long either,' he said. 'I returned to Bastwick Hall at the start of the festivities with Mrs Chesterfield and the others.'

He said it smoothly, nonchalantly, but I could tell my question had vexed him.

I pressed him no more on it though as I did not want to alienate my only friend, and it was an easy enough lie to disprove – I just had to ask someone in Mrs C—'s retinue if he did indeed accompany them back to the Hall.

We finished our discussion in sombre mood.

When he had departed I lay on my bed once more and thought again of leaving.

But if I left now, wouldn't that only confirm my supposed guilt?

As I mulled it over, I remembered the sections on human sacrifice in Gosterwood's histories; how the ancients would kill people at the commencement of building works.

Was this what the locals thought had befallen the girls?

I went over to the windowsill where the books were lined up and flicked through them to see if there was anything more in them about ancient sacrifices.

I found yet another passage that gave me cause for concern:

It was believed the most powerful spirit to sacrifice at the end of a building's construction was that of the creator or architect,

*that placing the creator's body inside his creation would result
in his spirit guarding it for all eternity . . .*

I stared at the sentence and read it over and over, recalling that
a similar ritual occurred in Ancient Egypt – the designers of the
pyramids were placed in them alive when the bodies of pharaohs
were interred, the building shut up and locked from the outside.

Was this the fate that was to befall me?

Would the death of the girls mark the start of building, and
my death mark its end?

2 May

I have spent the last few days trying to decide if I should stay
or return to London.

To return would soothe my mind, but the loss of income would
make it harder to find a way back to my family.

I cannot determine what to do, so I stay until I make my decision, and in the meanwhile, work progresses, and the scale of it
pulls me to remain here.

The site buzzes with life, with foremen, charge hands, labourers,
drivers, deliverymen, with horses and giant iron machines – more
of which arrive by the day – sending constant chains of smoke
and steam into the air.

Lines of wagons cross the countryside bringing building materials from York, Scarborough and Whitby, so much of it that ever
more sheds are being put up to store everything.

It all feels colossal and majestic, and to know that I am a part
of it fills me with pride.

Is this what it felt like to work on constructing the great cathedrals, the pyramids, the landmarks of Rome?

Does this make Mrs C— our Caesar? Our Pharaoh? Our
Empress?

3 May

The cabins for us to stay in on the building site have been completed and we moved in this morning.

I'm glad to be free of Lunham and its suspicious inhabitants.

Now I can rest easier and this makes me feel as if I should remain and see out my task.

I spent the evening unpacking my things and arranging them around my cabin, which I share with another four men, none of whom are from the village.

Once everything was in order, I stepped outside to smoke a cigarette under the mild, moonlit sky.

6 May

My walk across the moor today was cut short when the air began clouding with fog, and I had to return to my cabin so I wouldn't be lost in it.

The fog up here is different from the greasy, suffocating fog back in London, which creeps into rooms through open windows, hangs about in corners like a black spirit, and leaves an oily sheen on furniture and floorboards that has to be scrubbed off.

Here, the fogs are born of the sea, salty and sharp, clean and bracing, and they come on with dangerous speed.

7 May

I thought moving from the village would ease my anxiety, but I have not been sleeping well in the cabin, for I have begun to have nightmares.

I have dreamt twice now that I am on trial for the murder of the girls.

Both dreams ended with me being dragged screaming towards the gallows.

12 May

In the afternoon I took a walk along the coast, sketching.

As I returned I skirted by Lunham and happened to see the missing girls' parents walking back from the seashore.

The father eyed me angrily; the mother looked a broken woman, ashen and stooped, leaning in to her husband for support.

To not know her daughters' fate must be the greatest pain there is.

And even though it is clear all three of them are lost, the woman cannot still fully dress herself in mourning black.

By the time I reached my cabin the sun was already low, clotting the sky with blood.

13 May

Last night I dreamt of the girls again, but this time I was not on trial.

I was standing on the moor, looking across it through reeds and grasses to the cave I entered all those months ago.

Standing in its mouth were the three girls, staring at me, calling me to join them.

As they did so, the blackness inside the cave started to shimmer.

When I looked through the shimmering, into the darkness beyond, I saw the space was filled with a forest of yew trees.

I awoke in an icy sweat, convinced the dream had solved the mystery for me – the girls had met their end in the caves.

But how could this information be of use?

How could it help clear my name?

For to reveal that I know the whereabouts of their bodies would only incriminate me further.

Even more worrying, if they are in the caves, they can't have got there accidentally – I'm convinced now that someone must have killed them and hidden them there.

Meaning there is a murderer among us.

14 May

When the sun was up I took a walk across the moor, and passed one of the caves littered about the locality; this one is some distance west of the site, at the bottom of a hill that is topped with a half-collapsed ring of standing stones.

I stopped and stared at its entrance and had to suppress the urge to go inside and search for the girls' bodies.

As I stood there I began to fancy the blackness at the cave mouth was shimmering, moving.

Just as it had in my dream.

I hurried back to the site.

20 May

At lunchtime, as we ate our rations and drank our tea – for nothing is done here without a constant stream of tea – a carriage arrived on site.

Mrs C— descended from it, followed by Miss T— and Gosterwood.

They were greeted by Mr Waylett, one of the foremen; a young, amiable man, freshly returned from navy service, where he lost a leg below the knee and now walks with the aid of a wooden peg.

The men I was eating with, on seeing the two ladies together, made jokes of a Sapphic nature, and drew parallels with old Queen Elizabeth, who apparently shared a bed with her maid.

I was surprised by the jokes, but when I looked again at the pair, I have to admit, I looked at them differently.

It was then that I noticed Gosterwood breaking off from the group and coming over.

'Good to see you, Francisco,' he said.

I rose and we took a walk around the site.

'I've been meaning to ask you,' he said. 'In the batch of books I lent you just the other week, you didn't happen to notice an envelope in there, a letter, by any chance?'

'No. You have lost one?'

'Mislaid, dear boy. Mislaid. You wouldn't mind awfully looking through them all, and letting me know if you find it?'

I nodded, and he gave me a queer look.

'Now, dear boy. Now.'

'Of course,' I said, realising how agitated he was.

We headed towards the cabins, but before we reached them a voice called out.

'Mr Gosterwood!'

We turned to see Waylett standing next to Mrs C—'s carriage.

'Mrs Chesterfield is returning to Bastwick Hall,' he replied. 'She asks that you accompany her.'

The blood drained from Gosterwood's face.

'I . . .' he stammered, and again his loss of composure surprised me.

But it only lasted a moment.

'Of course,' he smiled, before turning to me. 'Have a look for that letter, please, old boy. And let me know if you find it.'

'It's safe with me,' I reassured him.

That evening I returned to my cabin as the sun was setting and the work site was a thing of beauty; the plain laid over with the blue shadows of twilight, dotted with the flickering orange fires the men make to cook their food, shining like stars among the velvet dark.

After dinner I worked some more on my plans, double-checking them against the lists of materials we have on site, so it was late when I settled into my chair for a smoke and a rest, and only then did I remember Gosterwood and his anxiety about his letter.

I looked through the latest case of books he'd lent me and found it, still in its envelope, with Gosterwood's details written on the front in an elegant hand, while on the back the sender was named as a Miss Emily Rowe, of Dover Street, London.

I slipped it into the pocket of my work coat and a sadness came over me, for I thought then of all the letters I have sent my family over the last few months, none of which has received a response.

21 May

Saturday.

A half-day.

As soon as the lunch bell tolled, the men lined up to get their wages and marched off to the village, to spend them all in the pub.

I walked in the other direction, towards Bastwick Hall.

It was a pleasant stroll of two hours or so over hilly moors, enjoyable in the afternoon sun.

The rolling pastures were full, the grasslands bursting with vibrant fresh growth.

Streams gurgled and sparkled.

Here and there cottages and farmhouses nestled in picturesque locations that would have made excellent subjects for landscapes in oil or watercolour, reminding me that I should make the most of the good weather and come out when I can to sketch.

Eventually I arrived at the manor house and walked down its drive.

The place is generously proportioned, of Georgian construction, in the style that dots the countryside hereabouts.

A maid showed me in and left me to wait in one of the building's reception rooms.

After a few minutes she returned and showed me up to Gosterwood's room.

It was pleasant enough; split into two sections by an ornate dressing screen, on one side was a bedroom, on the other a space with a writing bureau, a coffee table, an armchair and a small couch.

Gosterwood was sitting on the latter, looking as worried as he had been the day before.

I passed him over the letter and he seemed much relieved to receive it.

I wondered if I should say to him that I had not opened it.

Back in Venice I would not see the need, for as a gentleman it would go without saying that I would not pry into another man's correspondence, yet I was unsure if such rules of propriety would be assumed in England.

As I debated with myself, Gosterwood did an odd thing – he lifted the reverse of the envelope to his eye and studied it carefully.

I wondered if there was some mark on it that would reveal to him whether or not I had opened it, for when his studies were complete, I saw a wave of relief rush over him; he grinned broadly and thanked me again.

'How about a walk, Francisco?' he asked, his voice regaining that booming, operatic quality.

'A walk sounds excellent.'

He rose and went over to the other half of the room to get ready behind the screen, where his bed and nightstand stood.

As he readied himself and we chatted jovially, I happened to notice a cheval mirror just off to the side of the screen.

Due to where I was sitting, and the position of this mirror, I could make out part of the space beyond the screen, on Gosterwood's side of the room.

It was thus that at one point I happened to see, via the mirror,

Gosterwood lean down, flip the carpet back, and carefully remove one of the floorboards.

He reached down and took out a box with a host more letters in it, and a pair of books.

Placing the letter inside, he returned the box and slipped the floorboard back into place, then paused.

I could still see his face in the mirror, but he was evidently not aware of this.

I happened at this exact moment to be reaching the end of a humorous story I was relating.

I laughed as I reached its denouement, but instead of laughing with me, Gosterwood rolled his eyes and winced, clearly pained by my company, by how foolish he found me.

And then he laughed, falsely, still unaware that I could see his true expression.

I was shocked and upset by this behaviour, for over the months I had been in Yorkshire, I had come to consider him as my one genuine friend.

Gosterwood rose then and returned from behind the screen all smiles.

He grabbed his cane and we set off; he in the best of moods, I in the worst.

As we walked he kept up a light-hearted chatter, hardly noticing my cloudy mood, and I began to think it was a stupid way to waste the day – being irked by my walking companion.

He is a pleasant fellow, and I find it hard to be upset by the man.

Gradually my animosity towards him lessened, and I started to enjoy the walk and the clement weather.

After some time we came across a wide road heading south, and to its side, way markers.

I looked at the place names and one of them surprised me.

'Thornwick Bay,' I said. 'The same name as Mrs Chesterfield's lady's maid.'

'Yes. That's where her father was found.'

I frowned at him.

'Her father was a foundling,' he explained. 'I've learned the story from the locals. It's quite the tale.'

He gestured next to the way markers, where there was a tree trunk, long since fallen, lying on the ground. We sat on it and rested our legs and looked out over the fields in front of us that ran all the way to the cliffs, and beyond them the sea, glistening in the afternoon sun.

Gosterwood took his cigarettes from his pocket and offered me one.

'This coast is known as the Smugglers' Coast,' he said. 'Not much of that type of thing goes on these days, but earlier in the century the place lived up to its name. One morning, a group of alum pickers discovered a baby on the beach in Thornwick Bay – a secluded spot quite some distance down the coast from here. The baby was dark-skinned, a mulatto, most likely the product of a liaison between a local whore and some far-flung foreigner who'd passed through on one of the smuggling ships.

'He would have been taken into the care of the ward, sent to the orphanage up near Scarborough, but the local parson took matters into his own hands and raised the boy himself, named him Thornwick after the bay in which he'd been found. The parson looked after him for a few years until he had to leave the parish, when he placed the boy with a childless couple in Lunham.

'As you can imagine, he didn't have a good time of it. Teased by the other children for being dark, for being a foundling, a bastard and a whore-son, he quickly learned how to use his fists. As an adult he fell in with a rough crowd and gained a reputation as an ale can. Then at some point he caught the clap, and it further added to his anger, his madness. But despite all that he married and had a child, just the one – our own dear Miss Thornwick, whom it is said he most wickedly abused.

'Miss Thornwick was bullied by the local children in the same way her father had been. And then her mother died mysteriously, and shortly after that the father laid a man low when he was in his cups and was sent to Whitby Prison – where he still is today – on a charge of assault. Miss Thornwick stayed on alone in the shack they lived in just outside Lunham, subsisting these last few years by dubious means. All until Mrs Chesterfield arrived and settled on her as her new lady's maid.'

I was astonished by the story; I could tell the girl was an outcast and there was something dangerous about her, but to hear all this still shocked me.

'Did Mrs Chesterfield know her history when she employed the girl?' I asked.

'I'm certain of it. Your colleague Waylett is a local man and he must have informed Mrs Chesterfield of it before she made her decision. It is from the same source I learned much of the story myself.'

'And still she hired such a girl? But why?'

'I don't know,' Gosterwood shrugged. 'She's an unsettling little thing, young Miss Thornwick, that's for sure, but there's no denying her beauty.'

17 June

Work progresses.

The foundations for the central section of the house have been laid and the first of its storeys is going up with the aim of making this portion habitable by year's end.

While most of the men labour away on that, other teams lay the foundations for the other parts of the house.

If everything continues without a hitch, and Mrs C— carries on supplying such a weight of money and manpower, the deadline will be achieved, something I would have thought impossible when I was working back in Venice.

18 June

An invitation to dine at Bastwick Hall.

After work I bathed as best I could using the water in the vats next to the cabins, then I changed into clean clothes.

A carriage came to pick me up and we drove to the same house where I had visited Gosterwood last month.

Present were Mrs C—, Miss T—, Gosterwood, and a few of the nameless businessmen who are always in Mrs C—'s company, bowing and scraping and answering yes to all her questions.

Also there was the priest from Heybridge, the same one who'd come to the work site to announce the disappearance of the Marsden girls.

Before the dinner, as we were milling about the withdrawing room, I noticed a curious bauble hanging in one of the windows and went over to inspect it.

Of blue glass construction, the size of an apple, it hung on a single thread just inside the windowpane, the candlelight glinting through its swirling azure glaze.

'A witch ball,' said a voice.

I turned to see the priest from Heybridge standing behind me, smiling.

'An old Yorkshire superstition, a talisman designed to keep out evil spirits.'

'I see.'

'Just think, if Mrs Chesterfield had settled on a witch ball instead of a house, how different things would be.'

We smiled and introduced ourselves and talked some more.

Rather than being a dull local man, I discovered the priest to be a lover of the arts who makes serious study of what he can, being in so remote a place.

He offered to lend me some art books which he has sent to him from libraries in Leeds.

As we discussed our tastes we were called into the dining room.

We ate a dinner of boiled lamb and potatoes so bad I only managed to eat it by smothering the gristly meat in the mint sauce that had been placed on the table.

Throughout the duration of the meal, I noticed Gosterwood was not his usual boisterous self, but unusually quiet, moody even, reminding me of the incident of his missing letter last month.

As the meal came to an end, the conversation turned to Mrs C—'s gun company.

One of the nameless businessmen mentioned the company accounts.

Another talked of the fortune they'd made the last two years selling weapons to the 'factions' in the Italian war.

At this Mrs C— and I shared a look.

I still have had no word from my family back home, and newspapers have been hard to come by up here, so I know nothing of how the situation is developing.

I spent the rest of the evening in a foul mood.

After we had eaten and the men had moved to the smoking room, I spotted Gosterwood standing by the windows, alone, a cigarette in hand, staring out at the moonlit moor beyond.

'Gosterwood, how are things?' I asked, walking over.

He turned to me with a frown, as if he hadn't expected anyone to approach him.

'Just studying the locality,' he said, waving his cigarette towards the view.

I followed his gaze for a few seconds, then studied my friend; he looked drawn, worried, ill.

As I was about to ask after his health, he spoke.

'You like living here, Francisco? At the edge of the world?'

'Not particularly.'

'What about the landscape itself? Do you feel any kind of . . . evil presence here?'

I frowned, remembering my first day here, when I had ventured into the cave and sensed a great malevolence.

I told him as much and he listened to me with a detached interest.

'A cave is a place of natural awe and dread,' he said.

'How so?'

'It reminds us of our place in the world. It existed before we ever did, and it will continue to do so long after us, fretting not whether we live or die, whether our species flourishes or perishes. This cold longevity reminds us we are born into a universe too old and vast for our comprehension, a universe completely uninterested in us.'

'That's only true if you don't believe in a God,' I retorted.

He took a moment to mull this over.

'If I was to ask you to imagine a house that was filled with storms, floods, infernos, dangerous animals, poisonous insects, a numberless array of the most hideous diseases; would you say this was a good house?' he asked. 'Would you say this was a house where you'd want to live?'

'Of course not.'

'But this house is exactly the world we're thrown into at the moment of our birth. A house full of danger. And the true horror is, there's only one way of escaping it. And maybe that's the most monstrous thing of all, and perhaps that's what scared you in the cave.'

He shrugged then turned to look out over the moor once again, signalling an end to our conversation.

I am not ashamed to say his words cast a further shadow over my spirits.

Even now, sitting in my cabin hours later, drinking my negus, writing my journal, I am coming up with counter-arguments to his vision of universal horror, yet every one rings hollow.

23 June

Another death.

The men were lifting beams into place for the central hall when a rope in the levering system broke.

A counterweight was propelled into the team in charge of the Shire horses and the full force of it caught one of them on the side of the head.

Despite his skull being half caved in, he survived for hours, lying on the ground, stupefied, mumbling for his mother.

It was not until the afternoon that the doctor arrived, though there was no saving him.

Thankfully Hartington came before he died and administered the last rites, or whatever passes for them in the Anglican Church.

The body was removed to the dead man's house in Heybridge.

Waylett informs me the poor soul was married and the widow is with child.

Mrs C— said she would see the woman taken care of, and I am sure she is as good as her word, but I couldn't help noticing her coldness when she arrived on site, the way she dealt with the incident as one would an unexpected household chore.

I've noticed too how the men become apprehensive whenever she is around; at first I thought this was on account of Miss T—, but now I wonder.

We inspected the broken rope and found it to be burned through – someone had forgotten to grease it.

Of course, no one admits to the oversight.

This latest death brings to mind the disappearance of the Marsden girls in the spring.

Still they haven't been found, still I dream of them, still I wonder if their murderer is living amongst us.

1 July

Sunday.

The men trudged across the moor for church services in Heybridge, or slept off the drink from the night before.

I lay in bed till late then decided to take a walk, for what else is there to do?

I took my sketchbook and watercolours and headed for the coast.

The shoreline here is composed of tiny coves and bays, most of them nothing more than a slash of pebbles between the cliffs and the sea, making me realise why this was called the Smugglers' Coast, for these inaccessible, secluded places must have made perfect spots for the trafficking of contraband.

In the churning chaos below me a colony of seagulls swooped, and breakers shattered themselves against the rocks in great echoing booms, sending up spray like pearls.

Further on, in the larger bays, the beaches glittered in the sunlight, and the wooden groynes which keep the sand in place stretched like fingers into the sea.

Between them the scene was busy with pickers of jet, sea coal and alum, even though it was past noon on a Sunday.

Something about the dark-robed figures weaving along the grey beach, their stooping and bending to fill their baskets, their gleaning what they could, put me in a sombre temper.

Despite all the sunlight the sea seemed gloomy, heaving and boundless, with the glassiness of death to it.

It made me think how all the world's seas are graveyards too, tombs of drowned men and animals, darknesses where the nameless dead are forced to dance until they break apart and are no more.

As I was finishing up my sketching I saw a lone figure stalking across the moor further down the coast, heading towards Lunham – Gosterwood.

I had not seen or heard from him since the dinner at Bastwick Hall a couple of weeks earlier and was curious about his current state, so I decided to try to catch up with him.

As I crossed the high ground above Lunham I saw him walking along the road that leads towards the church.

I thought this strange, for the man has often expressed disdain, contempt even, for organised religion.

A few minutes later I entered the village myself, feeling most apprehensive, worried that I might be set upon.

But the streets were empty; perhaps everyone was home eating their Sunday lunch.

I walked up the muddy road that led to the church, and stepped inside softly.

Gosterwood was the only person in there, hunched over on a pew, sobbing to himself.

He did not notice me enter, and I was thankful, for I was unsure how to approach the man, so I stood there a few moments and observed him.

His tears were those of a heavily disturbed soul.

I do not know why, but I had the feeling that he was crying tears of remorse.

I turned and slipped out again.

Was I a good friend for granting him peace in his moment of turmoil?

Or had I left simply because I was too cowardly to deal with a difficult situation?

I fear it was the latter.

As I made my way home I wondered what it was he could be so remorseful about.

18 August

I lose myself in work.

The central portion of the house is coming together; the skeleton of the Great Hall is complete, the rooms surrounding it are being built, exterior walls go up, joists are laid, windows and doors are fitted.

10 September

Work progresses.

The season wanes.

Gosterwood will not return my notes.

15 September

This afternoon we noticed a long line of heavily laden drays approaching the house.

'The marble for the friezes,' Waylett informed me.

When the first of them had arrived, Waylett and I inspected the stone.

It is of the highest quality, brought all the way from Aquitaine.

'It must have cost a fortune to buy and have shipped here,' I said.

'Aye,' Waylett laughed. 'Aye, it did.'

I ran my hands over the cold, ancient marble.

17 September

The moor's grasses turn yellow with the first wane of the year, but the heather still blazes with dazzling purple and pink.

20 September

A letter arrived!

News that my family is safe!

They tell me they are well, that they have received a few of my letters, and have posted replies; with the blockade ended, this is the first to actually reach me.

I lay on my bed and my mind drifted back to Venice, to the beauty of my home, to its golden sunlight and warmth.

I cannot describe my good cheer.

25 September

A walk through the woods inland from Heybridge.

Above me the trees held in place a blazing canopy of red and gold leaves, a fireworks display frozen in the sky.

Below me the leaves already fallen were like a jewelled mosaic.

3 October

When we stepped out of the cabins this morning, we saw the work site had undergone the eeriest of transformations.

Some kind of ice had coated the land, forming crystals, so that everything looked as if it had been dipped in a milky glaze.

The frozen droplets caught the pink of the sunrise, making them glow in the warmest fashion.

According to Fernhurst the phenomenon is caused by a type of ice known as 'rime'.

As we ate our breakfast he and the other men explained to me the difference between rime, hard rime, hoar frost and black frost.

The distinction is easy enough to make, but all I can think of is what this race of men must have gone through to have different names for different types of frost; like the Esquimaux and their hundred names for snow.

13 October

The season has turned in just a few short days.

Both land and sky are so frozen through I can smell the very scent of the cold.

3 November

No matter how much I stoke up the braziers, nor how many layers of clothing I wear, nor how many blankets I throw over myself, still I am run through with the cold.

I am in a constant drunken haze from all the brandy and negus I drink just to keep it out.

Yet I seem to be the only one so badly affected.

Even in these icy depths, many of these Yorkshiremen go about in vests and hardly notice.

Truly I am among the Cimmerians.

15 November

On the moor, winter prepares her theatre afresh,
plucking the trees,
putting beasts to sleep,
the stage left empty for darkness and frost.

1 December

Winter descends from the sky as heavy as a falling god.

2 December

Has it really been almost a year since I arrived in Yorkshire?

A year of hardships, but in less than a fortnight we move into the house, for the central section is now complete.

I am amazed at the speed with which it has been built; a similar building in Venice would take three times as long.

Mrs C— has had to squander vast amounts of money to have it constructed so fast; if she'd gone slower, she could have had it for half the cost.

But that is not her way.

It seems anything is possible when you have an iron will and a bottomless purse.

6 December

Exterior work has been wound down for the rest of the winter.

Thank God, for the cold would do us all in.

7 December

From first light, wagons piled high with furnishings do not stop arriving; the road from the house to the station is practically filled with them, every inch.

A line of men transports them inside.

They are at it all day.

11 December

The move into the house is complete!

We are finally ensconced in the bosom of the beast.

I spent the afternoon arranging my things in my room, lying on my bed, *an actual bed*, a rosewood four-poster smothered with thick duvets and a coverlet of the finest embroidery.

Once I had been sated of my room, I walked the corridors of my creation.

Even though it is far from complete, it is still the most beautiful house I have ever built.

In fact, the incompleteness only speaks of how magnificent it will be when the interior work is finished – the tiling, the wood panelling, the moulding, the painting, the embossment of the ceilings, the varnishing of the floorboards.

Just being inside it gives me a sense of pride, a warmth I've never experienced.

In the evening we celebrated with drinks in the withdrawing room, though a more formal celebration is planned for tomorrow.

I noticed that Gosterwood was not present, and I found it most strange.

Is he still in his room at the manor house?

12 December

The 'celebration' to mark the occasion of our moving into the house was as dull as I had expected it to be, and yet it was also the most excitement I have had in months.

Present were Mrs C—, Miss T—, some of Mrs C—'s nameless, faceless businessmen, the Reverend Hartington and other local dignitaries.

Also attending were the men who owned the businesses Mrs C— has been using to construct the house – the building merchants, furniture designers, deliverymen.

I found this most strange, for such a class of people would never be invited to a similar occasion in Venice.

Is this the way in England?

Or is it a peculiarity of my most peculiar employer?

Gosterwood was not in attendance, of course.

I discussed his absence with Hartington, the priest from Heybridge, asking if my old friend might still be at Bastwick Hall.

'Oh, no. Mr Gosterwood moved across with the others,'

Hartington said. 'You must have missed him. By all accounts he went straight to his room, locked the door and renewed his odd behaviour of the last few months.'

'What odd behaviour?'

'You didn't know? He stays in his room, feverishly reading books. He only comes out when he has to, and when he does he looks quite ill. In body and mind.'

'Do you know what ails him?'

'Unfortunately not.'

'And his feverish reading?'

'That I know a little more of. The man came to me in the autumn asking for information on book dealers and libraries. He knows I travel up to Leeds frequently and have subscriptions with libraries there to have books sent down by mail. He was asking which dealers he could trust, which libraries had the most extensive catalogues. I gave him my opinions and suggested that while he set up his own subscriptions, he could use my accounts to get any books sent to him early. He agreed and the next day he turned up at the church in a fever with a list of books. I consulted my dealers and a few titles were obtainable and were sent down, but most of the volumes they'd never heard of. I passed along those that arrived and Gosterwood locked himself in his room to pore over them. A few weeks later he returned them.'

A pained look crossed the priest's face and he hesitated, as if deciding whether or not to continue.

'Then a week or so ago,' he said eventually, 'on my last trip to Leeds, I visited the offices of one of these dealers on some unrelated matter. He mentioned Gosterwood was now one of his best clients, and laughed about the man's demands. He said he was looking for certain rare books from the 1600s and was offering a small fortune to any dealers who could furnish him with them. Not just in Leeds, but in York, London and Edinburgh, too. Then the dealer showed me one of the notes Gosterwood had sent him. It was the work of a man already brought low by his obsession.'

'But what is it he searches for in these books?' I asked.

'No one knows. But the books he orders are almost all on occult subjects. And it's become an obsession, as I said. I just hope it doesn't consume the man any further.'

I was saddened at the fate that had befallen my friend.

Then I wondered guiltily about my own role in it.

For while he had hidden himself away in his room at Bastwick Hall, and had steadily deteriorated, I had been immersed in my work on the house and had put him out of my mind.

He had not replied to my notes, so I had stopped sending them, assuming he no longer had time for our friendship, but perhaps I had simply misread the signs of madness.

Would a better friend have done more?

'Have you spoken to Mrs Chesterfield about all this?' I asked.

'Oh, yes. I tried for some months to offer the poor man counsel, suggesting he talk to me about whatever ails him. But he shunned my attempts in the most violent and offensive way, so I entreated Mrs Chesterfield to call a doctor. She agreed and the doctor arrived some weeks ago. He recommended Gosterwood go back to London, or to a sanatorium to recuperate. Mrs Chesterfield offered to pay for it all, of course.'

'And Gosterwood refused?'

'Positively screamed the house down.'

'And Mrs Chesterfield didn't insist on it?'

The priest shook his head.

'So why would she keep him here when it is clearly having such an ill effect on his health?' I asked.

Hartington paused before replying.

'I think it's because *he* wants to stay here,' he said. 'For all her odd manners, Mrs Chesterfield is very traditional in some ways.

She believes Englishmen have certain rights, certain personal and civil liberties. Liberties our country has been built on. Why should those rights be taken away just because a man has an illness of the mind? Would you take away a man's freedom if his arm was broken? It's a view quite popular among the English, particularly the common people. When madhouse doctors arrive somewhere to take away some local who has been judged insane, more often than not, crowds gather to attack the doctors, to fight them off, so that the mad person may stay on, and not have their liberty snatched away. Sometimes during such instances, riots have started, especially in the poorer districts of our cities.'

Hartington shrugged and gestured in Mrs C—'s direction, as if to remind me that the woman was not of aristocratic lineage, but the daughter of a London shopkeeper, who might well be supposed to share the common people's view.

Just then the notes of a piano echoed across the room, a few sleek chords in a minor key, solemn, lingering, beguiling.

Hartington and I both turned to look for the source.

In the far corner of the room was a grand piano at which sat Miss T—.

Once the last of her practice notes had faded away, she began playing a piece of music I thought I recognised, but could not place.

It had a haunting melody, as elusive as the girl herself, and she played it with great skill.

'Mrs Chesterfield's work,' Hartington said, nodding at the girl. 'Strange to think barely a year ago she was illiterate. Your employer is paying to have her schooled in all the ladylike arts. So much so it makes me wonder if young Miss Thornwick is being groomed to be a lady's maid, or an actual lady.'

We smiled at each other and carried on listening to the mesmeric, echoing music.

'I feel as though I've heard it before,' I said.

'Bach,' Hartington replied. 'A tricky piece. Especially for a pianist with only a year's training. I doubt if one in a hundred students could manage it. She's incredibly talented.'

I nodded in agreement and it was then that I noticed a hush had descended on the room; everyone else in there was as bewitched by Miss T—'s playing as Hartington and I.

I turned back to the girl and as I continued to watch her through the warm glow of candlelight, she became even more alluring; the wildness of her upbringing mixed with the refinement with which Mrs C— was now endowing her, has created a beguiling and most unusual deportment.

She has the steeled beauty of a battlefield flower.

18 December

It has been exactly a year since I arrived in Yorkshire.

What to do to mark the occasion?

I decided to have a drink in the pub in Heybridge, where I am less hated than in Lunham.

I sat alone.

I raised a toast of weak warm ale to this strangest birthday – my first year as a Yorkshireman.

I raised another to my family in Venice.

21 December

Snow falls from the heavens.

Winter has laid its melancholy on the earth.

22 December

As I sat at my desk I could hear the men below singing Christmas carols.

Their rough voices lent the songs a texture, an earthy elegance, that arrested me in my work.

I drank my brandy and listened to the music, mixing with the eerie whistle of the caves.

I know tonight I shall dream of the girls once more.

23 December

The house fills with mirrors, as was my wont.

I was worried Mrs C— would reject this element of my design, for the common superstition is that looking glasses trap the spirits of the deceased.

But she agreed wholeheartedly, and now the house is filled with new passages of light, and planes of reflection that multiply and slice.

24 December

Christmas Eve.

The locals went home to their families, Mrs C— and the others took coaches to the church in Heybridge.

I stayed alone in my creation.

I walked its corridors.

I marvelled at its beauty.

As I strolled one of its hallways I stopped at an enormous mirror of Venetian glass positioned so that the room's entire length was reflected in it, including the mirror at the hallway's opposite end.

The effect is to make the room appear as if it is receding infinitely.

I stared at my reflection and saw how wild I looked, how I have changed in the last year.

And then I had the feeling of a presence staring back.

For a moment I fancied it was the house studying me thus; the mirror the eye to its soul.

It felt as if we were interlocked by that plane of glass, trapped in our self-reflections.

25 December

Christmas Day.

In the afternoon an elaborate lunch was held to celebrate the festivities.

The chef has finally arrived from Paris and the food is edible now, thank God.

It was a pleasant occasion, but I did not enjoy myself much, for my thoughts were with my family back in Venice; I recalled the banquets we used to have at Christmas, the music and wine, the laughter and dancing.

It was all I could do not to make a fool of myself and start crying at the table.

31 December

A horrible day.

I went for a walk along the coast, where a sweeping salt wind filled the air.

After about an hour or so I saw a figure up ahead, sitting just by the cliff edge, studying the waves below.

When I realised it was Gosterwood a chill fear sliced through me that he was there to dash himself onto the rocks below.

I ran to him as fast as I could and when I got close enough, I shouted at him, but he couldn't hear me over the howl of the wind and the racket of the seagulls.

Eventually I reached him and put my hand on his shoulder, expecting him to flinch from surprise.

But he didn't.

He calmly turned to look up at me and I saw his eyes were tearful and more haunted than ever.

Then he smiled.

That warm smile of his I had not seen in so many months.

'You seem worried, Francisco. Did you think I was about to jump?'

'No,' I lied. 'But you look upset. What's wrong? Why are you crying?'

It was as if by mentioning his tears I'd reminded him that he had been out of temper, for he deflated at my words.

He paused, then let out a long sigh.

'Everything is wrong,' he muttered. 'I have made a mistake. A terrible mistake.'

And with that, he turned back to look out over the sea once more.

I sat beside him, worried about how close we were to the edge.

Here and there, dotted along the clifftops, were cairns with posies of withered flowers, the last dots of summer's colour, commemorating where someone had slipped or thrown themselves to their death.

'What's this mistake you're so worried about?' I asked.

But he would not answer.

He continued to look into the sea below and started mumbling to himself, having already lost the lucidity he'd displayed when I first arrived.

I let him babble on in this fashion for some time, while all about us seagulls swooped and shrieked over the crashing noise of the waves, then I suggested I walk him back to the house.

'Back there?' he said fearfully, gesturing towards the moor.

His movement was so quick I was scared he might lose his balance and fall, so I grabbed his shoulder to be sure.

At my touch, he stared at my hand, and then looked me in the eye and started sobbing.

'I've made a terrible mistake, Francisco,' he repeated, but this time in a surer voice. 'I thought *I* was the vampire. I thought *I* was the one who was fooling them.'

'I don't understand.'

'Don't you see? It was *they* who brought *me* here.'

He sank into incoherence and began babbling once more.

Again I let him continue till he calmed down, then I attempted once more to coax him back to the house.

'No, Francisco. It's another mistake.'

'You need to rest. Your bed is there. You will rest and feel better.'

'There's no rest there. There's no safety. It's all a lie. Everything she said is a lie.'

'What lie?'

He paused and stared at me, as if realising something.

'You believe them when they say it's a house to repel ghosts?' he asked.

'I don't know what to believe.'

'This is not a house to *repel* ghosts. Francisco, promise me something.'

'Anything.'

'If something happens to me, promise me you'll take my books and show them. Promise you'll show them before it's too late. I'll not be able to rest in my grave if I know the house will continue to grow, and they succeed in what they are doing.'

As he pleaded with me the madness disappeared from his eyes, and was replaced by a steely look that appeared to me completely sane.

'I promise you. But what are they doing here that is so bad?'

'The house,' he said. 'Their building of it will be the end of us. The madness will spread. I will stay and fight, try to stop it. But if something happens to me, you must have my books.'

226

I nodded, and this seemed to calm him and we both looked out across the vast, muttering sea.

In the distance fishing boats and merchant ships rose and dipped in the grey swell, drained of their colour, lost on the horizon.

And then, on the very edge of the Earth's curve, there was a break in the clouds, and a sunburst poured forth, a shaft of golden light illuminating the vastness of the scene, the bitter fathoms of the sea.

We studied it and smiled.

Then I gently took my old friend's arm and walked him back to the house.

As we did so he alternated between long sullen silences and feverish mumbling that rose and fell like the boats we had seen out at sea.

In these moments I looked into his face and saw nothing but madness.

As we approached the house, and he realised where we were, he became increasingly agitated until he started pulling away from me, looking about wildly, shouting.

If Waylett and some of the staff hadn't come out to meet us, I doubt I would have been able to bring him inside.

They took him off to bed, and Waylett promised to call the doctor.

I returned to my room in a state of despondency.

Poor, tortured soul.

How the madness has seeped through his very being.

I recalled his words about how he thought he had fooled everyone.

It was the first time I had heard him admit his charlatanry, how he had bamboozled Mrs C— into coming up here.

Perhaps it is his guilt that has driven him mad.

227

1850

1 January

God prosper the New Year to those I love.

Wherever they might be.

2 January

I tried to visit Gosterwood in his room this morning, but was not admitted as a doctor from Heybridge was in attendance.

Apparently my friend is suffering from a 'brain fever' and needs solitude and rest.

I pray the Lord might give him strength and relieve his burdens.

3 January

I had more nightmares last night.

The girls.

They always come to me when I am vexed by some other mental turmoil.

Outside my window the moor is drowning in mist.

5 January

I stayed in my chamber all day to continue my work on the plans for the East and West Wings.

I only left to go to the dining room to eat, and to visit Gosterwood once more.

But again I did not get to see him, for he is up and about now, and had gone for a 'restorative walk' when I called.

I thank the Lord that he is recuperating.

14 January

The days pass in a blur of creation.

2 February

Sad and distressing news – Gosterwood is gone.

I heard it from Waylett this morning, when I asked after the man, for I had still not seen him since the episode on the cliffs on New Year's Eve.

'Mr Gosterwood is gone, *signore*.'

'Gone where?'

'No one knows. He wasn't in his room yesterday morning and he hasn't been seen since.'

I sought out Mrs C— and found her in her office.

'I assume he'd had enough of the place and returned to London,' she said.

'Why?'

'You saw the man, surely? He was under considerable mental strain.'

The emotionless way she spoke left me under no impression that she was hiding something.

I studied her closely, making my suspicion clear, and after a few seconds she sighed and her demeanour softened.

'I suppose you should know before you hear it from someone else,' she said. 'We had made arrangements to have him sent to a sanatorium. The best in the country, I'm told. We had witnesses to his madness make reports and then had two doctors come – there have to be two to avoid cases of fraud – and they interviewed him as to his state of mind. With their expert opinion we applied to a court to have him admitted, but . . .'

She raised her hands into the air.

I understood the inference; Gosterwood had realised he was about to be committed and had run away before it happened.

Was Mrs C— lying about this as well?

I studied her but found no reason to think so.

Why had Gosterwood absconded when only a month ago he was so hell-bent on staying?

And why did Mrs C— finally decide to have him sent to a sanatorium when she'd spent so long ignoring Hartington's entreaties for her to do just that?

I think back to the episode on the cliffs and how he looked at me in that moment of lucidity and told me to take his books if anything happened to him, and let the world know.

But *what* was I supposed to let the world know?

3 February

I spent all night lying in bed, trying to come up with an appropriate course of action and eventually I struck upon an idea – I recalled my visit to Gosterwood in Bastwick Hall, how he had hidden some articles that were important to him under a floorboard.

Had he made use of a similar scheme here in this house?

I wondered whether, if I sneaked into his room and checked the floorboards, I might find under them letters or books or other documents that could shed some light onto what has happened to him.

With a renewed sense of hope, I set myself to executing the plan.

4 February

It is late into the night now and my heart is racing.

This afternoon I left my work early and crept into Gosterwood's room.

I inspected the floor until I found a loose board.

When I levered it up, I saw my supposition had been correct – in the space under the board was a wooden box, the same one I had seen in the manor house.

I took it out and saw it was full of letters still in their envelopes, and some other unbound sheets of paper.

I stuffed all these into my pockets and raced back to my room, locked my door and laid everything out on my bureau.

I looked at the sheets of paper first: some contained a long directory of antiquaries, libraries and bookshops, all scribbled down in Gosterwood's hand; but most were filled with lists of book titles and authors.

As I had expected, the books were mostly on the topic of old Celtic religions, but towards the end were a great number of histories of the English Civil War, and the witch trials which were conducted at the time.

A sense of foreboding came over me as I was reminded of the Civil War artefacts we had discovered when clearing the plain, and of the human sacrifice uncovered in the marsh.

I put down the papers and picked up the bundle of letters.

They were all addressed to the same woman as the letter I had seen previously – Emily Rowe, of Dover Street, London.

All but two of the envelopes had postmarks on them, meaning Gosterwood must have sent them to this lady, and then she had sent them back.

Did they have a falling-out to make her return them?

As for the two without postmarks, I can only assume these to be the most recent, that Gosterwood was intending to send them just before his disappearance.

Putting propriety aside, I opened them up and was surprised to find they were written in French.

I spent the rest of the afternoon and most of the night reading through them all and I am shocked at what I've learned.

Now I understand why he was so desperate to retrieve the letter he had mistakenly left in my possession.

Now I fear for my own safety.

PART THREE
The Gosterwood Letters

Emily,

The lawyers in Leeds are demanding we 're-assess' their rate of commission.

Re-assess! The bastards!

They must have belatedly realised I am stuck in this godforsaken place and so have found opportunity for extortion. They sent a note suggesting one of their minions travels here to discuss the matter. They know full well the need for secrecy so it can only be an attempt to rattle me. Needless to say, I told them where they could go with their minion.

The only way to deal with such speculators is to hit them hard, and hit them fast. For if you show even the slightest whiff of appeasement then they *really* come looking for blood.

And yet, now I have sent back my angry response, I wonder if they will buy the bluff, or if they'll realise that such barking is done in the absence of any real bite. For possession is nine points of the law, and until all the legalities are completed, we are on shaky ground.

Either our scheme here succeeds and we become filthy rich, or we are discovered and end up in a filthy prison!

But if they want to turn this into a game of wills, so be it. I'll show them I'm strong enough.

For who gets wealth, that puts not from the shore?

And with that in mind, Emily, I hate to ask, but you must send me more money. Please. Post it to the inn as we arranged previously. You know that when the trick is finished we'll both be hideously rich.

Adieu,

G.

Emily,

Many thanks for the money, although once the innkeeper took his cut, it was not so great as you may suppose.

Life here in *ultima Thule* drags on interminably. I drum my fingers waiting for the lawyers to respond, trying not to go mad. I'm so agitated I can't even work on my *A Psychic History of the British Isles*. How foolish I was to assume that coming here would allow me to focus on it.

How I miss London. When I think of all those months I spent scouring the country looking for a suitable place. Perhaps I should have gone for the farmland in Cornwall. At least then I would have had more pleasant surroundings.

I say that things are interminable, but there is one glimmer of hope – little Miss Thornwick. She has a beguiling beauty to her and I'm wondering if Chesterfield has designs on the girl. It's delightfully tawdry, and so must be true.

This morning I had to go into Lunham to check for letters from the damned lawyers and who should I see but the young girl herself. As she was passing along the path just in front of the church she was set upon by three local girls, two of them twins (I have always found twins unsettling for some reason).

I stopped to watch the encounter as this is what passes for entertainment up here. It started with the three girls jeering at young Thornwick, and then they surrounded her. Thornwick hissed some insult at them that I couldn't make out. Then the girls spat at her and called her a 'witch' of all things. Then curses started flying both ways, and all hell broke loose. Thornwick lashed out at the youngest of the girls. (A mistake, I think. For I'm told in situations like this it's the big ones you're supposed to round on.)

Soon enough the four of them were rolling about in the mire, clawing and tearing each other's hair out. Thornwick gave a good account of herself against superior numbers, but when a few adults eventually came to separate them poor Thornwick was left sitting alone on the ground, muddy, bloody and sobbing.

It was quite the spectacle. I went on my merry way and stopped at the inn to pass the time with the owner. He's oafish and ignorant, but then that's the fun of it, I suppose. His wife was out so we adjourned to the cellar and then returned to the bar for an ale.

I asked him about the girls, but he remained tight-lipped, choosing instead to go on a diatribe about how badly Chesterfield's choice of maid has affected her standing amongst the locals. It was as if the poor man thought old Chesterfield actually cares what they think.

On the way back to Bastwick Hall I bumped into Waylett, one of Chesterfield's cronies. He's a local so I mentioned what I'd seen and he seemed completely unsurprised. Apparently the three girls are the daughters of a John Marsden, and there is a long history of animosity between them and Thornwick.

In fact, there's much animosity between *everyone* and Thornwick.

The girl is wild, and her father is wilder (a bastard of a ship's whore). The man is currently in Whitby Prison on a charge of assault. I'll write you more of the tale when I have time.

Adieu,

G.

Emily,

News to report:

Last night there was a festivity to mark the commencement of work on the house. Chesterfield paid – a bonfire in the village square, food and drink for all. By my reckoning the plebs from every surrounding parish showed up to stuff their faces. They are a loathsome breed, especially when drunk and boisterous, and having what they deem 'a good time'.

I prowled around the festivities, seeing if I could find any like-minded boys and girls, when who should I spot running through the shadows in the empty part of the village but the young and beautiful Thornwick!

She ran furtively away from everyone, as if on a clandestine errand, so I had no choice but to follow her. I caught up with her on a dark, deserted path, and wondered if this was where I could make my advantages known. Yet when she heard me and turned, I saw she was covered in blood – red smears across her dress and her face – and a wild, unsettling look in her eyes.

All of which startled me greatly (and you know how difficult I am to startle).

'What are you doing?' I asked.

'Visiting a friend,' she said. (Not a very good liar.)

'You are covered in blood,' I said casually, lighting a cigarette and offering her one.

She glared at me, those beautiful dark eyes flashing in the gloom.

'I helped with preparing the meat for the feast,' she replied.

A silly lie, so I remained undeceived. I wondered who it was she'd attacked and my thoughts naturally turned to the Marsden girls.

'I was meaning to pass on my compliments to the chef,' I said. 'I'll be sure to single out your preparations for special praise.'

At this she knew the game was up, and she stared at me for a long moment.

'What do you want?' she asked. (Though she knew full well.)

I decided to toy with her, things being *with more spirit chased than enjoy'd*, etc.

'I'll let you know when I'm ready,' I grinned.

The glare on her face was priceless. Then she nodded, turned and ran.

I sauntered back to the festivities, looking for the innkeeper, but the man was busy serving drinks. A shame, for my blood was up. I returned to the square, where the locals had thrown a straw man onto the bonfire and were passing out yew tree branches. I know not why, for it is the wood of a rowan tree, not a yew, that is supposed to ward off evil.

I watched for a few moments, expecting my spirits to be lifted, for this bacchanalia certainly contained traces of the *old religion*. But something about it made my blood run cold. I had the unsettling feeling that I had somehow travelled back through time, and worse, that I had witnessed this scene once before (maybe in a past life) and that in that precursor, it was *I* who was burning on the fire.

I sought out my horse and returned to Bastwick Hall.

Adieu,

G.

Emily,

Work has barely begun on the house and already it has been consecrated in blood, for it appears the three girls I saw arguing with Thornwick have disappeared. On the very night I saw the young wench covered in blood.

Imagine that: old Chesterfield's maid (and the target of her affection) is a cold-hearted, beautiful murderess.

The thought of having her excites me more than ever. And now I have the advantage. I remembered where I had seen her running that night, and wondered if she had made her way to the village along one of the less-travelled paths that lie between it and the work site.

I journeyed the same path this morning, and not far from the works, near some standing stones, I saw what looked like the site of a struggle: a mess of boot-prints; bloody marks on the rocks; locks of hair caught in a hawthorn bush, matted with gore. Further on were some stout yew tree branches, broken and likewise covered with blood.

Did Thornwick lie in wait for the girls and kill them here when she knew everyone in the surrounding fifty miles would be at the festivities? Did she dump their bodies into the foundations' shafts, which she knew would be filled in the next day by hung-over workers?

If so it was an excellent plan, and I wonder whether I have met my match in the girl. If circumstances were different, perhaps I would have offered her a position in our little enterprise.

But then, I puzzle over why she came all the way back to the village with signs of the fight on her. Did something go wrong?

I have set my mind to discovering everything.

And to make sure she's not arrested before I have my pound of flesh, I cleared the area of the evidence, and muddied all as best I could.

G.

Emily,

More news on the dead girls. Hilariously, the authorities (or what passes for them up here) are blaming it on the Italian. The poor fool. I encouraged them in this belief, and even offered to be there when they talked with him. He accounted for himself well in the interview so that after we left, *I* had to be the one to point out the inconsistencies in his story to the *gendarmery*.

They promised to keep their eye on the man, though I have the feeling no one really wants to pursue the matter further (apart from the dead girls' family) for fear of upsetting rich old Chesterfield.

Is it terribly mean of me to play with them so? But I am so starved of excitement here.

Adieu,

G.

Emily,

Further correspondence from the lawyers in Leeds.

The landowners are now saying the covenants might not be in order and they want to review them, and, not surprisingly, my own lawyers have agreed.

Bastards!

First they tried to up their rate of commission, and now this.

They must all be in on it together.

You warned me it was a mistake to hire lawyers in the same city. I see now we should have worked with the men you suggested.

Perhaps this is all still part of their delaying tactics.

Well, they won't grind me down.

It was *I* who led old Chesterfield here.

It was *I* who convinced her this land is a site of special powers.

It was *I* who made her buy up countless acres of worthless moors for four times their value.

These lawyers and landowners will be richer than Croesus, all because of *my work*. And now they want to play the fool with me?!

I shall journey up to Leeds and catch them by the neck if they don't finalise everything soon and send me my money.

I decided to go for a walk, thinking it might calm me down, but as I was crossing the hallway, who did I see coming out of the withdrawing room? Little Miss Thornwick. Now was the time to relieve my stress, and here was the perfect vessel.

'Miss Thornwick,' I said. 'It's time.'

Her eyes opened wide and her lip quivered. But she made no pretence of ignorance, for which I admired her.

'Now?' she asked. 'Here?'

Foolish girl. Next to where we were standing was the entrance to the storage room underneath the stairs. I grabbed her and pushed her inside. She stumbled and fell against a table laden with cleaning supplies and stacks of napery. I closed the door behind me and all was dark till our eyes adjusted to the gloom.

I waited for her to cry, to sob, to plead.

But she did nothing, just stared at me through the blackness.

'Come now,' I said.

She paused a moment, looked about her, then pulled herself up onto the tabletop, dislodging a half-dozen items which fell to the floor with a clatter. Then she hitched up her skirts, her eyes on me the whole time. Her nonchalance quite unnerved me, as did her forthright look, for I've encountered dockside whores who had more shame than this one. It surprised me, although I have always fancied that country girls are wiser than their years.

I wondered again if there wasn't something between her and old Chesterfield. If she was so easy with me, why not with the woman who would make her a lady?

But when the deed was done, I saw there was blood on my undershirt – had I deflowered the poor girl? Or simply been too rough with her?

As I buttoned myself up I noticed she was smiling at me through the darkness.

'What are you grinning at?' I asked.

'It's nothing, sir.'

She said it with such derision, such an air of superiority.

'You shouldn't have a great deal to grin about, I think. We both know what you did on the night of the bonfire. It won't take much for me to remember a few details and relay them to the police and you'll be hanged for murder.'

She flinched and it was my turn to grin.

'Maybe in future you'll think more carefully when exacting revenge on your bullies,' I said.

She frowned, and then that infuriating grin returned to her face.

'It wasn't for revenge, sir.'

'Then what *was* it for?'

'The land, sir. The land demanded it.'

And with that, she turned and left, leaving me flummoxed, and I am not ashamed to say, perturbed, for a feeling of mortal peril was clotting in my chest.

I exited a few seconds later, making sure no one saw me, then I made my way out of this damned manor house and spent three whole hours walking the moors, but it did nothing to relieve me. For all its beauty, this is a treacherous land: rolling fog, marsh, miasma, ague, hemmed in by sea and sky, both of them symbols of death. The contemplation of it put me in an even more maudlin mood, for Thornwick said she had killed for this land. I cannot stop wondering what she meant. It is hard not to draw a parallel between this beautiful treacherous place, and the girl herself.

Yours,

G.

Emily,

Good news! A letter from Leeds. They have relented. It seems their talk of having to 'look over the covenants' was all bluster. Their lawyer writes to say that everything is in order. Clearly my tactic of not giving an inch has worked!

The monies will be transferred as soon as we have moved into the new house, for Chesterfield's agreement with the landowners states the bulk of the money will be transferred to them then. Once that transfer has occurred, our share will be released from the escrow account at Coutts into your shadow account, and then, my dear, we shall be rich and free.

No longer shall we have to dupe the slovenly rich, for we ourselves shall be rich!

Ah, why should life all labour be?

I danced in my room at the thought of it. I dashed off a letter in response. Now all there is to do is wait.

Adieu,

G.

Emily,

Life continues to pass by in a bliss. The house is being constructed quickly and soon we shall move in.

I amuse myself with the barman and Thornwick, though our congress progresses perfunctorily. She has become used to me. Perhaps she even admits to enjoying it. (You were the same, too, in our early days, dear Emily, were you not?) At the end of our coupling, however, she always smiles at me in that beguiling way, as if it is *she* that has got the better of *me*.

In the meantime I pass the hours when I can with Hartington, the local vicar, and Varano, the Italian architect. He's dreadfully Continental – in that pompous way so many of them are – but I am so starved for company here. I have sounded him out subtly *vis-à-vis* the ancient ways, but he's a cold fish.

In the evenings I even work on my *A Psychic History of the British Isles*. I have made it through all the research books at my disposal and so have contacted antiquaries in London to acquire more, for each book references its own sources, and these in turn reference others – as each account illuminates, its illumination throws new areas into shadow, so that these too must be illumin-ated. Since I have so much time to spare, why not make this the most thorough history ever written?

A little learning is a dang'rous thing;
Drink deep, or taste not the Pierian spring.

The only dark spot in all this is that twice a week I must con-duct a seance for old Chesterfield. These are now attended by Thornwick, and it makes the pretence that much harder. The way she looks at me when Chesterfield isn't watching, the contempt at how I make my living, the amused smirk. But what do I care? In a few months we'll be rich and sipping champagne in the south of France.

Adieu,

G.

Emily,

Time passes and I steadily go out of my mind.

I found myself in Heybridge this morning, passing by the vil-lage green, where a gaggle of local girls were playing, dancing in rings, singing the following song:

Hush-a-bye baby, on the tree top,
When you grow old, your wages will stop,
When you have spent the little you made
First to the workhouse and then to the grave

It should have made me laugh, but for the mention of the workhouse. Suddenly my mind was back in Romford and my heart was thumping. Do memories of the workhouse ever assail you, Emily? Or have you well buried that past of ours?

I must admit that those experiences are never far from my thoughts. The slightest thing can cause it all to come flooding back, as if those memories are lying in wait for me, lurking, seeking any opportunity to waylay me. It's no exaggeration to say I still live my life under the moving shadow of those workhouse years.

The stench of the place, the dirt, the hordes of tramps and paupers and vagrants. The feeble-minded screaming and soiling themselves and laughing at their own nudity. The freezing cold cells and greasy walls. The inescapable stink of drains and shit.

And yet, it was there that we met. How different would our lives have been if I had not come over to speak to you that evening as we waited outside to be admitted? You on the point of being sent to Australia, me smuggling tobacco in my socks. What would we have become if you had not kept your promise and met me when we were both released?

For that was when our luck turned, when every trick we tried came off. Each one bigger than the next. First we duped the execrable poor, then the bay-windowed middle classes, then the slow-witted rich. And now our greatest gamble yet. It has to come off. It has to.

G.

Emily,

Disaster! I have mislaid one of your letters. One of your purple ones.

Will you ever forgive me for being such a fool?

I took it out of its spot under the floorboards in a moment of desperate need and now I can't find it. I searched my room wildly until I remembered that I had dropped off some books with the Italian a few days ago. Perhaps, without thinking, I put your letter in one of the books which I subsequently lent him?

Chesterfield was visiting the work site this morning so I hopped in her carriage. When we got there she bothered the foremen with her usual pettifogging and I used the opportunity to seek out the Italian. I tried to act composed, as if the letter and its contents were a mere trifle, and not something that could see me ruined.

The fool swallowed it, of course, but before he could look for the letter I had to return to Bastwick Hall.

Now I pace the boards and pray that the Italian has it and not Thornwick.

How stupid I have been.

G.

Emily,

Good news! The letter has returned. The Italian came by my room this morning to drop it off. I don't fully trust him – he is southern European, after all, which is only a boat ride away from African savage – so I made a careful check of the envelope and I am certain it has not been tampered with.

Aside from the physical evidence, the man himself is prim and self-righteous to a fault. This is exactly the kind of situation in which he would exercise the 'gentlemanly values' he seems so proud of, even as they so clearly drain his life of interest.

When I had returned the letter to its place, we went for a walk, and I made discreet enquiries on how the work at the house was progressing, and when we might move in so that the money can be released. By the man's estimate, we are looking at a moving-in date of Christmas.

So many more months in this desperate hole.

Adieu,

G.

Emily,

A fearful episode with Thornwick!

I was happening past the withdrawing room when I heard her practising her piano. (I am not sure if I have told you, but old Chesterfield is paying for tutors to teach the girl all manner of things.) I stopped in the hallway and listened and thought I recognised the piece, but could not place it as Thornwick's playing was most erratic.

It's strange, for I've heard the girl play often and she is exceptionally good for a beginner. When I passed the time of day with her piano teacher, he remarked that she had a preternatural talent. Which made me wonder why her performance today was so poor.

Never one to miss an opportunity, I opened the door and stepped inside.

She did not notice me at first and played on for a few moments. As I looked her over I was startled to see there were tears pouring down her face. Suddenly she saw me and with a jump, ceased her playing.

'My dear Miss Thornwick, your playing is most cacophonous today, whatever is the matter?'

I grinned at her and that wild glint appeared in her eyes. Then she hissed something under her breath. It reminded me of the way she had hissed at the three Marsden girls before they fought in the Lunham mud.

'What was that? Come now, girl, speak. You should be receptive when a gentleman furnishes you with such attention.'

'A gentleman?' she muttered. 'You're nothing but a charlatan, and a cheap one at that.'

How her speech has changed over the months, for her elocution tutors have worked their magic, improving her diction, cleansing her vowels of the brutish thickness of Yorkshire. Now when she speaks, she almost sounds like a respectable young lady.

'A charlatan, am I?' I replied.

I walked over and leaned against the piano. It was only now that I was up close that I saw how truly upset she was, how full of anger and hate.

'I know what you're up to,' she said, her eyes narrowing.

'And what is that?'

'You came here to steal from Mrs Chesterfield. You brought her here because you had an agreement in place with the land-owners, to sell her all this land at an inflated price and pocket a commission for yourself, because for all your airs and graces, you don't have a penny to your name. *Gentleman*, indeed.'

My heart jumped. How did she know? How *could* she know?

'Oh?' was all I could stammer out, like a fool.

'You did not pick this land,' she hissed, rising. 'This land picked you. It was the land that made you come up here. The land that tricked you and Mrs Chesterfield both. The land has been waiting for you to do its bidding since ancient times. *Terra suum templum aedificabit.*'

She said the last in a voice barely above a whisper and it took me a few seconds to realise that she'd spoken in Latin. I felt a chill fear run through me, for the words themselves were innocu-ous enough – *the land to build a temple on*. But the phrase had a familiar ring to it. Was it perhaps from one of my research books? Had she been sneaking into my room and reading them?

As she watched my confusion, a sly grin spread across her face.

'Go and look in those books you are so proud of,' she said, as if reading my thoughts. 'Vain and fragile man. It was all written down long ago, and its truth was spoken of by the women who tended this land before me, even as they were hanged.'

Filled with dread, I stumbled towards the door, wanting nothing more than to get away from her. On seeing me thus, I expected her to gloat, but she did not. She sat at the piano and launched once more into the piece she'd been practising, attacking it with a wild fury. In that anger she played it perfectly, even though it was fiendishly hard, and under normal circumstances, beyond the skill of a beginner.

It was only when I was rushing back up the stairs, with the music reverberating through the house, that I finally realised what she was playing – Liszt's first *Mephisto Waltz*.

I returned to my room in a daze. How did she know this whole escapade was set up to dupe Chesterfield in a land deal? Is Thornwick in league with the landowners? She is a local girl so may well know them, may well have given them favours of the type she so clearly offers Chesterfield.

I quickly jotted down the Latin words she'd whispered in case I forgot them, then rushed back downstairs to the library. As I moved through the house the whole place was still ringing with that infernal piano piece by Liszt. Even the chandeliers were shaking with it.

I reached the library and found a dictionary and double-checked my translation; I was right – *the land to build a temple on*. Again I had the sense that I had seen the phrase somewhere before. I raced back upstairs and searched through my books. But I could not find it.

I left the house and walked the moors for some hours to cool off, and eventually my heart was the better for it.

Then I had an idea and went over to the works and sought out Waylett.

'Latin, sir?' he said when I asked if a tutor had been employed to teach Thornwick the language. 'No, sir. No Latin. Just English, for the girl is quite illiterate. If her studies go well, next year she'll begin on French and Italian. And maybe after those, then Latin and Greek. Why are you asking?'

I made up some flimsy reason.

'I hear she is making good progress with her reading and writing,' he said. 'Despite all that has happened to her recently.'

'What has happened?'

'Oh, I don't suppose you'd know. Her father is dead.'

'I thought he was in prison.'

'He was. But last week there was a break-out. And then a few days ago he was found dead in the shack upon the moors he used to live in with Miss Thornwick. It's a desolate spot. A good place to lay low, but one the police were sure to check.'

'How did he die?'

'Bludgeoned. The talk is he came back to reconnect with his old accomplices, but they double-crossed him. Some old grudge resurfacing perhaps, or maybe some secret they wanted kept hidden. Or perhaps he came back for revenge and they got the better of him. Either way, he was found in there with his head caved in.'

This explained her tears and wild manner this morning. I thanked Waylett and returned to Bastwick Hall.

Terra suum templum aedificabit.

Where did she stumble upon the phrase?

I stayed up late into the night, thinking and smoking. Not even your purple letters could get me to sleep. And as I lay there, her words ran through my head, over and over – *You did not pick this land, this land picked you . . . its truth was spoken of by the women who tended this land before me, even as they were hanged.*

After a few hours, I thought of something; a story I had read in one of my books. Something about a witch trial in the area. Was this what she was referring to? I spent the night going through my books once more, but could not find the reference.

I must know the meaning behind her words, or all is lost.

G.

Emily,

I've exhausted my list of books and still I can find nothing. But I must find out what Thornwick meant so that I can have power over her in the battle that is looming. At the moment we are locked in a Devil's pact because we each know the other's secret – she is a murderess, I am a swindler – so we have not acted against each other. But we would be fools for assuming it will remain so. Any day the circumstances might shift and the police might come to arrest me, or old Chesterfield throw me out.

We have an adversary here – a very capable one, *a lusus naturae* – and so I amass an arsenal to use against her at the appropriate time and try to uncover all I can about her.

Either Thornwick has been sneaking into my room to read my books, or she is in league with persons unknown, or . . .

I don't even want to write down the third option, for I have made a career of duping those fool enough to believe in the supernatural. But when night comes on, as surely as the sun sets, I become convinced that the only explanation is the third one – that she *knows* something. Truly knows.

G.

Emily,

With our fate in mind I've approached the Reverend Harting-ton. The man has subscriptions with several libraries and dealers around Yorkshire, so I've asked him for their details, hoping that maybe, since the subject matter is local, I might have some luck with them.

In the meantime will you help me too, please, Emily? Ask around the book dealers and libraries in London for the volumes in the list I've enclosed.

Hopefully,

G.

Emily,

I try to imagine what our life will be like when this last scheme of ours has come off, when I've defeated Thornwick and you've ditched that rich fool you had to marry and you and I are independently wealthy and living abroad – summers in Monte and Biarritz, renting a *pensione* on Lake Como for the season, trips to Bayreuth for the *Festspiele*, to Paris for the *Salon*. Autumns spent wandering the *Strassen* and *Plätze* of Vienna, waltzing through coffee-houses and museums, feasting on *Sachertorte* and *Glühwein*. Browsing the wares of booksellers in Hamburg, watchmakers in Geneva. Springtime in the Alps, in Tuscany, on the Amalfi coast. Winters touring the ruins of Rome, Athens, Constantinople.

I keep my mind fixed on the life we shall lead, and from this gain succour for the battle ahead.

G.

Emily,

I've found a clue! It was in the memoir of a churchman who worked in the locality around the time of the Civil War. He refers to local girls being hanged after they were caught conducting rituals on the moor, worshipping something that was trapped in its caves by the same ancients who raised the standing stones as warnings.

Now I have a range of dates and some details, I can instruct the book dealers more closely. I know you have warned me against it but I cannot stop.

Will you play your part, too, Emily? Please? Ask the circle in London for any history which even glances upon the war years in Yorkshire?

Please.

G.

Emily,

Autumn deepens and as I look forward to the funds finally being moved I become more fearful. What if Thornwick is waiting for exactly this moment to make her advantages known? It is when we will be at our most vulnerable.

What if she too is playing a waiting game?

After yet another sleepless night I went for a walk at dawn to clear my head, and when I looked up I saw that I was passing by a cave entrance. I suddenly recalled what the Italian had said about feeling an evil presence in those caves. To disprove it all I did something stupid; I entered the cave to assure myself there was nothing in this landscape that I should fear.

How wrong I was.

Emily, I cannot begin to describe what happened, for I lost myself. I remember walking in just a few yards, and then turning back to find I could no longer see the mouth of the cave. I was so disorientated, I did not know which way to go. It felt as though I wandered those dark caverns for hours. I despaired I would ever get out again, for the space seemed to grow as I traversed it.

In the darkness fusillades of lighting shimmered, revealing something too briefly for me to comprehend. What is it that creaks through the fabric of our world? For some reason my mind fixed itself on a line of Euripides:

Out of the dark door of the pit of death I come, the shadow land where no god walks.

I became so despondent, I fell to the ground and cried.

After I know not how long I opened my eyes and found myself back on the moor, but miles from where I had entered the caves – at a crossroads on the outskirts of Lunham. I am not sure what happened, for I can't remember a thing. And to make matters worse, I recalled the old custom (which in Yorkshire only stopped a couple of decades ago) of burying suicides at crossroads, in unmarked graves, pinned to the ground with a wooden stake through their hearts to stop their ghosts from wandering.

The thought of it sent me rushing into the village's tiny church. I sat in its pews and cried like a baby. Eventually my terror subsided and I cleaned my face and left. My only saving grace is that no one saw me.

Despondently,

G.

Emily,

Nothing to report. I stay in my room searching through my books, looking and not finding. How are things progressing with you?

Hopefully,

G.

Emily,

Today Hartington knocked on my door and stepped inside, even though I shouted at him to go away. When I asked what he wanted he said he needed to check I was all right. I burst out laughing at how ludicrous it was. And thank God I did laugh, for if I hadn't, I would have throttled the fool. I screamed at him to get out and the man looked positively deathly. But he did as commanded and I got back to my work.

Then a few hours later there was a knock at the door again, and who should it be but Chesterfield and a doctor, there to 'appraise my well-being'. It was only then I realised the mistake I had made with the vicar. We are so close to the end now, and I have let appearances slip, for they would have me down as a madman. Perhaps that was Thornwick's plan all along – unsettle me until I am committed to a sanatorium.

And who would believe a madman when he accused her of murder?

I let the doctor come in and 'appraise' me. He asked me about my work and I explained that I was writing a history – *A Psychic History of the British Isles*. I told him this was my life's work and I had become obsessive about it, but now I was nearing its end. The fool swallowed the story and went to inform old Chesterfield that I'm in good health.

And with that, I returned to my research.

G.

Emily,

I have important news!

I've made a breakthrough. I see clearly now everything that has happened. We've been dealing with a network of accomplices. It was not Mrs Chesterfield who hired Thornwick as a maid, it was them! The landowners and the lawyers up in Leeds!

They realised they needed a girl on the inside so they inveigled Thornwick into the household. Of course her employment was strange, we all thought so at the time – it was because she was there with an ulterior motive!

This revelation led to a further one; the book that backed up Thornwick's babble about ancient evils and wise women – it arrived here via an antiquary in Leeds!

The same city the lawyers are in!

Can you not see they are ALL in it together?

It's a network of accomplices.

When Thornwick said I had been duped, she meant by tricksters.

Knowing this, I've decided to take the bull by the horns and confront Thornwick so as to force out everything she knows. Yes, it is a brutish way to go about it, but it is simple and effective, and I kick myself for not having done it earlier; *time's wingèd chariot* hurries ever nearer.

I know you will try and dissuade me, but we have no other choice.

Thornwick is the Devil who haunts this house.

I have sent her a note to sneak out of church service this Sunday and meet me in the churchyard.

I will let you know how it goes.

Hopefully,

G.

Emily

I met Thornwick in the churchyard this morning and I fear it has only made things worse.

I got there early and waited on a bench under a yew tree, watching the tombstones huddled together in the rain. Eventually she came out of the church and wound her way towards me. I rose and confronted her.

'I want to know what you meant last time we spoke,' I said.

'You want a lot.'

I slapped her and I can't tell you how good it felt to inflict on her a physical blow as repayment for the mental blows she has inflicted on me.

She glared and then she licked the blood off her lips, smiling at me most lasciviously.

'You told me the land had brought us here,' I said. '*Terra suum templum aedificabit.* Where did you learn the phrase? Who taught it to you?'

'You would not believe me even if I told you.'

At this my heart jumped, for here was proof that she had accomplices. I slapped her again, harder, and this time she did not respond with such feigned nonchalance. I saw that flash of malice in her eyes.

'What is it to you where I learned the phrase?' she hissed.

'I want to know everything about you and your accomplices.'

At this she grinned.

'Poor fool. You still have no idea. My accomplices are all around us,' she said, gesturing to the tombstones.

'Is it to do with the caves?' I asked. 'Is there something in those caves?'

'I see you have been reading your books, sir. It is all true. Everything you fear. All those things that keep you up at night, that send you sprawling through your worthless books looking for answers. They are *all* true. You have been made a fool of by coming here. You have been made a laughing stock by locking yourself in your room and calling for more and more books. Even your sweetheart in London thinks you stupid and mad.'

'How do you know—'

'I know much, sir. Which you have never credited me for because you think that poverty is the equal of stupidity. And yet it is you who are the poor one. Conniving for money, debasing yourself.'

'How do you know?!'

'I am a wise woman! A witch from a long line of witches. And just as the land bewitched me, I have bewitched you to help me build a door to the underworld. A temple. It will take a generation to build and it will cover this land and when it is anointed it will be ready to release what it has so unjustly held captive for all these thousands of years.'

'Release what?'

'Take a look around you,' she said, gesturing once more to the ranks of the dead. 'And know, sir, that you have assisted us, unwittingly, for you have no wit, despite all your desperate striving. This is where it has brought you, so weep, just as you have made so many others weep.'

258

She turned and stormed back towards the church, weaving through the tombstones and rain.

Emily, please, please, reply. What am I to do?

G.

Emily,

Well, this is splendid, Emily! Truly, splendid!

Yes, it was foolish of me to confront the girl. But to doubt me now when we are so near the end just because I didn't follow your good advice?

Trust me, I am NOT going mad!

Our encounter in the churchyard happened exactly as I recounted it to you. Verbatim!

To say it is all in my head is ridiculous.

G.

Emily,

We have moved into the house. It is complete. The chain of transactions should be triggered now. Send me word as soon as you have the money.

G.

Emily,

Please God, write back to me.

Not replying is bad enough but to send me back my letters as well?

(I notice you did not return *all* my letters, but kept the more incriminating ones. For a rainy day, I presume? Well, I suppose it goes to show how expertly I've taught you.)

All I ask is that you please confirm that the money has been transferred and you have received our share?

G.

Emily,

You may think yourself clever by not replying to me, or maybe you take pride in your cold-heartedness, I cannot say. If our romantic entanglement is at an end, so be it. But need I remind you that our legal entanglement is ongoing. The accountants and lawyers are well aware of what should happen, but just in case you need reminding of your obligations, I state them plainly – you *must* move on the money that has entered your account.

Please confirm receipt of this letter and acknowledgement of your duties.

G.

Emily,

Please respond.

Please.

Love is not love which alters when it alteration finds!

There is not a soul in all this country I trust. There is only you. There has always only been you. Ever since the workhouse it has just been you.

Please.

I have had the worst news imaginable!

I have got to the bottom of the mystery and now I know there is no hope.

Yesterday one of the antiquaries in York sent down a book I have been searching for; a bound volume of clerical documents from the diocese.

Now I've read it I feel sick.

Amongst the documents is a short letter written to the Church authorities by a clergyman at the time of the witch hangings.

It proves every one of my fears true.

PALACE OF SHADOWS

I know you will disbelieve all this, so I have copied out the letter in its entirety here, changing only some of its archaic language so it is easier to understand.

Read it and ask yourself, how could any of this possibly be?

G.

PART FOUR

Addendum to the Special Report
of Father Gregory Robbins into
the Activities of Witchfinder James
Beresford at the York Assizes,
December 1646

Father Thomas Kent,
Lincoln Cathedral
Friday, 17 December 1646

Sirs,

I include the below account as an addendum only to be seen by yourselves and those in the council. My hesitancy in setting forth the details in an official document will become clear.

As you know from the earlier report sent to you by Father Gregory, we were delayed in our journey and only arrived in York on the evening before the trials drew to an end. Understanding there was not much time remaining, we quickly settled in at our rooms then parted ways – Father Gregory went to the inn where the witchfinder was staying, and I went to interview the accused girls, who were being kept in the castle dungeon.

Although the seal of my office should have granted me unfettered access to them, gaining admittance for the interview was a delayed and difficult process. But eventually I was led through the dungeon by a crapulous, buff-coated gaoler.

We arrived at the part of it reserved for the female prisoners and I saw it was a hellish, lightless place; stinking, mired, damp, cold, the silence broken only by the drip of water, the skittering of rats, the moans of the inmates.

'Are all the six girls kept in the same cell?' I asked the gaoler.

'Nay. The five are kept together, the leader kept separate. She's the one you'll want to speak to. You'll get no sense from the other five.'

'Why not?'

'The leader has them under her sway. They'll not speak to you unless she says, and even then only what she commands them to.'

'How can she command them if they are kept separately?'

'How do you think? Witchcraft.'

The man led me to the very end of a corridor and stopped outside a cell door, in which was inset a small, barred window. He
peeped through it, then took the ring of keys that was hooked to
his belt, and unlocked the door.

We stepped into a large, square chamber that would have been
pitch black were it not for the gaoler's torches. The stench in here
was even worse, thick with the odour of urine and faeces, seamed
with mould and a suffocating dampness. I saw that the stones
underfoot were covered with straw, and that there were bales of
the stuff lining the walls.

'Don't worry,' the gaoler said. 'She's the only one in here, and
she's chained.'

He turned and approached the door through which we had
entered. Thereat he slipped one of the two torches he'd brought
into a holder on the wall.

'When you are finished,' he said, 'take the torch and return the
way we came. I'll meet you at the end.'

And with that he trudged out.

I turned back to look into the cell but could make out nothing
in the darkness.

Then I was startled by a girl's voice:

'I have no need of a priest. I am hellbound and there is no one
who can stop it.'

She had a Yorkshire accent, but she spoke with such clarity and
force it was easy to understand what she said.

'I'm not here to offer you spiritual counsel,' I replied. 'Though I
will if that's what you desire. Why do you say you are hellbound?
You admit your crimes?'

'I admit my actions.'

I frowned, but made no comment on her words. Instead, I
explained to her why I had come. A few seconds passed and
there was a scurrying sound from the depths of the cell, and the

girl appeared out of the gloom, walking into the torchlight. I saw there was a chain around her ankle, which led back into the darkness.

Despite the grime on her face, and her sallow, prisoner's complexion, she was a beautiful thing, with dark hair and eyes.

'You are here to investigate the witchfinder?' she frowned.

'We are.'

'The witchfinder is a fool and an abuser. He hangs innocent women for his own profit.'

'So the rumours say. And that is why the Church is investigating. But in your instance, you say he is right to hang you? You admit to practising the curious arts? To being a witch?'

She paused and smiled.

'I am a witch from a long line of witches, if a witch is someone who worships a god older than yours, a religion truer than yours, a belief more compassionate than yours.'

'There is no religion more compassionate than Christianity.'

'Then why I am to be hanged for not believing in it?'

I stumbled to think of a response and she smiled at me.

'You admit to conducting rituals on the moors as you have been accused?' I asked.

'Yes.'

'To worshipping the Devil?'

'Not the Devil.'

'What then?'

'Nature. The spirits of this land. The old ones.'

I frowned at this, intrigued. Even though I knew she was drawing me from my purpose – the trial, the actions of the witchfinder – what she said was so curious, I wandered from my path.

Again she smiled at me knowingly.

'You are yet another learned man so ignorant he knows not the depth of his ignorance,' she said. 'How is it there are so many of you in such high positions in this realm?'

'If I am ignorant, enlighten me.'

She studied me for a few seconds, as if to judge whether or not I was in earnest.

'Many centuries ago,' she said, 'long before Viking or Saxon or Christian or Roman ever set foot upon this land, they roamed. Until they were trapped under the earth. In the caves that cross the moors where I grew up. Trapped by foolish, scared men, who raised standing stones as warnings without realising they were simply making markers to their own folly.'

'And it is these imprisoned spirits you worship?' I asked.

'We *tend* to them. Just as we tend to the land.'

'They cannot be so god-like if they were trapped by men.'

'I could say the same about your Christ.'

Again I stumbled for an answer, again she smiled at my hesitation.

'How do you tend to them?' I asked.

'We sing and dance. We honour the ground. We bide our time.'

'You are waiting for something? For them to return?'

'Just like you wait for your Christ's return. They will be released from their captivity, though I will not be alive to see their arrival. But I go to my grave content in knowing I played my part. That I passed on the rituals to the next generation, that they may worship the land and be seduced by it in turn.'

'How then will these "old ones" be freed?'

'A queen shall come. Tricked by the land. Like so many others. She will do its bidding. She will build a temple that attracts souls. Over decades their numbers will grow. And then, on the eve of a new age, when a man has come from the east and a sacrifice has been performed, the temple shall be anointed, and the weight of all those trapped souls shall be heavy enough to break the ground that imprisons the old ones, and they will be free. The giants who roamed Albion will roam once more.'

'All this just from building a temple?' I said. 'Buildings are not so powerful.'

'No, but the spirits they contain can be. Just like my spirits haunt the land, so, too will they haunt the temple. *Terra suum templum aedificabit.*'

I was shocked by her use of Latin. Then I realised she must have simply heard the phrase somewhere, and memorised it. Maybe she didn't even know what it meant.

'Who taught you that Latin?' I asked.

'My mothers.'

Again she smiled at me through the gloom, her beguiling beauty flickering in the torchlight.

'And what of the accusations of murder?' I asked. 'That you killed a man in a sacrifice, that you pierced his skull with branches to make him like a beast?'

'He chose to be sacrificed. He came to us on his knees, for it was his wont for us to command him. His soul was food to the spirits. As were all the thousands of souls who died on the moor in the foolish battle fought there in the foolish war that destroys our country. It was us who brought the war there, so that the old ones may eat. For they are not just ancient giants, but gods of war.'

I am unashamed to admit that her words chilled me to my bones.

I struggled to clear my thoughts, realising again that she had drawn me from my path. Time was running low and we had not yet spoken of the trial and the witchfinder's methods so I set myself in the right direction and got her to talk about the matters at hand. I was surprised to find that she happily complied with this. She explained how she had been captured, what the witchfinder had done to her, the trial she had been through. On every point of the law and its execution – the accumulation of evidence, the interview of witnesses, the logic of the witchfinder's deductions – she pointed out inconsistencies, errors, omissions, all the deficiencies and suspicious practices that riddle the man's method. And she did so in such clear language, with such fault-less reasoning, I had no doubt that she was a singular creature of high intelligence.

This section of the interview is available in the official report, and confirms the witchfinder as a most evil man, ready to hang the innocent for his profit, though in this one case, perhaps he has happened upon actual witches.

Now, sirs, you will see why I did not include this preliminary part of the interview in my report. But for the sake of the folk who live on the moors where she was captured, I share with you what she said, that you may make appropriate provisions for the welfare of their souls.

As you know, the next morning she and her fellow accused were found guilty. Despite it being some days before they were hanged, I did not have the opportunity to speak to her again, though I fain would have, despite her scornful, unsearchable nature.

With our report completed, Father Gregory and I travelled to Lincoln Cathedral, to undertake the next task on our docket, and from where I write you this letter.

We happened to begin the journey on the same day of the hangings, leaving early, so we missed the spectacle. And yet, when we were already far to the south of the city, in the empty land that lies between it and Selby, Father Gregory and I saw smoke ahead of us, and came upon a yew tree, burning. We looked at each other worriedly, for no other plant or tree thereabouts was on fire, and the air was so wet as to make it an impossibility.

270

PALACE OF SHADOWS

We shared a look of unholy worry, then continued on our way, contemplating the unknowable judgements of God.

I smell that burning scent still.

Your most humble and obedient servant,
Father Thomas Kent

PART FIVE
The Gosterwood Letters

Emily,

Did you read the letter from the churchman? Do you see now?

The words spoken by that girl hanged for witchery two hundred years ago, are the exact same words spoken to me by Thornwick!

She used the same Latin phrase, the same self-identification – 'a witch from a long line of witches'.

She even prophesied Chesterfield coming here and building a house. A temple. And that it would come about by Chesterfield being duped by someone. By me!

How is that possible? How is it possible that a maid, a peasant girl, an *illiterate*, can know what was written in the most obscure Church books centuries ago?

There can be only one explanation.

She *knows*.

It's all true.

The people who lived here millennia ago trapped something in the caves underneath these moors, and ever since, others have been working to free them. And the house will be the conduit for their escape.

Terra suum templum aedificabit.

Good God, what have we got ourselves into?

But I know now what I must do.

I must do away with her.

This afternoon I went in search of the girl and found her in the music room, which was echoing to the sound of Bach. When I stepped inside Thornwick looked up at me and ceased her playing.

'What do you want?' she asked.

'I want to join you. I've been in the caves. I've felt it. The presence. The power. I want to be part of it.'

She studied me for a few moments, clearly disbelieving, so I laid on yet more of my subterfuges.

275

'What I felt in those caves, I found precedent and prophesy of in my books. I know now that you were right, and I was wrong. I want to be initiated into everything you are doing. And I want to be initiated in the caves, where the power is at its strongest. Will you meet there tonight? I beg you.'

And with this, I got on my knees, debasing myself, so she would truly believe me.

When I looked up, she was smiling.

'Very well,' she said. 'At midnight come to the caves a little north of the house, where the stones have fallen in a circle around the entrance.'

I nodded and thanked her, stood up and left.

The poor fool – for all her scheming she is still just a naive country girl.

Now it is an hour till midnight. Out on the moor, a mist is descending. All is black and blue and grey. I have stolen a knife from the kitchen and I will also take the stoker from my fireplace to bludgeon her with. I have secreted both in my greatcoat. When the deed is done I will drag her body far into the depths of the cave and leave it there, for no one ever goes into those places because of the old superstitions.

And when I have returned to the house, our problems will be over. The demon shall have been slain and we'll be drinking champagne in Monte Carlo within the month.

In bocca al lupo,

G.

PART SIX

The Journal of Francisco Varano

1850

4 February

I finished reading through the last of Gosterwood's letters in the small hours and when I was done I knew not what to do with myself.

I rose from my desk and stared out of the window, gazing at the infinite blackness of the universe above.

May God have mercy on his poor tortured soul.

For surely the man is dead at Miss T—'s hand.

Surely she didn't go to the caves that night out of naivety, but with the same murderous intent as he, for their entente could only last as long as Gosterwood stayed sane – the madder he became, the more chance there was of him letting something slip about her murder of the Marsden girls.

I fear when they met, he in his dazed, weakened state, that she had the advantage.

Perhaps his body now rests in the same cave as the Marsden girls.

I should have called him my friend but it is clear now that he saw me as nothing more than a clown to amuse him, as with everyone he came across.

It seems this Emily is the only person he ever truly cared about.

Maybe that is what blinded him to the ultimate truth; that the lawyers *were* in league with a secret accomplice – Emily herself.

How could he fail to realise that his 'loved one' was the one who was deceiving him?

She suggested they use her lawyers, and when he chose lawyers

279

in Leeds instead, she must have contacted them directly, and by keeping Gosterwood at the house indefinitely, they duped him out of his share.

Most glaringly, how could he fail to see that the moment we moved into the house and she received the money, she broke off relations with him?

And yet he continued writing her letters even after she'd abandoned him.

Was he, the ultimate charlatan, so blinded by love?

Perhaps deep down he knew he'd been betrayed, and rather than face up to the truth, he sank ever further into his delusions. Poor fool.

He took Mrs C— far from her home and stripped her of her family and friends so it would be easier to bleed her dry, but he didn't realise the place he'd brought her to genuinely *did* have spiritual power.

The charlatan was driven mad by his lies turning out to be real.

How did he not grasp the irony of it?

There is something altogether pathetic to the way his thoughts constantly switched; sometimes convinced Miss T— was in league with the lawyers, sometimes in league with the demons entrapped under the moor.

Terra suum templum aedificabit.

For all Gosterwood's pride in his learning, he failed to properly translate even the simplest of Latin.

The phrase's meaning is not 'the land to build a temple', but rather 'the land shall build its own temple'.

Perhaps if he had correctly translated the words he would have been surer of the conspiracies that haunted him, though I doubt it would have saved him.

My course of action now is obvious – I shall search the caves. If

I find his body there, I shall have proof that Miss T— is a murderess many times over.

Without the body I only have Gosterwood's letters as proof, and just as he himself observed, no one will believe the ravings of a madman.

6 February

Even though the horror only happened two days ago, it seems as if a lifetime has passed, and my memories are already dimming.

I recall walking over to the caves through a stinging, icy rain, so that by the time I arrived my clothes were soaked.

I waded through knee-deep mud to get to the cave entrance, and looking back now, I wonder what insanity compelled me to do so, for it was a miracle I was not pulled into the marsh; the rain having turned the ground into a mire, the water pouring into the cave mouth.

When I stepped inside, I took from my bag my lamp, lighter, spare bottle of oil and coil of rope.

I lit the lamp, then hoisted the rope onto my shoulder, and walked into the depths of the cave, through the dark, over rocks slippery with rain.

Just as I was thinking that surely Miss T— could not have dragged Gosterwood's body any further inside than this, and that I should turn back, I saw ahead the path veering sharply to the right.

I decided to check around this corner before making my return.

If I only I had not been so foolish.

When I walked around the bend I nearly fell to my death, for just beyond the turn the ground fell away abruptly into a chasm that stretched all the way across the floor of the cave and some twenty yards into the distance.

I breathed a sigh of relief for I only just avoided falling in.

I stepped as close to the edge as I dared – a dangerous endeavour, for the rainwater was rushing past my feet, pouring into the chasm.

I lifted my lamp high over the abyss, then peered into the depths below.

I could not see the bottom.

If Miss T— had dragged the bodies of Gosterwood and the Marsden girls all the way here, and pushed them into the chasm, they would never be found.

Just then there was movement, a stirring in the air.

I stumbled back from the edge as a sulphurous vapour rose up from the depth of the chasm.

It filled my nostrils with a wretched stench that made me dizzy and delirious.

Looking back now I am reminded of the ancient oracles at the Temple of Apollo in Delphi, the priestesses who stood above a crack in the rocks of Mount Parnassus, whence noxious gases were also released that made the priestesses hallucinate and see visions which were taken as predictions of the future.

Did the gases here likewise have the power to induce such visions?

Fearful that my dizzy stumbling might cause me to fall into the chasm, I turned and headed back the way I had come.

And this was when the terror started.

As I journeyed back to the mouth of the cave, I realised I was passing by features that I had not passed on my way in – forks, grottos, side passages, waterfalls and lakes.

I walked through cavern after cavern, endlessly looping through the darkness.

At some point I stepped through into a space larger than a cathedral, filled with a forest of yew trees, its ceiling hundreds of yards above me, illuminated by a pale green glow that emanated from the rocks themselves.

Surely the chasm gases had made me hallucinate.

Or was the cave revealing itself to me, just as it had on my first visit?

Once again I had the sense of an evil presence that was making those caves stretch and grow.

Visions flashed before me, in flickers and snatches, like those of the brain fevers I suffered as I child.

I saw a horde of demons; powerful, giant, snapping and lashing, trapped in the bedrock of the Earth, miles below me.

I felt them straining to be unleashed, their malign influence stretching across unthinkable gulfs, with the power to warp reality itself.

These were the ancient giants the witch-girl had spoken of in the churchman's account.

I realised then that this evil would seep into the house, just as she had predicted; it would possess the building and all who lived in it, meaning what I had built here wasn't really a house, it was a portal, a conduit, a sacrificial temple that these demons would use to free themselves.

It had been anointed with the blood of the Marsden girls, and it would be anointed with my own blood, for I, too, would be sacrificed.

The creator trapped inside his creation.

In that moment, my courage and my disbelief both broke.

I turned to run away and that was when I saw them.

The girls.

With blood on their necks and all over their clothes.

They did not speak to me, but communicated still.

Join us, they said. *Join us and build.*

I turned and ran as if all the demons of hell were on my heels.

I screamed prayers.

I slipped in the water and the light of my lamp went out, then I slipped again and hit my head.

I know not how it happened, but when I awoke, I was lying on the moor, miles from where I'd entered the cave.

7 February

Today I went to see Mrs C— and tendered my resignation.

'But, *signore*,' she said. 'Why would you want to leave now? Your work is only half done. There are the two wings to build, the sculptures to adorn the house. And once those are complete, years more work extending the house backwards over the moor.'

'I want no part of it.'

'But why?'

I had decided before our interview that it was my duty to inform her of the peril she faced, even if it made me look foolish.

'I believe there is evil in this land. And that is why the house is being built here. I believe you have been duped. First by Gosterwood and then by Miss Thornwick, who are both agents of the evil that resides here.'

'Duped by the land, *signore*? I do not understand.'

'Gosterwood was lying to you. The house is not being built to repel souls, but to *draw* them here. Evil attracting evil. So when the weight of all those souls is heavy enough, they will unleash a malevolence that was trapped here long ago. Look . . .'

I handed her Gosterwood's letters, which I'd brought with me to her office.

'Gosterwood's correspondence,' I said. 'Read it for yourself. It proves all I say.'

She frowned at me, then took the letters and started reading through them.

After ten long minutes she sighed and looked up at me.

'*Signore*, these are the scribblings of a madman. A poor tortured soul slowly losing his mind. You know that he tried to kill
himself a few weeks before his disappearance? And he would
have succeeded if a maid hadn't found him. This was why we
finally called in the doctors. Yet he makes no mention of this
episode in his letters. An episode that was witnessed by many
people. Nor the numerous interviews we had together, in which I
pleaded with him to seek help. And as for this last episode, Miss
Thornwick was with me the night he disappeared. All night. It is
you who has been duped, *signore*, by these . . . *fabrications*.'

She solemnly folded up the letters and passed them back to me.

It was as I had feared: she had dismissed the letters as the ravings of a madman.

Without his body, there was nothing to back up Gosterwood's
claims.

'*Signore*, I have heard these stories about ancient evils before,'
she continued, her tone soft and soothing. 'Rest assured they
are false. There *are* dead souls here, but they are coming on *my*
say-so. Because *I* have willed it. I know, for I have seen them.
The unknowable dead. I see them all, crawling over the moors
in their thousands. A legion of the mutilated and maimed. I see
them scratching through the dark, scaling walls, trying to rip
down the house. They scream in a hundred foreign tongues. They
want their revenge, but they will be denied. Because when they
get here, *signore*, they will see that what I have built for them is
not a temple, or a sacrificial altar, or a prison to trap them, but a
home, a palace for them to rest in until the Day of Judgement.
A palace for me to rest with them. I am not trapping them here,
I am supplying their weary souls with refuge, their journey's end
after a long, bloody pilgrimage.'

She smiled and it was as though the Devil himself was beam-
ing at me.

I shook my head, fighting the terror I felt.

'You are wrong. You are being duped. And I can have no part of this. I have to leave.'

'I would advise against such a course of action, *signore*. The house still has use for you. And when the house wants something, it's best to submit or you might force it to do something drastic to keep you here.'

I shook my head again and handed her my letter of resignation.

'A shame,' she said. 'You shall see out the week of your notice?'

'Of course.'

She nodded, and with that, the interview was over.

12 February

A letter from home.

My family are dead.

13 February

Still feeling sick and dazed and utterly alone.

Still crying.

Mother is dead; Father is dead; my sister, too.

I don't know the details, only that Austrian soldiers were involved, even though the siege ended months ago.

Was it a reprisal?

A tragic accident?

Were they trying to arrest Father and something went wrong?

I have had no news from them for so long, and now when news does arrive, it is the most devastating of all.

16 February

I have not been eating or drinking for I can keep nothing down.

This leaves me woozy and yet I cannot sleep.

Strange visions flicker: standing stones and mirrors, bonfires and caves, witch balls and rowan trees, dreams of forgotten dreams.

It is the brain fevers once again.

18 February

I awoke this morning to find myself out on the moor.

The country is thick with snow and I wandered out wearing only my nightshirt.

When I awoke I was halfway between the house and the caves.

Had the girls been calling to me in my sleep?

14 April

In bed eight weeks with fever.

My thoughts scatter away before they form, dissolving like snowflakes falling on a fire.

I need to write this journal so that I may remember what is happening to me.

17 April

I cannot fight this house, I cannot destroy it.

I tried to leave and it killed my family to make me stay.

20 April

I wake to find myself surrounded by familiar faces.

'How do you feel?' the doctor from Heybridge asks.

'Fine,' I say. 'The fever is gone.'

'You need to rest, *signore*,' the doctor says. 'The fever has broken but you are still very weak.'

He turns to the others.

'Here is the medicine,' he says. 'Three spoonfuls taken every three hours. Day and night.'

Miss T— volunteers to administer it.

21 April

I wake, I rise.

The door to my room is locked from the outside.

The windows are bolted.

Outside, ghost owls swoop between skeletal trees.

Gosterwood was right; it's a cold, uninterested universe, caring not if we live or die.

This is the true horror.

22 April

I dream of the house, not as it is now, but a future version of it. Infinitely vast, tumbling over the moor.

Its rooms flicker in and out of nothingness, its staircases rise and fall through endless dark.

A maze of a house with swarms of corridors shifting like the things beneath the caves, warping reality as they writhe, testing it, looking for a way out.

23 April

I set down here what I cannot trust my memory to hold:

We are not building a house to repel the dead, we are building a house to attract them.

To draw them here in their millions.

To open the gates of hell.

24 April

I come to understand the nature of true terror.

It lies not in the dead things of the past, but in the limitless horrors of tomorrow.

The future for ever stretches ahead, the abyss from which all nightmares are called.

26 April

I awoke to find Miss T— in my room, going through my chest of drawers, looking through my possessions.

I am glad I followed Gosterwood's example and started hiding my journals and books under the floorboards.

I passed out and when I awoke again, she was gone.

29 April

I awake.

Miss T— hovers.

She holds the spoon to my mouth.

'You were wandering the moors again,' she says. 'If the bogs do not kill you, the fever will, for each time you sleepwalk, the fever returns. How did you get through the locked door and the bolted windows?'

I shake my head, for in truth I do not know.

'You need to be more careful,' she says. 'The doctor suggested we tie you to your bed to stop your sleepwalking. Why do you wander so?'

I tell her the truth – that the dead girls call to me from the dreamery of the moor.

'Why is it that in the house I can hear them scream,' I say, 'but when I go looking for them on the moors, the world is silent?'

'The Marsden girls found eternal life on the moor. And now they beckon yet more souls to join them in their singing. So the horde can grow ever stronger.'

'How do you know this?'

'It was I who killed them.'

30 April

Again I dream of the future house.

The impossible house.

A house that plays tricks on reality, as if to spite it, to exert its mastery.

I walk its paths, I feel its strength, which will lie not in locks and barriers, but in its bewildering endlessness.

Passageways melding into passageways into yet more passageways so ceaselessly it inspires absolute dread.

So it shall be with this house, because so it is with all.

Whether through microscope or telescope, reality's edge scurries away from us as we near, so no end to it can be seen.

What better symbol for this than the impossible house?

1 May

The house is alive and hungry for souls.

It lured us here even before it was built.

It drove us insane, and now it feeds off our madness.

2 May

My thoughts skitter away half formed.

Memories shatter, leaving only shards of being.

Is it fever or madness or medicine that slurs my mind?

3 May

Mist on the moors. Sea-dusk air.

An ocean of clouds barring entry to heaven.

4 May

A disagreeable sensation of cold.

PALACE OF SHADOWS

Am I Varano or Etherstone?
My self fragments.
And thus I become reality.

5 May

The fever has broken.
I can feel it dissolve.

6 May

They tied me to the bed each night and it saved my life, for surely I would be dead otherwise.

I must have struggled against my bonds for there are scars across my wrists where the rope has burned my skin.

7 May

My mental faculties feel almost fully recovered.

Now the fever seems like a nightmare that I can barely remember.

I read again the journal entries I made in my illness and while some I can understand, others I can make no sense of, yet every one of them chills me to my core, fills me with vague, terrifying sentiments.

What catacombs I built in the shadows of my imagination.

What corpses rise from the soil of sleep.

8 May

Mrs C— came to see me this morning.

'You have had quite the time of it,' she said. 'The grief when one's family dies can be overwhelming. I still suffer from it.'

'And were it not for your care I should be dead, too.'

She eyed me for a long time before speaking again.

'Is it still your intention to leave the house? You are welcome to stay till your recovery is complete, but of course we would like you to stay longer.'

'I still want to leave, though I am not sure where I will go. I have lost my true home with my family gone.'

She nodded. 'The war in Italy has been long and costly.'

'Costly for the victims,' I said. 'But profitable for you.'

'These profits are just more sins for me to carry on my back.'

I wondered then if my family been killed by bullets fired from Chesterfield guns.

'You accept responsibility for my family's deaths?' I asked.

'I accept responsibility for the death of every person my guns have killed. As I told you previously, this is why I am building this house. This home. For all those victims. Just like your family.'

I stared at her, not quite grasping her meaning.

'My family?'

'Do not look so shocked, *signore.*'

'No,' I muttered, a feeling of sickness rolling through me.

'It is the truth. The souls of your family will make their way across the Continent to join their brethren, to come to the house that you have built for them.'

'No!'

'You say you have no home now. But your family is coming here. So *this* will be your new home. Do not look sad; you will be reunited with them. In the most beautiful palace in all the world. A palace that you will build for them. And you and I, our families, all the dead, will live here until the end of days. For though they come here seeking revenge, they will instead find a home. They'll walk its corridors, dance its ballrooms. So you must stay and help us build it. Your family deserves no less.'

She smiled at me, then rose.

'Take some time to come to terms with it,' she added. 'And when you are better, finish your work.'

9 May

I cannot get her words out of my mind.

And despite putting all my wit and will into rejecting her proposition, I know she is right; my family *will* come here, attracted by this evil land and the temple it has built for itself.

I can sense my family growing near and I am horrified to say that the thought brings me comfort.

10 May

This morning Waylett took me out for some fresh air.

It was good to be outside, good to talk to Waylett, to be distracted from Mrs C—'s nightmare vision.

We walked about the front of the house and when the men on the site saw me, they smiled and cheered and wished me a speedy recovery, which further buoyed my spirits.

I saw that work was well underway on the two wings.

The scrubland that had previously been used as a storage site for building materials is now being turned into a garden and an avenue of elms.

'Where is the marble being stored?' I asked.

'Around the back of the house. I can take you if you have the strength?'

I nodded and we walked around to the rear of the house, making our way to the sheds where the marble is now kept.

'It's all still here, *signore*,' Waylett said. 'We've left it all untouched for you.'

When we stepped inside I looked up at the giant slabs slumbering in the shadows.

In the emptiness of the stone, I saw the fault lines distort and stretch – just like the rocks in the caves.

I saw them take on the form of demons, saw the stone become the very beings of my nightmares.

I looked down the line of slabs and saw all of them alive.

I decided then to build their house.

But not for them, for me.

A home for me and my family.

And when I am done I will let them kill me, so my spirit will stay here, the ghost that haunts its own creation.

I will be trapped here for all eternity, but I will be with my family.

It is the only way.

15 May

This morning I felt it – I am strong enough to start.

I sent word to Waylett and he came to my room and took me again to the marble stores.

My family will be coming to the house, and I will build them the greatest house the world has ever seen.

The impossible palace of my dreams.

I will build them a new Venice, with corridors for canals, and rooms the size of cathedrals that will grow and stretch each night, will spread across the moor, all the way to the borderlands of the past.

Mrs C— was waiting for me in the marble store, smiling.

I pressed my hands to the marble, caressing it, felt the demons writhing inside, waiting to be freed.

I turned to look at her and she gestured to a work table, where a set of stonemason's tools was laid out.

She picked up a chisel and passed it to me.

Work, her eyes said. *Work and never stop.*

I took the chisel from her, and a hammer, and with that I sealed my fate.

My submission is complete.

I have made no preparatory sketches, I have made no measurements.

I have no need.

I can work from the nightmare visions I see whenever I close my eyes.

For dreaming and life have become one.

I lift my tools to the first of the slabs, and something guides me, as I knew it would, something puts its hand on mine, and warms my skin on this cold moor.

PART SEVEN
Memoir: Samuel Etherstone

27

From that point on, there was no need to translate Varano's journals – the final sections were the meaningless ramblings of a man rapidly losing his mind. The last entries were barely discernible as language at all, mere scratches and daubs and strange geometric symbols. So, too, the architectural sketches, which descended into the expressive scribblings of a soul in torment. Even the dates stopped following any logical order.

It had taken me the best part of three days of almost continuous labour to complete the translation and now that I had finished, I felt numb and heavy, but also intensely alert, for what I had read suggested that I was in immediate, mortal danger.

I rose from my desk, and just as Varano had done when he'd finished Gosterwood's letters, I walked to the window and studied the world beyond. The last light of day was fading and through the gloom, storm clouds were moving in from the sea.

I lit a cigarette and let the opium calm me. I closed my eyes and swayed. I had put together a grotesque tapestry that revealed the bloody, murderous history of the house, feeling as though I had borne witness to not one, but two men's descent into insanity.

I dwelt on their sorry fates and then on their portrayals of Miss Thornwick, trying to square the beauty of the girl as they had described her, with the twist-faced crone she had become. I had seen the marks of syphilis on her the moment we first met – the painful disfigurement, the discoloured teeth from the mercury used to treat the infection. Could the syphilis have so destroyed her looks?

Gosterwood mentioned that Miss Thornwick's father suffered from the disease. Did he pass it on to his daughter? And if so, was it passed down congenitally? Or through rape? For Gosterwood also mentioned local gossip that the father maltreated the girl.

Certainly she was already afflicted with it when Gosterwood was raping her, for why else would she smile at him after every assault? How could he not realise that each time he took advantage of her there was further chance of him catching the illness, and going mad from it? He was so worried the girl was driving him mad through her schemes, he did not realise it was the consequence of his own cruel violations.

But I had no pity for the man. A swindler and abuser and a rapist of children, for Miss Thornwick was barely in her teens when he started forcing himself on her. Were it not for the fact that she was a killer herself, I might reserve my sympathy for her, ill-used as she was by both Gosterwood and her father.

I sighed, for despite everything I had learned, so much still lay in shadow. Had Miss Thornwick killed her victims with Mrs Chesterfield's knowledge? Did Gosterwood really end up murdered and dumped in a cave as suggested in his letters? Or did he manage to flee as suggested by Mrs Chesterfield? And what of Varano? Did he go sleepwalking into the moor and drown in the marshes? Did Miss Thornwick discover he knew about the murders and so kill him too? Or was Varano's own premonition about his death correct? Did the poor tortured man finish his work and allow himself to be sacrificed, so he could spend eternity in the house with his family?

There were no answers in these journals and letters, and why would there be? Their text was as distorted as the house itself. For if one thing was clear, it was that this was a tale of women – of a witch, a maid and a widow – warped by the fact that it had been told by men. How different would the narratives be if their protagonists had been allowed to tell their own tales?

The words of the condemned girl in the witch trial were initially spoken to a churchman, who transcribed them into a diocesan report, which was then re-written in an anthology, which was then copied into French by Gosterwood, then translated back into English by me. The light of their meaning had been reflected across the planes of so many dark glasses that it was impossible now to know what was distortion and what was truth.

I thought again of the journal entry Varano had made when he was in the midst of his fever:

Am I Varano or Etherstone?

How could he possibly have written this? The very thought of it filled me with dread. Worse, it confirmed the sense I'd long had that somehow our fates were intertwined, our very characters, and thus it further underscored something even more pressing – that I was in immediate danger.

I returned to the bureau and flicked through the translation, making a note of all the sections which had chilled me when I read them.

First the snippets from Gosterwood's pagan histories:

A victim was sacrificed at the start of construction to consecrate the ground, and the building would be anointed at the end of construction with another victim.

It was believed the most powerful spirit to sacrifice at the work's end was that of the creator or architect . . .

The calendar also played a part; sacrifices were thought to be more powerful if they occurred on dates of astronomical or

*calendrical significance: the equinoxes, the solstices, the night
of the New Year . . .*

And then from the churchman's account:

> *On the eve of a new age, when a man has come from the
> east and a sacrifice has been performed, the temple shall be
> anointed, and the weight of all those trapped souls shall be
> heavy enough to break the ground that imprisons the old ones,
> and they will be free. The giants who roamed Albion will
> roam once more.*

Was the dawn of a new age the new century that was looming
over us? And who was the man from the east? Me? Thurlby?

I could not be sure, but still I feared that I was to be the sacrifice. That once the mausoleum was completed on New Year's Eve,
I would be killed to anoint it, to mark the end of construction,
and so would be unleashed the horrors below the moor.

Viewed through this lens, all the oddities of the last few
months started to make sense. The contract stipulating that I
was not to be paid unless I stayed till the New Year, that I must
keep to my room so nothing would befall me in the night. Mrs
Chesterfield's rush to have the mausoleum completed. The opium
cigarettes to keep me disorientated and docile. The gilded cage of
my room and studio. The promise of unimaginable wealth.

It scared me to think now what might have happened had I
not stumbled across Varano's journals. But of course, I did not
stumble across them, I was *led* to them by the apparition in the
mirror, and on the beach.

I stared out over the sea and planned my escape. I would have
to go to dinner as usual that night and act as if nothing was
wrong, for if I deviated from my regular behaviour, my hosts

might become suspicious, and I might be locked up in my room like Varano.

If I got through the dinner, then afterwards, when everyone was asleep, I would sneak out of the house and steal away across the moor. I would forfeit my payment, but perhaps I could still leave with something to show for all this madness.

I went to the wardrobe and dragged out the case with the cine-matographic camera. I inspected it and saw it was of the same type I had used previously with Fitzpatrick. The problem would not be in using it, but in not being seen while I did so. I would have to do the filming on my way out of the house that night. But would there be enough light in the nighttime for it to capture anything?

I smoked more of Mrs Chesterfield's cigarettes and stared out at the oncoming storm, which now obscured the line that separated land from sea, so that the two realms merged, making all a borderland.

28

As far as I could tell, no one in the dining room realised that anything was amiss, even though I was having trouble eating my food. Perhaps Sarah might have noticed if she had been there, but she'd been taken ill with a cold and was having her meal in her bedroom. I sorely regretted not being able to say goodbye to her, but I got through the dinner without anyone remarking on my behaviour, or casting me strange looks.

When we'd all said goodnight I returned to my room and continued planning my escape. I packed everything I needed into a bag then I took the camera out of its box and assembled it. I used one of the five reels I had to test that the camera was working, and all seemed to be in order, though I did not know if it would actually capture anything useful in the nighttime dark. I checked the window and saw the earlier storm subsiding. Maybe the skies would clear enough to allow a little moonlight through.

I decided I would use three of the remaining reels inside the house, and one from the top of the hill that stood between it and Lunham. It meant adding a few extra minutes to my journey, but the delay would hopefully make me a rich man, and still leave me plenty of time to get to the village long before sunrise. My plan was to catch the fishermen there before they set out and pay one of them to take me to Filey, using the stipend I had been saving this entire time.

If I reached the station in Filey by dawn, I could be on the first train back to London before anyone realised I was gone.

When the hands of my watch turned to midnight, I rose, put on my coat and flung my bag over my shoulder. I picked up an oil lamp in one hand and the camera in the other. I went to the window to check if the storm had abated, but was disappointed to see it had not. Rain was sheeting down onto the rooftops and the empty moor, and the moon was all but obscured. My spirits sank, for there was no hope of the camera capturing anything under such conditions.

And then there was a boom of thunder and a flash of lightning, and I realised I might have a chance after all. For if I set the camera running and awaited the lightning flashes, I might be able to obtain at least a few seconds of sufficiently exposed film. I put the camera on its tripod, and positioned it in front of the window to capture as much of the house as possible, its carpet of roofs that ran all the way to the distant hills. Then I set it running. So long as there were a few lightning flashes in the time before the reel finished I would have something to show for my efforts.

After a few long moments three lightning strikes lit up the skies and I felt a rush of relief. But the feeling only lasted an instant, for in those momentary flashes I saw that the surrounding land was no longer deserted. On all sides of the house, from the coast to the moor, the ground writhed with a horde of unworldly shapes, a tide of bodies. In their hundreds of thousands. Perhaps in their millions. Rushing the house, trying to breach it.

The lightning faded, and the moor was empty again. As quiet as a tomb. The pale spectral army no more.

Had I hallucinated the vision? Or had I genuinely glimpsed something out there in the darkness? I was filled with the same strange sensation I'd had on my first night in the house, when

I'd sensed something outside in the storm light but could make nothing of it.

Then the lightning flashed once more, a fusillade of strikes, one after another, and the feverish vision of the horde reappeared, and this time I could see it in all its detail – bloodstained, butchered, limping, shrieking. As if the entire sickening legion had freshly trooped out through the gates of hell. Some wore the red coats of the British Army, but most were garbed in foreign dress. There were French Légionnaires, Prussian lancers, Cossack horsemen, Boer infantry, Mongols, Ottomans, Chinese and Japanese. Some were naked, or clothed in mere shreds. Some held aloft the banners and ensigns of their regiments. Some held guns and barbarous swords. Some clutched leather reins that trailed behind them, connected to nothing but the severed heads of horses, bumping along the ground. Some hobbled, cradling their own spilled guts. Some had their skulls caved in, their torsos cratered, their limbs bare stumps of bone gleaming in the night, skin blackened as if by brimstone.

And in amongst these soldiers were civilians – children, widows, craftsmen, merchants, dead mothers clutching dead infants. Some were wailing, confused, as if they'd just awoken into this nightmare. But most were as enraged as the soldiers, clawing to get into the house, their fingers splitting against its walls as they tried to tear it down, brick by brick, tile by tile.

But the house stood firm.

Implacable and malign.

All this I saw in the few seconds of illumination afforded me by the lightning flashes.

And then the lightning faded, and the vision disappeared from view.

All was as it had been. All was peaceful. The moor was empty.

A screaming fear sliced through me. My thoughts scattered.

The energy flushed from my limbs, but I knew I had to move. I grabbed the oil lamp and camera, and without even turning it off, spun and ran out of my room. I had no thought but to escape, to leave the house, to get as far away as possible.

I ran as fast as I could, heading for the Great Hall. As I turned into the passageway with the floor-to-ceiling mirrors set at either end, I heard a low groaning sound, as if wood was being pressured, as if walls were stretching. When I reached what should have been the end of the passageway, I realised with a shock that there was no doorway leading into the next corridor, and where the mirror should have been, the passageway seemed to continue on as far as I could see, its floorboards thickly covered in dust, torches blazing in holders along the walls. I turned to go back the way I'd come, but the passageway behind me now stretched endlessly in that direction as well.

I realised then that this was one of the house's hidden spaces.

Knowing not what to do I ran down the corridor regardless.

I must have been running for at least ten minutes, but there was still no sign of an end. There was just the same black point in the distance, the same torches on the wall flickering past, their light rolling, streaking, hypnotising.

I stopped in a fit of despair. Should I turn back and retrace my steps? Or would the passageway extend itself in the opposite direction? I looked around and had the sense that I was the first person to ever traverse these spaces. And I knew then with certainty that this place would disappear before daybreak and I would be trapped here for ever. What should I do? How could I escape? I could think of nothing.

As I was about to give up all hope, I heard footsteps walking up the corridor behind me. I let out a sigh of relief for the sound meant a human presence; whether alive or dead, it did not matter – I was not alone in all this infinity.

The footsteps became louder and louder, but still I could make out no figure coming towards me. Surely I should be able to see who it was by now? Yet everything remained motionless.

And then the dust motes closest to me rushed about, as if moved by some passing object, and I felt a breeze against my cheek. And then the footsteps were past me, going off in the opposite direction.

But I had seen no figure.

A shiver of fear ran through me so intense that my muscles burst into life, and I was running as fast as I could. Maybe I was screaming. I could not tell. I bounded down the corridor, the light of my oil lamp whipsawing, the oil at risk of jumping up and extinguishing the flame.

I ran on and on until my legs became weak and my chest was burning.

Eventually I noticed a bend in the distance, a corner that I had not previously passed. I ran towards it, turned and saw I was in a part of the house I recognised.

A wave of relief coursed through me.

A few steps further on was a descending spiral staircase that led back to the section where my room was. My room. I could return there and wait it out till morning. Without thinking I stepped onto the stairs and before I knew it I was falling down what felt like a slope. My oil lamp smashed, my camera slipped from my grasp and tumbled downwards after me.

Eventually I came to a stop after what must have been a fall of at least two storeys. I lay in the darkness, my leg throbbing. Then I opened my eyes and saw the oil lamp and the camera were in pieces, scattered across the floor around me. I was lying at the bottom of the staircase, which I realised now had no steps on its upper side – it was just a curving slope winding down multiple floors. The steps were on its underside. The house had turned it upside down.

I looked at my body and saw it was covered in blood, that my right leg was twisted at a sickening angle. Only then did I feel the pain of it ripping through me. I gritted my teeth and searched for a way out. The room I'd landed in was thickly encrusted in grime, with a stale, musty smell to it, but warmly lit by candles glowing in sconces. The walls were gilded and adorned with ornate plasterwork. Giant windows looked out onto an inner courtyard. I heard a soft, ghostly waltz playing and I realised where I was – a ballroom. A golden Venetian ballroom. I'd fallen into another of the rooms from out of time.

Couples were dancing past me now, through me, unaware of my presence. And although they were dressed in the finest of clothes, they were tattered and stained. And they reeked of death. Their flesh rotted. Their bones gleamed through their opulent rags.

The sound of the waltz grew louder. And I saw that there was a man dressed all in black at the far end of the room, his back to me. He was the only other person in there who was not dancing. He looked tired, slumped. In his hand he held loosely a stonemason's chisel. I realised who he was and I feared what might happen if he turned and our gazes met.

And then I looked beyond the man, through the windows on the far side to the inner courtyard beyond. I recoiled in shock as I realised how immense the courtyard was, and how it was filled with staircases, all made of some translucent stone, glacial and grey. They floated supernaturally in the vast emptiness at the centre; a landscape of steps sliding and merging into each other, doubling back, twisting upside down in strange loops and spirals, their geometry so senseless it bewildered and confused my eye.

And across this bizarre, undulating prairie of steps, a multitude of figures moved, trudging as if stuck in a maze. Going up one set of stairs and then onto another, and then, against all laws of perspective and gravity, coming back to the staircase they had started on. There were women dressed in maid's uniforms, men dressed as builders, as clerks. All the poor people who had died in the house. An army of lost souls trapped in an abyssal, Sisyphean march.

I recoiled in horror and screamed. But none of them turned their heads to look at me, even though they were so close. They just carried on walking their endless midnight walk, marching shoulder to shoulder, swaying, trapped.

Then something moved and I heard the groaning noise again. The very sound of the house. I knew it was sending this room back to that other world whence it came. If I did not leave it in the instant, I would be stranded here for ever.

I sat up and an indescribable pain pulsed through the wound in my leg. Despite this I dragged myself to the nearest door and through into the next room.

I took a few moments to regain my breath, and turned to look behind me, through the open doorway I had traversed, expecting to see Varano there, staring at me.

But there was no doorway behind me, the wall was completely blank.

The other room was no longer there.

Then I felt the house start to spin about me, and with the spinning came blackness, consuming all.

29

I dreamt of armies dead and alive. Of metal birds raining down fire.

Explosions rising up over the Earth in giant clouds shaped like mushrooms.

I dreamt of millions marching across the plains of Europe, trenches the length of continents, whole cities destroyed by flames.

I dreamt of death and war taking over the world, of the Earth become hell.

I dreamt of a black figure looming over me.

I dreamt of a flickering flame.

Orange light.

A room. My room. My bed.

The pain in my leg, pulsing.

The black figure feeding me syrup.

Voices of doctors.

Daylight and mirrors.

Slowly, through the drip of dreams and pain, I realised I was not dead.

I had been saved.

I was in my bed.

The black figure loomed once more.

'Take it,' she said. 'For the pain.'

I drank the syrup and the pain dissolved, and I sank once more into the trench of dreams.

30

Time passed and the fever world fell away and I awoke to see it was morning. A man whom I guessed to be a doctor was busying himself at my bedside table. I tried to speak, and it took all my effort to shape the words and express them.

'How much time has p-passed?' I stammered.

The man seemed startled by the sound of my voice and turned to look at me in surprise.

'How much time?' he repeated. 'Do not think of it. You must rest. You did yourself a serious injury.'

'How much time?' I asked once more.

He paused, a frown spreading across his brow.

'I have been attending you since the night of your fall, some eight to ten weeks ago. You've been in a fever most of that time.'

'No,' I said. 'It's not possible.'

Ten weeks would mean I had slept through the entire autumn, Christmas too. It was not possible. Had they been drugging me?

'What day is it?' I asked.

'December the twenty-ninth. We are almost at the turn of the century.'

He smiled at me, as if this should make me feel better, but my mind reeled. The mausoleum. Had it been completed? Were they just waiting for New Year's Eve to conduct my sacrifice? Did I only have two days left to live?

313

'You were found with a broken leg and a fever,' the doctor explained. 'A bad break. "Comminuted", as we doctors say. Multiple fractures and fragments. Still, we managed to set it and the fever seems to have broken. You'll be up and about in a few weeks' time.'

I couldn't take in what he was saying, too agitated by the thought that my situation had become immeasurably worse. I needed to leave as soon as possible, but how could I?

'Am I to be given a crutch?' I asked.

'Oh, not till the New Year, I'm afraid. I've ordered one for you, but it will take a while to arrive. In any case you shouldn't be upright for at least another week. You need to give the bone some more time to set. Like I said, it was a bad break, and no doubt the fever set back your recovery.'

He left soon after that and I was shocked to hear that he locked the door on his way out. I looked around the room frantically for something with which to fashion a crutch, but could find nothing. I sank into my bed and cried and eventually fell asleep, despite my anguish, for the doctor must have administered morphine syrup to me before he went.

When I awoke it was dark outside and the door was opening. I looked up and saw Mrs Chesterfield entering.

'How are you faring?' she asked.

'Well.'

She nodded and walked over to the gas lamps on the wall, turning them up so that the room was flooded with orange light. Then she sat in the chair to the side of my bed and looked me over with her deathly pale eyes. It was only then I realised that Miss Thornwick was not with her, and that this was the first time we'd ever been alone together.

'The doctor said your leg should heal well. You had a lucky

escape. Did no one warn you not to walk through the house at night?'

'I was warned.'

'Then what were you doing out there?'

'Sleepwalking. Ever since I have come to this house, I have been sleepwalking.'

'Sleepwalking with your coat on? It was sleepwalking that led to Signor Varano's death. You need to be careful.'

Did she suspect I had been attempting an escape? That I was trying to film the house? My bag and broken camera and reels had all been left in that room from out of time, and so had disappeared with it, back into its unknowable realm. Or at least, I hoped they had.

'As a precaution, we've locked your door,' she said, gesturing behind her. 'For your own safety. We had to resort to similar means when Signor Varano started sleepwalking as well.'

'But you didn't know I was sleepwalking till I just told you.'

'No, but we suspected it. I've long noticed the similarities between you and Signor Varano. I've long thought you might be kindred souls, joined somehow. It was not a great leap of logic to assume you might suffer from the same affliction. The windows here have also been locked and all the keys taken away. As you know, it's best that you're not about the house at night.'

She looked at me in the stillness, and the jets of the gas lamps flickered. I realised more than ever that I was trapped and alone.

'Tell me, Mr Etherstone, what did you see on your nighttime ramble through my house?'

'I saw nothing.'

'Come, now. I can see it in your expression. What scared you so much that you missed your step? Or did the house shift so that you fell? Did it show itself to you? Its secret rooms and passageways that defy reality? This was Signor Varano's genius and madness, built into the very fabric of the moor. And you have enhanced it.'

'No.'

'Yes. The mausoleum is complete. Now all that remains is to consecrate it. Signor Varano sacrificed himself for this house, because he came to understand what it meant. And you will sacrifice yourself too. Isn't that what artists do? Sacrifice themselves for their art. Here you will achieve eternal life, Mr Etherstone. Inside your creation, you become the art itself.'

'So you will have me killed? For this mad scheme of yours?'

'I said nothing about killing you. You'll sacrifice yourself willingly when the time comes, just as Signor Varano did.'

'No, you worked Varano to insanity and death. To say he died of his own free will is a lie. You led him to it.'

'I did no such thing.'

'The Marsden girls were killed at the commencement of building, and now I will be killed at its end. A blood sacrifice to complete the house's creation.'

She stared at me in shock.

'Rumours,' she said. 'Just rumours. No one knows how those girls died. Whether through accident or malice or by their own hand, no one will ever know. But now that they *are* dead, they are a part of the house, and they revel in it. They rejoice in their life eternal. So much so they go out onto the moor to sing yet more souls to us.'

'Those girls were murdered by Miss Thornwick,' I said, 'who has heartlessly duped you all these years. This house is not attracting souls so they may live with you eternally. It is attracting them so they may unleash what has been trapped beneath these moors.'

'I have heard these stories before,' she said. 'And they are just that. Stories. Idle, simple superstitions.'

I remembered then that Varano had also attempted to free Mrs

Chesterfield from her delusions, to warn her of the danger. He had even shown her Gosterwood's letters, and still she would not believe. Her philosophy had been set in stone, and no amount of good evidence would change it now. I realised there was no chance of talking her round.

'Do you remember the seance you attended, Mr Etherstone?' she asked. 'You were convinced your wife was in the room. So much so you brought poor Alice out of her trance calamitously early.'

'What of it?'

'Did you not stop to think how your wife's spirit happened to be present in the house?'

'I don't understand.'

'She killed herself, did she not? With poison. You're aware, surely, that the Chesterfield company also produces poisons. It's an efficient way of using up some of the by-products of our munitions manufacturing process. If it was Chesterfield poison that killed her, then she, too, would be part of the horde brought here to the house, would she not?'

'That cannot be,' I whispered.

'It can and it is. Your wife is here. One of our company's many victims. By choosing to stay with us, you would be choosing to stay with your beloved. Would that not be a beautiful thing? To be reunited with your dead wife? Here, in this house that is as much yours as any other's?'

She was laying the same trap for me that she had laid for Varano: the suggestion that the house had taken those whom we loved and the only way to be with them again was to sacrifice ourselves.

But as she continued to speak, I no longer listened to her words, for I could not concentrate on anything but the thought

317

that Rose was trapped here, among the horde, and had been all these long, terrible years since she had died.

Suddenly disparate senseless things that had bothered me since my arrival flooded my mind: Alice instructing me to leave; Rose's voice at the seance; the figure in the mirror in Varano's room, guiding me to his journals; the apparition on the beach, doing likewise.

They had all been Rose. She *was* here.

She had been warning me to leave since I'd arrived, speaking through Alice, and when that hadn't worked, she'd guided me to Varano's journals so that I could see for myself.

She'd been here all along, trying to protect me.

And yet, she herself was trapped, and suffering.

And I could do nothing to help her.

With the knowledge of it, I broke down sobbing, and through my tears, I saw Mrs Chesterfield rise.

'Rest, Mr Etherstone, we are expecting much from you.'

And with that she left my room, locking the door behind her.

31

I was still weeping some time later when I heard keys in the lock. The door opened and Miss Thornwick stepped in, followed by Edith, the maid, carrying a tray of food. Miss Thornwick gestured to Edith and the girl came over and laid the tray on my bedside table. I looked at her and she gave me such a sorry look I was convinced that she knew something was gravely wrong with my situation. But there was also something else in her features – fear. She was scared of Miss Thornwick, too scared to even speak to me. I turned my gaze upon Miss Thornwick then and saw she was eyeing us closely, making sure that no communication passed between us.

Edith took the bedpan from under my bed, then left the room. Miss Thornwick sat in the chair by the door and watched me through the gaslight. I sat up and slid the tray from the bedside table onto my lap. A supper of vermicelli soup and buttered bread. I took a few sips of soup, casting occasional looks at Miss Thornwick, her twisted expression, the sneer set into her face by the disease. I wondered what she had looked like in her youth, the beauty mentioned by Varano and Gosterwood. I thought of her telling Gosterwood that she was a witch, descended from a long line of witches. I thought of all the people she had murdered.

'You have been crying,' she said.

It was the first time in all those weeks that I had actually heard her speak. She had a remarkably soft voice. Gentle and warm. No hint of a Yorkshire accent remained after all her tutoring.

'What is wrong?' she asked.

Again I found the very sound of her voice unsettling, the mildness, the sweetness of it.

'I know what you mean to do,' I said. 'I know how you have fooled Mrs Chesterfield all these years. *Terra suum templum aedificabit.*'

She flinched, shocked at the extent of my knowledge. But the slip in her usually cool demeanour only lasted a second; soon enough she regained control of herself, and she smiled a thin, evil smile.

'Mrs Chesterfield wanted to be fooled,' she said. 'She has always thought the world revolved around her. I let her believe it. And I gave her a good life. She will be dead soon of that tumour in her brain, but she will not suffer. I was good to her.'

'And Gosterwood and Varano? Were you good to them too?'

'Gosterwood,' she repeated. 'I have not heard that name for many years. I was not sorry when he disappeared.'

'You killed him.'

'The moor killed him. Gosterwood abused me cruelly; it was right he was punished. But I never harmed Varano. I liked him. I tended to him through his madness. I doubt anyone will know for certain how he met his end, but I'm sure it wasn't on the moor, by drowning in any marshes. Much more likely he died by his own hand, by wandering into one of those infernal, flickering rooms he built so he could be with his family. Not so sad a fate as the rumours would have us believe.'

'So the only people you sacrificed for this house were the Marsden girls?'

Again she flinched but quickly regained her composure.

'I know you killed them at the start of this mad project,' I

320

pressed. 'And you mean to kill me at its end. On New Year's Eve. To complete the temple and release the evil that lies beneath these moors.'

She smiled when I said this, then slowly raised her eyes upwards, as if she was a saint looking up into a holy light.

'To think it has been thousands of years in the making, and I will be here to witness it,' she said. 'That I was instrumental in bringing it about. And you shall be, too. When your blood is spilled on the mausoleum, these great works shall be complete, and the old ones will rise.'

'And who are these old ones that you would murder for?'

'The old ones? They are spirits of nature. Gods of war. Destroyers of time and illusion. They are the giants of old Albion that strode this land when it was still green and pure, before men imprisoned all with their laws and religions and philosophies, and made the world small by bounding all that they could not comprehend.'

As she spoke her eyes glazed over, her attention drifting out of the room, to some far-off long-dreamt paradise. Then after a few seconds her reverie seemed to pass.

She looked at me, then nodded at the tray on my lap.

'Eat,' she said. 'It will improve your mood.'

I realised there was no point engaging her further. She had confirmed my worst fears. I was to be killed and a great evil was to be unleashed upon the land.

My thoughts turned to stopping the completion of the building, to thwarting at the last hour a conspiracy that had been aeons in the making. And most importantly, freeing Rose. But how could I accomplish all that when I could not even save myself?

I took up my spoon, and even though the very thought of eating any more made me feel sick, I ate, so that I might recover some strength and clarity of mind.

When I had finished, Miss Thornwick rose and walked to the bureau, where there was a box of medicines. She took out a spoon and a bottle of what I guessed was morphine syrup. She approached, poured the syrup onto the spoon and I took a dose. Then she returned everything to the box and sat in her chair once more. As I began to feel the dulling effects of the medicine, I heard the door opening – Edith coming to return the bedpan and collect the tray.

Again the girl looked worried. Again Miss Thornwick watched her hawkishly. This diligence gave me hope, for it signalled that Miss Thornwick didn't trust Edith, and that therefore, maybe I could.

When they had both gone I tried to focus through the delirium of the morphine, attempting to put some plan together. But the drug was too much, and I slipped away, my mind drifting to the visions I'd experienced in my fever – trenches the length of continents, metal birds raining fire, mushroom clouds towering over the Earth. Even though they made no sense to me then, still they inspired profound dread.

Through the terror my memories travelled back further. To that ballroom I fell into when I broke my leg, the sight of Varano through the dancing corpses. I realised now why I had been so scared of him turning to face me, of our gazes locking – we were one and the same. Kindred spirits connected through time by the house, just as Mrs Chesterfield said we were. The future that awaited me was Varano's past, just as his future was my past. Both of us were trapped in a strange, inescapable loop that had arisen from nothing and defied time.

For the entire house was really just a series of loops, of self-references. Varano had seen the demons in his visions and set them down in stone, and then I saw the demons in stone and they appeared in my dreams, which I replicated in the mausoleum.

Miss Thornwick planted words in Gosterwood's mind that made him run to his books, where he saw her words written down centuries before she spoke them to him. Thus the text made Miss Thornwick's revelations real. It was the reflection that confirmed the reality. And so it was with everything connected to the house, the demons and the art, Mrs Chesterfield and her ghosts, Varano and I, Miss Thornwick and Gosterwood – it was all self-reference and strange mirrors.

That was where the house's power lay. Not in spectres, statues or walls, but in the way it merged with itself, in its sheer impossibility, its endlessness. A man trying to discern the secret of the house was like a man confronted with a set of Russian dolls that became ever smaller until they reached an unseeable realm of atoms and nothingness. This was the house's security, and also its horror. It was an endless loop. A mirror of time. An impossible object.

32

When I awoke, daylight was streaming into my room. The grogginess brought on by the morphine was abating, and pain was beginning to pulse through my leg. I knew that I only had these few moments to come up with a plan, for soon Miss Thornwick would return and dose me with the drug again. I set my mind to it as best I could, trying to find some way out of my predicament.

As I weighed up my limited options, I heard the key in the lock. Edith and Miss Thornwick entered, bringing my breakfast. Again Edith looked unsure of herself and Miss Thornwick watched her diligently. As before, Edith put the tray down, took the bedpan and left, and Miss Thornwick stayed and observed me while I ate.

When I had finished she rose to administer my medicine. I knew I had to stop myself from being dosed into sleep again, so this time I only pretended to swallow and kept the syrup in my mouth. I waited for Edith to return and for the pair of them to leave, then I spat out the drug into the bedpan, and put my escape plan into action.

I pulled the sheets off, sat up and shifted my legs over the edge of the bed. They throbbed as the blood rushed into them, a dull ache coursing through my knees as they flexed. It was now over two months since my injury and still the break was painful. Had the fact that I had been bedridden with fever delayed my recovery so much?

I leaned forwards, grabbed hold of the bedpost, and rose. My head swooned and I nearly keeled over. But I stayed upright, keeping my weight on my good leg. Slowly I put some pressure on the broken one. The cast took much of the weight, but still I could not press down on it fully. I needed a crutch if I had any hope of getting out of the house. But first, I had to write a note I could slip to Edith. By holding myself up on the bedpost, then the windowsill, I made it to the bureau. I sat and once more my leg pulsed with pain. I took paper and pen from the drawers and wrote two notes, one for Edith, one for Sarah, the latter folded into the former.

Then I looked about my room once more for a way to fashion a crutch. Maybe I could pull up a floorboard? Or the slats from the bed? My eye alighted on the doorway into my studio. The easel.

Again I rose, and using handholds on the furniture, I made it to the studio. I approached the easel and examined it. The wooden beams that supported it would work. I set about dismantling it, until I had one of the beams free, then I used it to pull myself up. I put the beam under my arm and took a step.

It worked.

With some folded cloth wrapped around the top of the beam to stop it digging into my flesh, I could finally walk.

I spent the next hour making small circuits of the studio, building up my strength.

Then I returned the beam to the easel, reconstructed it, dragged myself back to my bed, and awaited lunchtime.

It felt like an eternity, but eventually Edith and Miss Thornwick entered. We went through the same procedure as before, but this time, when I'd finished eating, I slipped the note underneath the plate, hoping desperately that Miss Thornwick hadn't seen it.

Again she gave me my morphine and again I held it in my mouth. Edith returned and when the two of them left, I spat the morphine into my bedpan. All there was to do now was wait, so I lay back in a sea of anxiety, praying that my plan would work.

In a state of restlessness I watched the sun travel through the sky and drop below the hills. As the darkness came on, my sense of impending doom grew ever more acute.

I heard the door opening again and once more the two women entered. Edith shot me a meaningful look as she laid down my tray, and I saw that she had placed something underneath one of the plates – an envelope.

As I brought the tray towards me I slid the envelope off it, hiding it under my bedclothes.

When the two women had left me alone again, I took the envelope out and opened it. Inside was a letter and a small key. I unfolded the letter:

Dearest Sam,

I pray this reaches you well. I am most disconcerted to hear what has happened to you. I was told that you had a fever and this was why you were in your room. However, when I tried to visit you, I could not enter, for one of Thurlby's men sits outside your room, keeping guard. I have been seeing more of them these last few days, involved in some mysterious work. I completely understand your call to escape! But you cannot do so via your door, for you will be caught instantly by Thurlby's man.

I spoke to one of Edith's colleagues and we managed to obtain a copy of the window key – apparently all the windows in the West Wing have the same key. From the ledge outside your room, you should be able to make your way to the gallery below. I will leave a window there open for you.

If, as per your note, you can leave your room tonight, I
promise you I will fulfil what you asked of me, and end this
horrible situation.
  Sarah

I folded up the letter and slipped it into the pocket of my night-shirt, warmed by a faint sense of hope. As per the schedule of the previous day, Miss Thornwick would return in the late evening to give me my nighttime dose before leaving me alone till morning. To fill the time I decided to practise walking around once more, to ready my clothes and to check the key actually worked in the window lock, for such was my anxiety.

After I had done all this, I returned to my bed and waited.

Miss Thornwick entered some time later to administer my nightly dose. Again I deceived her. I waited for half an hour then I hobbled over to the studio. When I'd built my crutch, I went back to the wardrobe and put on my clothes, having to rip my trouser leg to get it over the cast. I filled the oil lamp and slipped it into my bag.

Then came the most difficult part. I walked over to the window, opened it and looked down. I would have to haul myself out and drop onto the ledge some feet below. From the ledge I could make it to the windows that looked into the gallery, and through them get back into the house.

I raised myself up onto the windowsill, dropped the crutch and the bag onto the ledge, praying the oil lamp wouldn't break, and then I let myself fall.

33

I landed on the ledge and my leg crumpled under me with a sickening crack. The pain was so strong a breathless nausea rose up in me. I took a few moments to let it subside then I looked down and was relieved to see that the crack I'd heard was from the top of my plaster cast breaking.

I rose unsteadily and made my way carefully along the ledge to the gallery windows. I peered through them to check if anyone was inside, for the thought of Thurlby's men prowling the house had unnerved me. But I couldn't see anyone. I checked the windows themselves and Sarah had indeed left one of them slightly ajar. I opened it and slipped through.

When I was inside, I proceeded to the Great Hall then turned for the interior of the house. Eventually I arrived at the lightless sections, lit the oil lamp I'd brought with me and stepped into the darkness. This stretch of the journey was even more difficult as I had to hold the lamp in front of me, but after what felt like an eternity, I reached the very centre of the house, and walked out into the clearing.

And there the mausoleum stood, gleaming in the moonlight. It was the first time I had seen my creation since it had been completed. And it was perfect. It rose into the night exactly as I had imagined, achieving the effect I had striven for. All the monstrous sculptures from my dreams were there, fearsome and breathtaking, and so possessed of life they seemed to writhe about in the glow of the moon, snapping their jaws, straining to free themselves.

I circled the mausoleum, studying the impossible objects I had included in the design, watching as their lines moved with my changing position, falling into alignment so that they created an illusion of unreality, before falling out of alignment and into chaos once more.

Eventually I found what I was looking for – the path that Waylett had driven through the house, in a straight line from its exterior to the mausoleum, so that building materials and man-power could be transported there directly. I saw with relief that the path hadn't been closed up yet, meaning my escape route was still intact.

I kept on circumambulating the mausoleum until I reached its opposite side and approached the wooden walls there, the tinderbox sections. Stepping through the closest door, I found the cabinet next to it and took out a bottle of oil. I stepped through into the clearing and smashed it against the wall. Then I moved on to the next door, the next cabinet, and did likewise. When a whole stretch of wall was thus doused in oil, I lit a match and set it on fire.

The flames spread rapidly, engulfing that entire section of the house, the conflagration already too great to be stopped.

I hobbled towards the passageway and when I reached its start, I turned to take one last look at the mausoleum. It was even more beguiling now that its backdrop was a huge, circular wall of flame, the dancing light of the fire making the sculptures look even more alive.

I set off down the passageway, the roar of the fire becoming steadily louder, the smell of smoke ever stronger. I realised the wind had picked up and was pushing the inferno towards me so I tried to increase my speed as best I could. And then I heard voices up ahead and saw a few bulky figures running in my direction, heading for the fire.

I looked around me for somewhere to hide. The passageway had been gouged out of the house in a straight line, ploughing through rooms however they lay, meaning its sides were made up of the ragged remains of whatever had been there previously. I searched these for any feature that I could hide behind, and saw, a few yards further on, a chimney breast protruding from a wall.

I lurched towards it and thank God, I managed to slip into its shadows just as the figures rushed past and I realised who they were – Thurlby and four of his men.

When they had gone, I peered out of my hiding place and saw their silhouettes further down the passageway, near where it opened out onto the mausoleum. They were standing, staring at the fire, gesticulating, shouting. Then Thurlby and two of the men ran into the field, while the other two lingered where they were. I was caught in an ice of indecision, for if I left my hiding place, and the remaining two came back, they would surely stumble upon me. But if I stayed where I was, the fire would consume me, for it was getting ever closer.

The seconds ticked by painfully and all the while the heat of the fire grew stronger, the smoke thicker. After what felt like an age, the remaining two men turned and ran off in the same direction as the others, disappearing into the field.

I hobbled out of my hiding place and was about to continue on when I realised I had left it too late – the fire was already upon me; the walls on one side of the passageway were aflame, not only where I stood, but ahead of me too.

As I took in my dire situation, a section of wall in front of me succumbed to the fire and crashed down into the passageway, sending sparks and firebrands rolling, releasing a thick fog of smoke into the air. I doubled over and coughed violently. I tried to open my eyes but the smoke was too heavy. I almost dropped to the ground as I waited for it to clear.

When eventually it did, I was shocked to see that the collapsed wall had blocked the passageway entirely. My only option was to turn into the house itself and hope to escape that way. I found a door in one of the nearest rooms, stepped through it, and tried to navigate as best I could, praying I was going in the right direction.

As I journeyed on through a series of strange rooms, the air filled ever more with smoke and ash, stinging my eyes, burning my throat. In the distance I could hear crashes as different sections of the house came down, the building breaking up and collapsing, joists and beams splintering, forces untethering.

And then I saw a figure coming the other way through the ashy shadows. I froze, fearing it might be Thurlby or one of his men.

But as the figure neared, I realised it was Mrs Chesterfield, striding along as quickly as she could, heading into the conflagration.

She went to move straight past me, so intent on her destination she hadn't seen me. I reached out and grabbed her arm. She spun about and looked at me tearfully, the reflected orange flames dancing on the white discs of her eyes.

'My house,' she muttered. 'My house.'

'You're going the wrong way. The fire is that way.'

'I need to get to my mausoleum,' she cried. 'They are coming for me.'

There was an almighty crash behind us as a section of roof collapsed.

'Do you not hear them?' she said. 'They are coming. The soldiers.'

I realised she was mistaking the sounds of the fire for the sounds of war, of an approaching army. I stared at her, confused.

For in our previous conversation she had insisted that she had never tried to shield herself from the vengeful dead. And yet, here she was, running into an inferno to get away from them. Had all her previous talk been a lie? Or had she faltered at the very last?

'You will not make it to the mausoleum,' I said.

'I must or they will come for me.'

She let out a sob and I realised it was the first time I had ever seen her displaying any true emotion. And then, with a strength I had not expected, she yanked her arm from my grip, turned and disappeared into the smoke behind us, heading further into the inferno.

I debated going after her, but I knew there was no way I could catch her, encumbered as I was by the crutch; I would only be dooming myself.

I turned and hobbled on, room after room, through the smoke and ash and the orchestra of destruction that surrounded me.

At one point I passed an open doorway on my right and saw it gave onto an unholy ballroom, where corpses waltzed among golden walls, even as those walls blazed with fire, and the room filled with a blizzard of soot. And in the centre was Varano, just as I had seen him before – dressed all in black, his clothes covered with stone dust, his back to me.

This time I was not worried that he might turn and look at me, I know not why. I studied him for a few more seconds then noticed something on the floorboards, just inside the ballroom – a broken cinematographic camera. My camera. The exposed film still inside it. And next to it, my bag.

Was it a trap? A way to get me inside just as the ballroom disappeared for ever into that other realm?

I took a chance, trusting Varano. I set down my oil lamp and entered the ballroom. Kneeling as best I could, I used the crutch

332

to pivot forwards and pick up the camera and the bag. Then I stepped back out.

A second later there was a great wrenching sound and the ballroom stood empty. The doorway gave onto nothing but a blackened room. No crowd of cadavers, no golden walls, just a wreck of a space, bare but for ash and fire.

I packed the camera into the bag, slung it over my shoulder, and picked up the oil lamp.

As I turned to continue on, I sensed a great rending in the air – time and space warping, the house flexing as the firestorm untethered it from those infernal rooms that flickered in and out of reality, marooning them in that other world whence they came.

I journeyed on and after a few minutes I heard a voice calling my name.

I looked into the darkness ahead and saw Sarah approaching.

'Are you all right?' she asked. 'I came back to look for you.'

'You shouldn't have.'

'I only came in a short way when I saw the passageway aflame. The outside isn't far. Come . . .'

She put her arm under my shoulder, and with her on one side, and the crutch on the other, we continued.

'Where's Alice?' I asked. 'Did you get her out?'

'I did. She's waiting on the driveway. I would have come to search for you earlier, but we were delayed. Alice's parents . . . they would not part with her.'

She said this in an anguished tone, making me wonder what scene had occurred between them.

A minute later we reached a set of exterior doors and stepped out into the gardens at the side of the house. We turned to each other and embraced tightly for a few long moments.

'Come,' she said eventually.

We walked around to the front of the house, our ears assailed by the roar and crash of destruction. It truly did sound like an army, like mortars going off, like war. I thought of Mrs Chesterfield, lost somewhere in that infernal battle, burned to death in one of the endless corridors that had failed to protect her.

When we reached the driveway, it was pandemonium. The staff were rushing in and out of the front doors trying to salvage what they could, people were screaming in the smoke and terror. A crowd had gathered on the gravel, on the lawns. No one tried to put out the fire, because they knew there was no point. All we could do was watch as the inferno grew stronger, as it roared like a crashing ocean, as the horizon of roofs succumbed.

Eventually the flames reached the stone section at the front of the house, making its windows glow orange. The metal struts holding the friezes in place began to buckle, and then the stones themselves started cracking in great booms until finally the sculptures dropped piece by piece to the Earth in showers of sparks, as the sky glowed and vast plumes of black smoke drifted across land and sea.

And as we watched I felt that same stirring in the air as when I had seen the horde of trapped ghosts. I turned and looked back across the moor, and in the ethereal orange glow cast into the sky by the fire, I saw them streaming away from the house, their forms becoming ever more faint as they escaped their prison, disappearing, vanishing into peacefulness. And as they streamed over the brow of a hill, I saw a lone figure among them stop, turn, and stare at me. And even though the distance between us was great, I knew it was Rose. As I remembered her, in all her beauty.

She smiled at me and I knew she was finally free.

AFTERWORD
Memoir: Samuel Etherstone

The fire didn't stop burning for a week, and for days afterwards a canopy of smoke and ash drifted through the air, falling to Earth in a gradual, lingering rain, across the moors, along the coast, out to sea. Almost everyone who resided in the house was accounted for, but a few were not. Mrs Chesterfield, Miss Thornwick, the Danbys, Waylett – none of them were ever seen again. I have never stopped feeling guilty for their deaths, but I reassure myself that had I not acted as I did, a great many more would have died, myself included.

In the immediate aftermath, Sarah, Alice and I found lodgings in Heybridge, where we assumed parental responsibility for the child, now that the Danbys were missing, presumed dead. Thurlby and his men, I heard, made a swift retreat to London, departing the very same morning of the fire. After we had spoken to the police and were told we were free to leave the area, we went north, back to Sarah's home town of Edinburgh. And there we stayed. We married not long after and adopted Alice.

I sent the film to Fitzpatrick in London and he said there was enough on it to interest his network of distributors, though whether he padded out the reel with the faked images he so often created himself, I cannot say, for I never viewed it. Certainly with the house no more, the reel contained the only extant images of it – except for those in my sketchbooks, and Varano's journals, all of which I have kept well hidden.

Fitzpatrick sent me a lump sum for my film, which Sarah and I used to buy the house in New Town where we still live. Royalty cheques came for years afterwards. I have no doubt that Fitzpatrick short-changed me on them, but they were enough to leave us well off.

The new century had dawned and not long after that Queen Victoria died and it felt as though we had entered a different age. Alice called us Mother and Father. We loved each other. We built a life and the years slid away. Alice never spoke of the Danbys, or anything that happened before the fire, and with time she healed and was no different to any other child. When she grew up she became an artist herself, trained at the school in Glasgow, and then the Slade, just as I had.

I never returned to London, except to put up headstones over Rose and Thomas's graves. I certainly never went back to Yorkshire. We stayed in Scotland and were happy. Sarah found teaching work and I started a photography studio, for I could never again bring myself to pick up a brush and resume my former vocation.

But as time passed, tastes turned in my favour. I heard now and again from Carmichael and other old friends in London that collectors and fashionable galleries were buying my works. They urged me to return to painting. To come to the exhibitions of my work there and in Paris. But I never could. It would disturb the fragile peace of mind I had managed to build for myself.

True art is that in which the artist lives, which captures something of their soul. My soul was captured in that house, and when it burned down, something died within me, something that could never be replaced. Maybe because of this, I sometimes feel as if I'm living as a ghost, even though I escaped the flames. Perhaps because I broke the loop and so, remaining outside it, I somehow stopped existing, like the tale Thurlby told about the mountain of skulls. Or maybe I simply died in the fire and all of this is yet another false mirror.

I am reminded of what Gosterwood told Varano, that every fraction of a second the universe is erased and replaced by a new one, ever so minutely different. It seems now that a million universes exist between this one and theirs, and the only remains of it are the memories flickering in ever-darkening minds.

Now and then I still dream of the house. Sometimes the dreams are benign, the house fantastical, all cloud-capp'd towers and faded pageant, as reassuring as a fairy tale. But most nights I awake in a sweat, having found myself trapped once more in its corridors, its infinite rooms and shadows. And in those twilight moments, it's as if the house still exists – and perhaps it does, somewhere.

Often I dream of my mausoleum. More often of the ballrooms where I saw Varano. I like to think he found release when the fire destroyed the house. Or maybe he really was happy there. Maybe he and his family are dancing still.

But my most vivid nightmares are the same ones I had when I was locked in my room with the fever upon me: the millions marching across the plains of Europe, trenches the length of continents, metal birds raining down fire, whole cities devoured by explosions rising up over the Earth in clouds like giant mushrooms.

For in the years that came we saw the Great War, and many of those visions became reality. Now I wonder if maybe I failed in destroying the house, if the gods of war trapped beneath it were unleashed after all, for it has been a century of conflict so far. I worry that there are yet more to come; wars where aeroplanes really do rain down fire, and mushroom clouds really do consume cities. I pray I die long before that. I pray that when it happens Alice escapes the worst of it. For as Mrs Chesterfield said, there will always be war, for there will always be empires, for there will always be men. Foolish men who have mechanised war and made it our God.

You would think from what I have written that my outlook is bleak, that my life has been blighted. But it is not so, for despite everything, I have lived a happy life since I left the house, having lived it in the bosom of a family, in the reassuring glow of love. I have come to realise that Gosterwood was wrong – we are not merely ghostly mirrors, alive only in our own reflections. We are also alive in the eyes of those around us, the people we love, and who in turn love us. For if man truly is an impossible object – a soul trapped in flesh and time – then the love which emanates from us is even more impossible still, warming us eternally in this cold flicker that is life.

Acknowledgements

I'd like to thank the following for all their help: Mariam Pourshoushtari, Stephen Reynolds, Jacob Lawson, Joseph Haywood, R-J. Berridge, Julia Pye, Fran Cooke, Cedric Sekweyama, Shemuel Bulgin, Jane Finigan, Francesca Davies, Susannah Godman, Anna Boyce, Maria Rejt, Alice Gray, Charlotte Tennant, Mary Chamberlain. Everyone at L&R, Mantle and Pan Mac, the North York Moors National Park Authority, the Yorkshire Wildlife Trust. As usual, special thanks to Ben Maguire and Nana Wilson.

About the Author

Ray Celestin is the author of the prize-winning City Blues Quartet, a series of novels which charts the twin histories of jazz and the Mob through the middle fifty years of the twentieth century. The first novel in the series, *The Axeman's Jazz*, won the CWA New Blood Dagger for best debut crime novel of the year, and was featured on numerous 'Books of the Year' lists. The second and third books in the series, *Dead Man's Blues* and *The Mobster's Lament*, were shortlisted for the CWA Gold Dagger and the Capital Crime Novel of the Year respectively. The final novel in the series, *Sunset Swing*, won both the CWA Historical Dagger and the Gold Dagger in 2022 and was described in the *Sunday Telegraph* as the conclusion to 'one of the finest achievements of recent crime fiction'.